FLAMINGO SCOTTISH SHORT STORIES 1995

Introduction by Tom Adair

Flamingo
An Imprint of HarperCollins*Publishers*

Flamingo
An Imprint of HarperCollins*Publishers*
77–85 Fulham Palace Road,
Hammersmith, London W6 8JB

First published in Great Britain by Flamingo 1995

1 2 3 4 5 6 7 8 9

The Publisher acknowledges the financial assistance of the Scottish Arts Council in the publication of this volume

A catalogue record for this book is available from the British Library

ISBN 0 00 649648 2

Set in Linotron Baskerville

Printed in Great Britain by HarperCollinsManufacturing Glasgow

FLAMINGO SCOTTISH SHORT STORIES 1995

Now in its 23rd year, and published for the first time in Flamingo, *Scottish Short Stories* represents the best of contemporary Scottish short fiction. The collection is introduced this year by Tom Adair, journalist and literary critic.

ACCLAIM FOR SCOTTISH SHORT STORIES:

A Roomful of Birds: Scottish Short Stories 1990:

'Continues to attest to the vitality of the short story in Scotland' *The Scotsman*

'A stunning collection of short stories from Scotland's finest contemporary writers' *Book News*

Three Kinds of Kissing: Scottish Short Stories 1993:

'An exhilarating display of skill and storytelling by craftsmen' *Edinburgh Evening News*

Looking for the Spark: Scottish Short Stories 1994:

'Diversity rules . . . in this collection. There are enough bright sparks to keep you burning the midnight oil' *Glasgow Herald*

'These short stories capture the intensity of a moment and leave indelible impressions. A rich, varied and sobering collection' *The Universe*

CONTENTS

INTRODUCTION

'In art, as in life, narrowness becomes arid,' wrote an Irishman, David Marcus, introducing, more than twenty years ago, a collection of Irish short stories. Stories from Scotland, England and Wales he declared, cavalierly, and somewhat dismissively, to be 'regional'. Denigration? Well, perhaps, but not in the class of the remark expressed to me recently by someone who deserves to remain anonymous: 'To be a Scottish short story writer,' he said, 'and to aspire to be any good is to be an admiral in the Czechoslovakian navy.'

This class of ignorance – of the politics of Europe, as well as of the fiction writing in current profusion in Scotland – is subverted, contradicted and blown to the stratosphere of baloney by the evidence of talent in this, and previous selections of Scottish short stories. Scottish, yes, but in no way regional. They espouse an eager artfulness, and an art which is neither arid, myopic nor narrow.

This twenty-third annual collection brings us tales which emerge from and melt into many landscapes – geographical and cultural, rural, urban; twists and visionscapes running to fantasy, heightened realism, folklore, the penetrating 'I' voice often present or implied, inducing complicity, even in moments when reality hangs by its fingertips. Viz: the audacious opening sentence of 'God's Own Country' by P. F. Brownsey – 'I saved Judy Garland by taking her hill-walking in Scotland.' While your mind conjures Judy, out of kilter in high-heels among Scotland's Bens, and incongruity overwhelms the story's chances, your eye and ear are already refreshed by the verve, comic shrewdness and ingenuity of what follows. Brownsey's story meets Yeats's demand (an unlikely association of talents) that a tale should 'engross the past and dominate memory'.

In many of these tales the glow of memory is itself a potent presence. Esther Woolfson's 'Rosh Hashanah' traces the past with fingertip stealth, exploring, through the adult sensibility of Henry, its narrator, the knotted years of his turbulent Jewish adolescence, a time fraught with inwardness, taboos, a reductive world which brings to these pages Aunt Adele, an unforgettable, thorny stick of unyielding, and sometimes comic propriety, denouncing *goyshke* contamination of all things pure. The subtle creation of the story's double perspective – through the adult narrator's quiet reinvention of his adolescent self – imbues the story with a rare and moving richness: a *mille-feuille* world.

Interleaved too, and graced by that spaciousness which coaxes the imagination to unfurl, is the compact, rapt, 'A Story of Folding and Unfolding', by Ali Smith – one of the newer names on the scene and full of starry possibilities – a portrait of loss, befuddlement and loneliness. In it a man, it seems in the wake of his wife's recent death, surveys the collection of her belongings: 'The room has the air and the smell of someone who's just left . . . her movement through the room displacing the settled air like a light breeze in humid weather . . .'

Ali Smith delves into the making of a love-match, evoking ghosts, erotic shimmers, the talc of intimacy, the settling dust of desire, providing 'a glimpse of the ring, the couple . . . the moments and materials of which love gets made.'

In sifting, discarding, reinstating and finally mulling over the choices from the two hundred or so early entrants, Alison Walsh, Douglas Gifford and I – like diviners awaiting the twitch, the telltale moment of reward – were ever susceptible to the prickle the real thing brings to the imagination's skin. As if the story, in that moment, across that instant of timeless time, releases its ghost, at once compelling us to pursue its implications – social, moral, psychological and narrative (what happens next?) – becoming a haunting. Hauntings proliferate.

In 'Heron' by Douglas Strang, Findlay is haunted by the 'grey shadow, with one bright eye staring' in the midst of a city park. Or again, in 'Beady Eyes', John Cunningham, confirming his growing status, crafts, in brilliant, telling detail, the sudden spooking of his narrator by a slipper left by his girlfriend 'to tell me she was watching, even when she wasn't there'. His subsequent journey from lover to lodger thrums with a rare obsessive pulse and lyric exactness. The lover staking his slice of the action in Jonathan Wood's 'And on the Seventh Day an Angel Came', is haunted by his past and hears the wingbeat of final reckoning in this tense, enticing tango of cryptic, economical dialogue interspersed with a gospel-hall soundtrack from over the street.

These darkish clouds are edged with a brighter, silvery lining in stories like Gordon Legge's 'The Paper', a comic exposé of library mores as Sandy pops in to read the dailies and gobs on the spine of one of the books. A sure survivor against the odds, he'd have wagered on 'Nan MacDonald's Gamble', a tale full of pathos, love and chance in which Jock, gone senile, is tuned to the future, predicting events of outrageous comic improbability. Will aliens really 'land on Glasgow Green on Xmas Eve'? Will Tom McKean, a feat of greater improbability, some say, 'win Olympic gold'?

In a vein more jugular than comic comes 'The Murderer', set in Toronto, full of sublimated craziness, typically angled into darkness, by Iain Crichton Smith, who, at his best approaches mastery of the genre. Two other established, prodigious talents, Dilys Rose and Candia McWilliam, in 'Rope' and 'Carla's Face' respectively, portray and vent the resentments of adolescence, and the merciless, often sardonic vision of life in those bird's-nest years from the safer vantage of middle age. But beware Ms McWilliam's delicious twist that brings a whiff of *grand guignol* to a story which beats with a sense of mortality on the blink.

These tales grace a book which hoards its delights. Among piquant surprises are the elegiac anger in 'Leaving Assynt' by Anne MacLeod, the narrative grip of 'The Unlocked Door', Stuart David's parable of faith, and of Hal Duncan's purring 'Slab City, April 12th'. Each story more than earns its place in what I find to be an enervating collection, ghostly, spritely, a peal of voices in the dark midnight of the mind. Prepare to be haunted.

TOM ADAIR

FLAMINGO
SCOTTISH SHORT STORIES
1995

MIRROR IMAGE

Ali Duncan

The face cloth leaves a smear of make-up as I rub the steam from the mirror. The whole flat's like a sauna, suppose I'll have to get someone in to fix that shower. More expense. It keeps turning so hot I could brew tea with it, and my buttocks sting where it caught me out again. I'm perspiring already, beads of sweat on my lip and tickling my armpits. Karen would say; buy a book! Do It Yourself!

I wipe the sweat with the mirror-cool cloth, spread it open in my palms and press it hard to my face. It sucks the heat from my eyelids, takes away the itch, but it heats too quick and smothers me. I let it fall into the sink and the mist-stripey mirror still shows the scar and faint network of red vessels in the corners of my eyes.

I reach for my make-up bag.

It smells when I open it, smells like my mother used to, though I can't place what of exactly. Mixture of powder, perfume, toilet roll. Musk.

I wonder what the E number for ox-secretion is.

I can't see Karen in the noise of the pub.

No one's up on the dance floor, so why the music and lights? Thumping and whirling with a raw, volcanic power. I feel somehow guilty. Someone should turn them off, they're such a fuckin' waste if there's no one using them.

I work my way round the dark edge of the room with

bright snakes writhing in my eyes, scared I bash my shin on a table. I glance too high and a strobe freezes a look in my direction. I turn away too quick, almost fall. I'm sure I heard:

– *Whit the fuck is that?*

Spent hours on this kind of Goth look, I know it's too young for me but I like the colours. Black. Everything black except for blood-red lips and carmine fingernails poking out from the black lace gloves I cut the fingers off.

I probably look like a witch. And these gloves used to make my hands look smaller.

– *Angie!*

Karen. She's alone at a table by the wall. At least I think it's her. I move towards the table, make out her face in the sudden clamour of light that kicks in with the next track.

Village People, for Christ sake.

She's half rising, half sitting, scanning the room. Making my back itch. I glance over my shoulder and there's nothing, at least nothing I can see to make her nervous. She's not usually like this. Not here, anyway, where you can hide in the noise and the dark corners away from the dance floor. Maybe it's because there's no crowd yet.

– Hi, Karen.

I smile at her, I think, feels more like a leer. Lean over to kiss her cheek, fingering my hair from my face and careful not to smudge the heavy layer of powder. She angles her head away. My nose brushes against her hair and I smell her perfume of hair spray and cigarette smoke. I half hope she sees the face I pull as I sit behind the low table that wobbles when I nudge my knees behind it, trying not to catch my tights on the melamine strip round the edge. Never seen any knives in here yet, but all the tables are scarred and frayed at the edges.

She already has a drink for me, a Long Vodka, beside her

half empty glass. On the other side there's a pint of lager in one of those straight glasses without a handle. I smile at her with an eye on the lager. She shifts slightly. The table's so close, so uncertain, that it shifts uneasily with her. There's a silence between us, just that unsure smile. She shouts to me through the music.

– WASN'T SURE WHO WAS COMING. WASN'T SURE WHO I WANTED TO COME.

What is this, some kind of psychoanalysis? She knows I drink vodka, whether I'm dressed up or not.

– HEY, THAT'S A BIT HEAVY. WE'RE NOT SCHIZOPHRENIC.

– WHAT?

I lean into her ear. I can almost taste the stale smoke, she's been in here a while. I shout,

I SAID WE ARE NOT SCHIZ o PHRENIC.

She heard this time but she doesn't know what the fuck I'm talking about.

Try again.

– WELL I KNOW I'M NOT BUT HE MIGHT BE.

She just looks at me, shakes her head. Maybe it's paranoid I meant. She's a nurse. Fuckin' nurses. Think they know more than the doctors. I suddenly need to piss, *my girdle's killing me*, I feel the mask crack at the corners of my mouth as I try to control a laugh. Who's in the gent's? I haven't been watching. I can't go yet.

I KNOW FINE WHAT YOU MEANT, ANGUS, IT'S JUST THIS IS SERIOUS.

Angus. This must be heavy. I'd better keep my mouth shut. She just needs a cuddle or something, a bit of small talk. Then I can make my excuses. Fuck off out of it to another pub. Plenty pubs in Glasgow don't mind people like me, though you've got to be careful. Some of the guys you meet are dangerous, they treat us the way they treat their women.

I reach for the lager, pick up the pint glass and put it

beside my vodka. The table shifts from one leg to the other and Karen says,

– I mean, Alan. He suspects something.

I twist to look her in the face and kick the table with my ankle. Karen grabs a glass before it falls. There's beer on her hand.

– You just missed him. Things got a bit difficult.

I look closer and there are signs of bruising under her make-up. Bluish shadows round her eye. This line comes into my head, heard it in a film, *you shouldn't do so much to your eyes, it makes you look like a tart.* Her face feels hot when I touch her cheek and she presses her head into my hand. A moist wave of skin swells beneath my thumb as I stroke her cheekbone, just below the bruise. I take my hand away, leaving my perfume on her, and hold her eyes with mine.

– Thought he was in Aberdeen.

She shrugs, breaking away from my gaze.

– It's OK. For you anyway, he doesn't know about you. He doesn't know anything really, just suspects.

So the lager was for Alan. Karen licks the beer off her hand, not as a man would but like a cat. Careful not to rouge her hand with her lips. I want to lick the beer off her tongue.

Alan might come back, though. He might be here. Now.

There are a few guys up at the bar but they're all businessmen or something, loud ties, loud voices. This is the place for business right enough, but not the kind you'd tell the wife about. They've been glancing over at us now and again, snickering amongst themselves like the bunch of wankers they are. I'm not sure now which of us they've been looking at. I want to know what happened with Alan, but I don't want to ask her. Maybe I'll ask one of those guys later.

What the fuck. I gulp down half my vodka, feel the better for it. Think straight. Alan can't know anything, really. Nothing I can't handle. I drain the glass and get her go up for another, slipping some money from the pocket of my long black coat on to the table.

She takes the glasses with her, each stained a different shade of red around the rim, mine looking like someone's cut their lip on it. I close my eyes against the dance floor lights and the people who've been drifting in. I don't want to see the girl I bought the make-up off, I knew her from here and I'm sure she recognized me. More fucking snickering.

I open my eyes and see Karen swivel on to a stool and lean heavily on the bar, talking to Mark the barman as he fetches the drinks. He picks up the old glasses, glances over. Karen says something and they laugh as he puts the glasses under the bar. I wonder who'll get my glass next and I start to get hard, thinking of my blood on someone's mouth, like I got Karen's blood on mine once. Try thinking about something else. Fuckin' sore sometimes, all that hard flesh and bollocks squeezed into a cache-sexe, not much room. Squash sex, more like. And I still need to go.

Shit, I might as well drink Alan's lager. Sure he won't mind. Karen's still up at the bar there, talking to one of the businesswankers now. Still laughing. Probably be there a while yet.

I check my pocket for a joint and head for the bog.

I don't know what's wrong. Not even sure there's anything wrong at all. The room's still dark, as dark as it gets when the moon's hidden high above the still cloud that touches the sea. I flick my eyelids Open Closed and poke the outside corner of my eye to see the white ellipse where my nose should be.

It's not what I see, it's what I feel. My mattress is gone. I'm lying on the bare mesh of an old bed frame and I'm in the quarry. I can't see but I know I am, I can feel the distance between myself and the cold grey slate of the cliffs.

I move my hand through the dark. The air feels thin and cold, not bedroom air at all. I paw the air above my face and make out a glow like I saw in the wake of the boat one summer night when dad took me night fishing.

But that had been moonlight. Full, bright moonlight, warm and calm so the sea looked almost solid, the wake of the boat crept slow and substantial as mountain ridges.

I can see now. I'm lying on a trap and facing the sea.

I try to stand and find a rope tied round my ankle, thin and cold like electrical wire. I kick at it and hear a scream. My mother, it's her hand, she's holding me down until she sees me looking, sees the look on my face, then she springs the trap.

Instead of falling back I fall up, up towards the light that starts to spread. I see it's not a disc of light but a tunnel and the colour I saw was made of every colour except they're all red. They're mixed at random as I enter the tunnel, but they quickly congeal into concentric circles, a kaleidoscope. The circles flash by as I fall at such a speed that I know I should be scared, but I'm not. I'm warm, and the wind I pass through is like the light wind that blows from the sea on a warm summer evening.

I fall for ever, and when for ever ends I see the end of the tunnel. It's not a hole, it's a pillow. A pillow with a dent in the middle and only the size of a baby rat, but I'm only the size of an ant anyway.

When I hit the pillow it's wet, not made of feathers and fabric as I thought it would be, but made of warmth and wetness. Could be water except I can breathe and I have to take in deep, quick throbs of breath, in and in and in until everything I've breathed in is about to burst out . . .

– Jesus, what . . .

The dark collapses on to my chest with a heavy flailing of arms so I'm confused, scared for a second until the bedside lamp clicks on and Karen's face appears inches from mine. Suddenly I'm staring into her wide open eyes, the pupils shrinking like a falling stone seen from above. She rips the duvet off me and starts to shove.

– Karen, what the fuck . . .

– Get out, Jesus, get out . . .

– Wait a bit, what . . .

I stumble out of bed out of balance, feel stupid with one foot on the floor and the other tangled in the bedclothes, legs apart and the smell of sex hot in my nostrils.

She's pointing at the wardrobe, stabbing at it with her finger as though she's trying to shake off a snot.

– For fuck sake, did you not hear, fucking hide, it's Alan, fucking *do* something . . .

Alan. Alan.

O my god.

Alan.

What the fuck do I do, I hear a bump from somewhere in the flat and make a dive for the space beside the wardrobe, don't want to open it for the noise it'll make.

Holy fuck. How did I get here anyway? I can't remember anything after the pub.

I close my eyes, like a bairn, and it helps. Maybe if I count to fifty, everything will change. Maybe if I hide behind my hands.

But I'm already hiding behind my hands, they're clasped round my crotch. The wardrobe feels hot and wet where my arse sticks to it like cling film on a glass.

Jesus, no. I'm starting to get hard.

I can hear Alan. Rattling cutlery, shouting, can't make out what though. More because he's incoherent than he's not loud enough. He's in the kitchen, on the other side of the wall I'm trying to blend into. Damp wallpaper, musty and chilly on my shoulder. I turn my head to the wall and feel the cold radiating from it.

I can't open my eyes yet, not till the pressure on my palm drops. Till I have to face the shame of it. The ludicrous fuckin' hiding place. Brian Rix had nothing on this.

Alan crashes out of the kitchen. I feel the waves of pressure off the wall, quick and light despite the noise, as he thumps the kitchen door against it. A thrill pops in my stomach like a bubble in hot mud and I start to get harder. Jesus. I hope Karen isn't looking. This is her fault. Shit, this is all her fault.

I open my eyes.

I see her in the mirror on the dressing table in front of me. She's in the bed, leaning heavily on one elbow, rolling a fag.

She's leaning away from me. The quilt's down about her waist, but her breasts are hidden by her arm, puckered in the low angle of light from the lamp. She's concentrating on rolling the fag, like she never rolled one before. She's not even looking at me, the bitch, even with Alan out the room. What's she going to do when he comes in? She's going to drop the lighter and scream or something; *Alan, who's that behind the wardrobe!?* She looks up as Alan does his door thing to the bedroom.

I wince as the door crashes into the other side of the wardrobe. My knee jumps, forces the back of my leg against the wood. I'm tense with cold or something, starting to shake a bit. Makes me notice the hot dribble of sweat down the inside of my thigh. Like some kind of animal pissing on itself. Alan can probably smell me, never mind see me, he seems so close.

There's quiet at first, except for the buzz in my head from the grass. It's like I'm not watching them in the mirror. I'm standing in the frame of the mirror, except I can see myself as well as them. I stumble slightly as I watch myself try to lean on the frame.

It's only a second like, while Alan moves towards Karen and sits on the bed, his back to me, bent over a bit. Seems like hours, hours spent watching his arse settle into the soft mattress. The bed sheets that needed changed, they felt itchy with cat hairs or smeg or something. The whole flat presses into my skin, cat-shit, dust and tapeworms. His right buttock starts to bounce in rhythm with the dull beat of his trainer off the storage unit under the bed.

Seems like hours as I stifle the nervous laugh that pokes at the back of my throat. The reflection of the clock by the bed shows the seconds ticking by where the hours should be. I concentrate on it until the numbers pop into focus in my head as if they're suddenly the right way round and I'm surprised to see them increasing instead of going backwards.

Alan grunts, stops his kicking, bends down.

He's seen my clothes on the floor, mixed up with Karen's. He picks up a pair of Docs, stands and waves them at Karen.

– Whose are these?

– Mine, says Karen, smooth as fuck, nice scornful edge to her voice as if to say; whose else? Alan drops them, picks up another pair.

– Well, who the fuck's these then?

She looks away. Shit, don't look over here.

– Well? *Well?* You've done it again, haven't you. You've fuckin' done it again. I knew there was something going on. Well, who's it this time? Eh?

Karen stares at her knee under the quilt. Lights her fag. Alan ruffles through the pile of clothes at his feet with his trainer.

– Come on, who the fuck is it? Shit, fuckin' obvious isn't it, you might as well say it. Unless you've turned into a fuckin' dyke. Come on, that bastard Angus, isn't it?

Jesus, this was like some game until he says my name.

Like some cheap cop movie. When the guy gets pulled out of the line-up, then he's in big shit. Except I'm the only one on parade.

– How long has this been going on?

He must know I'm here. Or maybe he thinks I'm *in* the wardrobe. I wish I was. In the wardrobe, that would be perfect. Brian Rix stumbles out of the wardrobe. But Vicar, where's his trousers?

– Fuckin' bitch.

He throws the boots across the bed, one of them flying into the wall beside her head.

– A-*lan!*

She sounds more irritated than scared.

– Alan, that nearly hit me!

He looks guilty, I can see he's not used to this, he's used to it happening but he's not used to controlling it. Without her make-up the bruise over her cheekbone gives her face a kind of lopsided look, like one eye socket's bigger than the other.

– Fuckin' bitch, how can you do this to me now? Christ, I can't work for worry.

Jesus, the petted lip.

– My fault! Listen, don't blame me. You sneak about, trying to catch me out. Why should I traipse after you, do your fuckin' washing, get your fuckin' mother to do it why don't you. You're looking for some fuckin' reason to fail.

There's an edge to her voice, an authority. I've seen her compliant before, charming, cheating, lying, but this is like bare-faced *shut up I'm in charge*.

I have a sudden urge to come out from behind the closet. A feeling that it would impress Karen. That my nakedness would shame Alan more than me. At the same time, I'm not sure they'd even notice. And I'm not sure who it is I should be trying to hurt.

– Wait a minute, this is fuckin' ridiculous.

It's as much a question as a statement. He can't quite figure why exactly he's right and she's wrong.

– Don't . . . I've worked fuckin' hard.

– I know. I know, Pooh.

Jesus, *Pooh*. Her voice is suddenly soft, intimate, sickening.

Alan, I'd fuckin' hit her now, mate.

– Listen.

She leans towards him, stubbing out her fag and exposing her breasts, nipples slightly erect.

– Listen, you've been through a lot. I understand.

Alan doesn't think so, he raises his arms, fists clenched.

– You're behavin' like a tart. And what's that crap about my mother?

Shit, Alan, you're giving this away.

He grabs the bottom of the quilt, shakes it like he wants to shake her, like he should fuckin' shake himself.

– Cover yourself up, for Christ sake, woman. And you too, ya wee bastard.

He opens the wardrobe. He pulls out a blanket and throws it in my face.

– Call yourself a friend. Some fuckin' transvestite you turned out to be.

– What the fuck you mean by that? You think it's some kind of fuckin' club or somethin'? Guys-it's-safe-to-leave-your-girl-with?

I'm in the living room, waving the blanket like a banner. I'm suddenly conscious of the nail varnish on my toes, chipped from wearing the Docs.

– What about me, where am I supposed to fit into this?

He goes into the kitchen, doesn't even pause while he says,

– Look, just get some fuckin' clothes on.

Karen comes out of the bedroom, tying up the dressing gown that's clean enough but always feels grubby. At least she looks at me.

– Better get dressed, Angus.

She glances at the kitchen door and raises her eyebrows. He's rattling things around again.

I feel a need to generate some respect somehow, self-respect at least, but I suspect the only way to do that involves some sort of fight for Karen, like dogs over a bone.

I wrap myself in the blanket. I hadn't realized how cold it was. Even in the blanket, I'm shaking. I sit on the sofa, tuck a woolly corner round my balls and crouch over, trying to control a spasm. Karen turns on the ceiling light.

The bulb's too big for the room or something. The harsh light makes the pale skin of my legs glow, highlighting the stubble, sparse and stiff like the hairs on a fly. I tuck my legs under me on the sofa without rearranging the blanket too much, without letting in the cold, and shake my head so my hair falls over my eyes.

I'll try and sit it out. Main thing is they don't chuck me out. But I hear Alan on the phone in the kitchen, can't hear what he's saying but I hear the word 'taxi'. There's no way he'll have asked for a driver I know, Jesus, it's bad enough when I don't look like shit.

I hide behind my curtain of hair, trying to ignore Karen. She's kneeling by the dead fire. Turn the fucker on, why don't you. I try to suggest it, but it comes out as a croak. She looks at me, loses her balance as she hands across the tobacco and papers. I suppose I could handle rolling one for her, though I don't want to face the cold on my arms.

I get damp, soft tobacco grit tangled in my pubes as I roll one up under the blanket.

Alan comes out of the kitchen and I look up, waiting for the crash of the door, but there is none. He pulls the door open with his foot and comes out with a mug held in each hand.

My legs tense almost to a crouch, I lift my buttock to loosen off a corner of the blanket, grip the edges. I test the air for:

bleach;

boiling water;

Christ knows what.

Tea, for fuck sake.

He puts down two mugs of tea. One for me, one for Karen. Goes back into the kitchen. I start to wonder whether he remembered mine's two sugars when he comes back out pulling on his coat.

– I'm going to my mother's. I'll talk to *you* tomorrow.

She ignores him. He opens the front door, a blast of cold air tugs at the steam off my mug, and before he bangs the door shut he shouts . . .

– AND YOU CAN PAY FOR THE FUCKING TAXI!

I'm getting colder. I eye up the tea. Pick it up, slop some on the carpet, my hands are shaking. Hold the cup in both hands, grateful for the warmth, and watch circles ripple on the surface. I scald my lip with the first mouthful but don't mind.

Two sugars.

We're both quiet for a while, can't think what to say. I'm almost scared to say anything, maybe she's forgotten I'm here. Scared in case she tries to get me back into bed.

I cough hard, get my lips in working order.

– What about the eye? It wasn't Alan, don't tell me that.

She leans across for the smoke I rolled for her. Maybe she thinks that's the price of an answer. I don't really want one. It wasn't me. It wasn't Alan. I don't give a fuck how many, never mind who.

– Listen.

She whispers, ignoring the question.

– He'll probably phone you tomorrow. Why don't we just tell him things got a bit out of hand, with the dope. Tell him you were just trying on some of my dresses.

Jesus. Why don't we just cut off my bollocks.

ROPE

Dilys Rose

The leather leashes are taut as rigged hawsers. The man strains to match the force of their muzzled heads and harnessed shoulders. They're taking him for a walk, these muscle-bound, rock-skulled dogs with boiled red eyes and drooling jaws. These are no pets in the ordinary sense; not cuddly beasts with which an animal lover might share a bit of harmless rough and tumble, not fluffy mutts which lope after sticks and balls and deposit them at the feet of an approving master, begging for claps on warm compliant heads and the game to begin again.

Nothing at all is compliant about this pair, nothing tamed except by force. It's in his every step, the strain of control, of keeping these power-packs in check; these bald brutes pitting their wills against his. His belted mac perfectly matches their own coats, close-cropped, colourless as putty.

To love animals like these takes something other than delight. There is nothing to love in these dogs unless you can count devotion to their transparent savagery, their naked ugliness; every step the man takes is one of restraint, of struggle for control. If the bitch's lead goes slack, if she pauses to sniff the soiled municipal turf or if the dog thrusts thuggishly at a whimsical, park-wise squirrel, it is all the man can do to keep them in check.

Like the dogs, the boy, too, moves from the shoulders, as if he sees some aggro ahead, something to square up to, as if he's going to hit something head-on, though there's only his dad's tightly-belted back, his dad clenched in the steel grip of his will, his dad's body hard, unyielding, buttoned up against the elements.

The boy doesn't mind the cold. The winter wind scrabbles through his outsize lumberjack shirt. He shivers at the thrill of it nipping his chest, scratching at his belly, his belt buckle. On either side of his dad he sees Cass and Tara's thin, bare tails twitch as they walk, stick up from squat, wagging bums, porking the foggy air like it's flesh.

Flesh: that word. He just has to say the word and he imagines Chantelle trotting ahead of him, Chantelle with her pale lips and arched black eyebrows, her pointy tits and long, long legs. He feels hungry. A burger would hit the spot; meat, melted cheese and a soft, spongy roll; something to put in his mouth. If he had something to put in his mouth he wouldn't have to think about Chantelle's body or dogs' tails porking the fog.

The boy needs a haircut; his thick fringe swings into his puppy eyes as he shoulders forward, shirt-tail flapping, trainer laces trailing. It will be his turn soon, his shot. His dad will wrap the leashes round his gloved palms until the dogs are half-choked, until their tongues go purple and slop out of their mouths. Then his dad will hand the dogs over to him. He has to go through this stuff with the dogs; it's crap and sometimes he moans about it but there's no point, there's no way around it. It's Friday and he wants money. His dad will hand over a fiver. – If you've shown some progress with the dogs, son. I want to see some progress. There was always this progress thing, this way his dad had of measuring him up, even though you never got to see it in his face. You couldn't tell anything from his dad's face about how he felt; it hardly moved. Even when he spoke, his face looked frozen and grey, like his coat.

You've got to have money in your pocket. Chantelle always has loads of money. In the lunchbreak, she flashes her cash about and treats her pals to cream cakes. One time he was standing right behind her in the baker's, in the queue for filled rolls and pizza. With all the jostling going on, it was easy to rub up against her short tight skirt, accidentally on purpose. He just about came on the spot.

Chantelle hardly knows he exists. And if she knew, if she knew what he does while he chants her name over and over? Jeer, probably, or pity him and one is as bad as the other. Chantelle doesn't go with schoolboys; Chantelle's into men. Men are into Chantelle. Boys are dross to Chantelle but one day he'd show her, one day he'd give her one, give it to her right up the crack. He'd get her down on the grass; she'd be laughing and trying to fight him off with scorn. He'd pin her down so she'd have to kick and bite and scratch but he'd be strong, and rock hard. Her skirt would ride up her thighs as he pulls down her pants in one easy movement and then he'd be up there, up inside her, pumping . . .

His dad is pushing his biscuit-coloured hair out of his eyes. The boy has forgotten the colour of his dad's eyes. They're just dark gaps, gashes in his face. His dad's eyes are not looking out or in, they're looking away, always looking away, even now when he calls him over, yanks him out of the Chantelle fantasy and back to the sweaty smell of the dogs, to their thonged leashes cutting into his dad's thick gloves, their short strangled pants as they gasp for more rope, his dad's faraway groan, his dad's hands clasping his own, the leather rope between them. There was always this thing between them, this thing handed from father to son.

As soon as his dad lets go, the dogs tear off. They're making for a tree – headbutting's a favourite pastime – but instead of charging it together, they split up at the last moment, forking at the tree and dragging him hard against the trunk, stretching his legs and arms like the bands of a catapult, scraping his nose, chin, belly against the rough bark. His bare hands burn. Why doesn't he get to wear gloves, like his dad? His eyes burn too, prickle with tears but he won't cry out, won't howl in pain, bawl at the dogs or his dad, won't let the shame show.

Folk are looking. Folk are laughing. His dad is laughing. The dogs are bastards, doing this to him when there are people about. People have stopped to look and point him out to each other. His dad's a bastard, standing there watching and laughing.

– Need a hand, son?

– Nuh . . .

– You've scuppered yourself, son.

– I'm okay, right!

– You need a bit more control, another wee lesson in leash management.

He isn't giving in. He's had it with giving in, had it with his dad's wee lessons. He'll just hang on like this, jammed up against the tree like a fucking clown until the dogs stop straining, until there's a bit of slack from one of them.

His dad's lessons took place out the back, in the concrete yard where dandelions and thistles burst through the cracks. It felt like prison, being marched around with the dogs, his dad ordering him about, barred in by windows on all sides. The dogs had their kennel in the yard and the run, well it was a big cage really, with a dirty great padlock on the steel door. His dad built it. He held pliers and hammers and bags of screws. When Tara had her pups – just the one litter – his dad threw in a couple of blankets. The pups were sold and then the vet sorted her. The vet said he could fix Cass too so he wouldn't strain so hard at the leash but his dad didn't want that. His dad thought that was cruel, though he whipped the dog often enough for it.

– Grip it like this son, close to the body, son, grip it like your life depended on it. Let them know who's boss.

He knows fine who's boss right now, who's always bloody boss. His dad just won't accept it, won't see that it's all he can do to stay on his feet, never mind trying to make the bastards walk to heel. But this is what they do; night after night they pretend that one day he'll take over, take his dad's place, put on the gloves and tighten the muzzles, clip on the leads and hit the streets, a team to be reckoned with.

It had to happen when there are all these folk out for the shows, drifting through the fog with their bouncy balloons and puke-pink teddy bears. He can see the lights, their colours milky in the fog, and hear a muffled mess of noise; squealing voices, roaring machinery, thudding music. Some of his pals have been to the shows already. Others will be there tonight. Pug told him about a new ride, the Magic Carpet, which swings up really fast and high and all the girls' skirts fly up. If you stand in the right place, you can see everything. Chantelle might be there. He'd like to watch Chantelle on the Magic Carpet, or anything else. He'd like to watch her being tossed about, squealing.

The rides make him sick and the sideshows are crap but he likes the food smells; burgers, onions, candy floss, pop-corn, all the warm, sweet, greasy smells. He likes the crowds, likes being in the thick of people, the closeness. And the noise. Once you're in there, the noise is like a wall, blotting everything else out. But the noise is too far away still to blot out the dogs, yapping and panting on either side of the tree and not fucking budging an inch.

– I've better things to do than stay here all night, son.

– Me too.

– Call it a day, son. Just call it a day.

His dad is flexing his fingers, as he always does, in a showy self-important way. His dad likes people to see his thick black gloves which make his hands look too big for his body, make them slow and clumsy and evil-looking, like the mechanical mitts of a robot.

The only chance to get free of this tug of war with the dogs is to go for one at a time. Cass is on his right. The dog is stronger than the bitch but his right arm's stronger than his left, so he wedges his left arm against the tree and tugs on the right with everything he's got and he can see it happening, he can see the bastard turn tail and trot towards him but it's too late to stop the pulling. He wheels round the tree, lands flat on his back in the wet grass and there's a shadow above him closing in, and the shadow raises its feet and stamps them down on his open hands. And then his dad's gloved hands reach down and clamp around the leashes before he lifts his feet.

The boy tries to shake the slimy leaves off his clothes but they cling on, like shreds of wet skin, and he has to peel them off one by one; they leave behind gouts of greasy mud. The shirt is ruined. It's his favourite; a real American skateboarding shirt from the best place in town. Weeks, no months, he'd saved up for it, served his time out the back with his dad and the dogs and now it's gubbed. He nurses his fingers in his armpits. He's finished with it all, finished. He'll never get to grips with the handling. And doesn't want to. His thumb's rigid. Maybe it's broken. Maybe his dad's broken his thumb. Maybe he should go to the hospital. He's surrounded by them. To the left, near the school, is the Royal. To the right, bang up against his old primary, is the Sick Kids. He was there a few times when he was wee, quite a few. He got to know the nurses and some of them were okay, kind, but he's too old for the Sick Kids now.

His dad and the dogs are plodding on. Their breaths echo, make holes in the fog. His dad holds his head high and stiff. The dogs, cowed by the whipping from their master, walk to heel, their hurt noses skimming the ground. The team dissolves slowly, melts away. The boy stays where he is. They're not his dogs. It's not his life.

CLEAN STREETS

Elizabeth Burns

In the dream there are white birds flying. But not flying, swinging – they're on strings and they're made of white china clay, not feathers, and they're swinging, swinging, up towards the glass roof and the blue sky. White birds shattering the glass and flying out.

I wake and see a slit of light in the crack between the blind and the window frame. The sheets are twisted. The room smells of our bodies. All summer I've been saying to Hal, 'Let's open the window,' but he doesn't want insects coming in, bringing germs. We use the electric fan, but I turn it off at night, I can't sleep for the noise. I get up now and switch it on. It starts its spinning and I hold out my arms, sticky with sweat, into the breeze.

Today is Wednesday. Today I'm meeting Kerry to have coffee and go shopping in the mall.

The birds in the dream: they're the ones that hang from the mobile in the shopping mall. That flock of white birds that come flying down to peck your face, to peck your skin away – The air in the mall tastes queer. It licks you cool all over, but sometimes I think I can't breathe it, and I run to the door for a gasp of outside, thick and warm and full of traffic fumes.

The air is clogged but the streets are clean, shiny clean. 'Cities stink,' my mother says, 'but not Toronto. It's the cleanest city on earth. You're lucky to be living there, Louise.' She says you could sit down on the sidewalk and eat your dinner off it. And the tiles in the subways! As clean as your own bathroom.

But they scrub everything so hard, it makes you feel dirty when you walk along the sidewalks or go down into the subways. And the heat . . . You feel dirty in the heat, even here, in these leafy streets with their own backyards, even here you feel dirty and it's hard to breathe. No wind all summer. Just days and days of heat. The sun beating down on shiny tarmac.

Hal wants air-conditioning in the house. He says we can afford it now Tim's gone.

'The fan's okay,' I tell him. 'The fan's enough, don't let's get air-conditioning, please Hal –' Don't make the air turn cold and queer.

I go downstairs to put the coffee on. The kitchen is gleaming clean and stuffy hot. I open the door and take gulps. Then I take Tim's card down from the wall and read it again while I'm waiting for the coffee. The Eiffel Tower. Hal said, 'If he wanted to learn French, why didn't he go up the road to Quebec? They'd teach him French. Why go halfway round the world when you could go to the next province?' But he wanted to go to Paris.

On the card he says he's heading south for the grape-picking. When I showed it to Hal, I said, 'Do you remember? Do you remember the fruit-picking?' 'Oh yeah,' he said, 'rained a lot,' and went out to the porch with his beer. But I could tell he was thinking about that summer. Picking peaches in the south of Ontario, in the farmlands where I grew up. It was so hot, and my skin was golden like peaches. That's what he said. I must have been strong then, outdoors all the time, up and down trees. I still try to get a tan, but it's not the same lying by the pool or in the backyard. Not like then, when the summer was warm and full of fruit, and Hal was a student down from Toronto and we used to lie in the peach orchards in the dark together. Then the bad weather came, and the peaches were over. After that, we worked on tobacco farms. Our hands sticky and black from the nicotine on the leaves. Washing yourself in a little outhouse and the farmer's daughters bringing out bread and spicy sausages for lunch. Staying in cheap motels on wet nights, getting up at dawn to look for work. Down in the town square, 'Is anybody hiring today?' Sometimes it would be too wet, and we'd hang out all day in a bar or a pool hall. Rain dripping into a tin pail. Going to bed in the motel.

We eat breakfast at the breakfast bar. Hal reads the paper. I stare at the Eiffel Tower. When he's finished, Hal goes and cleans his teeth, then he kisses me goodbye and it smells of spearmint.

I go up to Tim's room. I like to give it a dust, keep it clean for when he comes back. When I've dusted, I lie on the bed for a while, looking at his posters. I think about the secret life, about how everything could have been different if I hadn't told Hal I was pregnant. He was already back at college when I found out. I wrote and told him. He said we'd get married and live in Toronto and he'd find a job. But in the secret life, I think about how it might have been, just me and Tim, still living in the country near the peach orchards. Tim growing up the way I had, barefoot on the dirt tracks, swimming in the creek, knowing the names of birds. Sometimes I'd whisper to Tim, 'Don't you wish you'd been brought up in the country?' But he'd just shrug. I wanted to whisper too, 'Don't you wish you'd been brought up without your daddy, just you and me?' That was the secret life, inside my head. We'd have managed, me and Tim.

I'm lying on his bed staring at the hot blue sky, when I remember about meeting Kerry at the mall for coffee and shopping. But I can't. Not the mall. Not today, not the cold queer air of the mall, and the swinging birds. Not today, please Kerry.

I call her and tell her I've got a headache.

'Oh well, I guess we can go another time,' she says, but I can tell she's not pleased.

'Why don't you ask someone else? Why don't you ask Heather?'

'Heather's getting her hair done. Anyhow, I thought it might be fun, just you and me, Louise . . .'

'I'm sorry, Kerry, I'm really sorry. I just don't feel so good . . .'

But I feel good when I put the phone down. I kiss Tim's postcard and fetch myself a Coke and ice and go out on to the back porch. I look over to Mrs Wu's yard with the yellow roses clambering up the wall, and I think about the first time I met her, back at the beginning of summer, when I was sitting out here, same as now, drinking a Diet Coke.

She came out of the next-door house, a little Chinese woman carrying a basket of washing. I waved and called and she came over to the fence. I pointed to the Coke, offering her some. She laughed and shook her head, but then when I went over with the glass in my hand, and held it out, she took a sip. Then she made a face.

'Go on,' I said, 'have some more. You'll get to like it.'

'No,' she said, 'no, no thank you.'

Then she pointed to my dress and nodded.

'You like it?' It was a new one, a print with daisies on it. She nodded, and touched the sleeve, feeling the way the heads of the daisies were raised up slightly from the cloth.

'Nice,' she said.

'Thanks!' I did a twirl to show her how the skirt swung out, and we laughed. I looked over at the huge pile of washing she had. Then I said, 'You want me to come over and give you a hand?' We both looked at the picket fence between us. Then, 'Okay,' said Mrs Wu, and reached out her hand to help me over the fence. As soon as I was in her garden, I glanced at my watch, but of course it was still early, Hal wouldn't be back for hours. We stretched the wet sheets out between us, then flipped them over the line. They dripped on to the parched grass.

'No machine,' said Mrs Wu proudly, pointing to the washing. Her hands looked raw from wringing it out.

Afterwards she'd made me sit down on her porch, and she'd brought out tiny white cups and a pot of pale yellow tea.

'Jas-mine,' she told me, saying the two syllables separately, the way she said my name, Lou-ise.

The tea tasted strange but I liked it. She filled my little cup again and again.

When Hal got home that night, he said, like he always does, 'What did you do today?'

'Oh, nothing much,' I said, because I knew I couldn't tell him about meeting Mrs Wu and going for tea. He'd been muttering about the neighbourhood turning into Chinatown these days, all these people moving in. I said nothing. I thought about the dripping washing and the yellow tea. The fan whirred in the silence.

That was weeks ago but he still doesn't know about me and Mrs Wu. I'm sitting there thinking about her when she comes out into her backyard, and goes to pick some roses. She smiles as she holds them to her face and smells them. I go over to the picket fence, and she shows me the flowers. Then she notices that I'm standing on the flowerbed in my bare feet.

'Shoes?' she asks.

'They're over on the porch. It's too hot for shoes!' I wriggle my toes in the dry crumbly earth. When I move I leave faint footprints.

Mrs Wu invites me over for tea. I say I'll go back for my shoes, but she shakes her head: 'Please come.'

The tea today is the greenish one with the smoky taste. We drink, and then Mrs Wu brings out something to show me. A bundle of photographs. Chinatown. She goes there a lot, she used to live there until her husband got rich and bought this house out in the suburbs. 'I want to be a real Canadian,' he told me one day when we were sitting out on their back porch. 'All Canadians together, eh?' And he shook my hand and patted his wife on the shoulder. He was drinking the same beer that Hal drinks.

But Mrs Wu likes to go back to Chinatown. Her eyes light up when she tells me about it. In the photographs there's some kind of festival going on: fireworks, and paper lanterns and green and red and orange dragons. There are pictures of her sons and daughters and her baby grandson, sleepy eyes and a shock of black hair. There are pictures of children with masks on, and kites flying in the dark. There are flecks of light that are candles.

'It's beautiful,' I tell her. All I've ever shown her are holiday snaps – Tim, white and skinny, standing by a lake, Hal fishing, me cooking steaks on a barbecue. Once a bear came in the night, we heard it thumping the roof of the car, and in the morning there were scratch marks to prove it. I told Mrs Wu about it but I don't know if she understood.

As well as the photos of the festival, there are the ones I've seen before, of the streets where her relatives live. I love these pictures, with the stalls of fruit and meat and shellfish, and things lying on the sidewalk, baskets and boxes and heaps of straw. In one picture there's a kitten, in another there's a dog eating a bone. In the window of Mrs Wu's aunt's house there's a pot of red flowers, geraniums maybe, and a faded blue curtain flapping out in the wind.

I look at these photographs again, and then I ask the thing I've wanted to ask all summer.

'Will you take me there? To Chinatown?'

Mrs Wu frowns for a moment. But it's because she doesn't

believe me, she thinks she's misunderstood. When she sees I really want to go, she smiles.

'Okay,' she says. 'Tomorrow, okay?'

'Tomorrow would be great.'

I climb back over the fence, excited as a kid.

When I get home, the phone's ringing. It's Heather, to ask if I want to go to the pool this afternoon. 'Sure,' I say.

We've spent a lot of time there this summer, Heather and Kerry and I, lying out on the poolside, getting a tan, flicking through magazines, gossiping. After lunch, I pack my bag and drive down. Kerry's there too.

'Feeling better?' she asks.

'Were you sick?' asks Heather.

'Just a headache. I didn't feel like going out this morning.'

'So where were you when I called? I was trying to get you all morning.'

'Oh, I was just resting . . . I go upstairs to Tim's room sometimes, it's not so hot in there, and then it seems like a long way to the phone when your head's splitting open –'

Why don't you tell them you were having tea with your nextdoor neighbour? Why can't you tell them about Mrs Wu?

Mrs Wu's become a secret life too. But this is a real one, not in my head. She lives next door. I help her fold her washing and she brings me trays of sweetmeats. She rubs suncream on my shoulders and I give her apple pies. It doesn't matter that we don't know each other's language.

With Heather and Kerry I swap magazines and recipes and novels. We have coffee and we go shopping. I've known them a long time. But they don't make me feel calm the way that Mrs Wu does.

It seems that she is always cool, even on these hot hot days. She stands in the sun with a handful of yellow roses and she never gets flustered, she is always calm, with her sleek black hair with the streaks of grey and her beautiful pointed nails. She sits in her backyard under a paper umbrella and nothing seems to bother her. She makes me feel big and crumpled. But when I'm with her, she soothes me with her cool hands that are like my mother's hands on my forehead when I was sick.

And she's a secret, even from Hal. He hasn't guessed, even when she came round one Sunday and he was there. She came over the fence to the back door, bringing back a plate I'd given her with a cinnamon cake on it, my mother's recipe.

'Very good,' she said, nodding at where the cake had been.

I hustled her out on to the back porch.

'Come tomorrow, okay? Tomorrow? I'm busy right now. But thanks for the plate.'

'Who was that?' asked Hal from behind the Sunday paper.

'Just the Chinese woman from next door come to borrow some tea,' I told him.

'I thought they drank some fancy kind.'

'She said regular would do. I gave her some teabags, just a few.'

'How did she get round to the back door anyway? Over the fence? Doesn't she know to ring the bell at the front?'

'It must be the way they do things,' was what I said. And then I went upstairs to Tim's room and lay on his bed and started crying for no reason at all.

I lie at the side of the pool and wonder if Mrs Wu goes swimming. If she swam she would be like a fish, tiny and dark with glints of gold, gleaming in the water.

When I get back from the pool, Hal's home. He comes in from the kitchen with a beer.

'Louise, have you seen the dirt in beside the refrigerator? That card of Tim's fell down and I went to pick it up. It's filthy in there. You need to do something about it.'

I stand there nodding while he talks.

'It's asking for trouble in this heat. Remember when we had the mice? It'll be cockroaches next. I don't want people saying my wife doesn't keep a clean house, I don't want people saying we've got roaches. You'll have to take more care, Louise. You've been letting things go since Tim left.'

'Yes, Hal. I'm sorry.'

He's obsessed with disease. It comes from working in those labs all day where everyone's in a white coat and their skin smells of disinfectant. Scrubbed hands, starched coats. He thinks we should live in a lab.

I think about my bare feet digging into the warm dry earth. The dirt track when you were a kid. My feet used to be tough, no shoes all summer.

I go over to the refrigerator to peer at the dirt. He thinks diseases come from foreigners, too, not just mice or crumbs. He wouldn't say that in his scientist's voice, but I know it's what he thinks. That's why he wouldn't want me mixing with next door.

I couldn't tell him I've shared bowls of rice with Mrs Wu, that we've eaten from the same chopsticks. She's trying to teach me how to use them. We giggle and I drop a lot of rice. She kisses me goodbye on the cheek. Her perfume is lovely. It smells of flowers.

'I'll give the place a good clean tomorrow,' I tell Hal, and pour myself a Diet Coke.

After dinner, we take our coffee out on the back porch. It's still warm and you can see the fireflies.

'Ground's looking dry,' Hal says. 'Needs the sprinkler.'

When he's finished his coffee he sets it up, spinning over the dry grass and the crumbly flowerbeds. You can hear the water falling like rain on the rhubarb leaves. Hal goes inside to fix himself a whisky. I take off my sandals and step down from the porch. I can feel the circle of damp ground made by the sprinkler. I go over to the flowerbed by the picket fence, and I can't help it, I step on the earth, just to feel it damp and muddy and squelching up between my toes, and I bend down and pick up a handful of it and rub it through my fingers. Then I stand up and the sprinkler brushes over me, showering me with water so finely sprayed it's almost ticklish. I stand there and it comes round again and again and again, drenching me.

Then Hal's footsteps on the wood of the porch.

'Louise? What are you doing?'

I come towards him.

'Jesus, Louise, you're covered in earth, look at your feet!'

I look down at them.

'I'm sorry – I guess – I was just so hot and it seemed like a good way to take a shower –'

'Take a shower? You want a shower? We have a bathroom, don't we?'

He's angry, that tight-voiced anger, and he's gulping his whisky.

'Yes,' I say, nodding fast. 'We have a bathroom. I'll go and take a shower.'

Clumsily I put on my sandals, so I won't leave footmarks on the kitchen floor, and stumble inside.

I take a shower and I dab on some of the perfume he gave me at Christmas, though I hate the sweet sickly smell of it. I put on the dress with the buttons all down the front. Hal likes that one.

I go back out on the porch. The moon's up, right over Mrs Wu's garden. You can hear the sound of a television from somewhere.

'I'm sorry, Hal.' I touch his arm. He looks at me strangely, as though I am not who he expected to find at his side. Perhaps it's the perfume.

I sit down and undo the bottom button of the dress. My knees feel big and bony. I do the button up again.

But then he's standing behind me, undoing the buttons

from the top. It's better this way. He can't see my face. He can't see the way I clench my teeth when his big cold fingers touch my breasts.

I try and remember how it was, I try and think, we are lying under the peach trees and everyone else has left the orchard. It's you and Hal and he's brown from the sun, from picking peaches all summer and he says your skin is golden, he says it's soft as peach-down, he is stroking you all over in the moonlight –

But he's rough and drunk and it hurts so much you cry out and he shoves his fist in your mouth, and pushes you down on to the boards of the porch, splintery under your bare legs. The way he pushes, he's edging you off the raised-up porch, and your head's hanging upside down, seeing the sprinkler still going, seeing the moon. 'Stop,' you're shouting, 'stop, stop, stop,' and his whisky mouth's over you, roaring, 'Shut up, shut up, you don't want the neighbours to hear, do you?'

The neighbours. Mrs Wu, Mrs Wu. Can she hear you screaming? Your hands clinging to him because you're scared he'll shunt you off the porch. Biting your own tongue. Trying to stop yourself shouting out. 'Oh Mrs Wu, Mrs Wu –'

I am the bird in the mall, flying, flying, hitting myself on the glass roof, swinging in the wind, clay on glass, clattering and tinkling. Something has fallen and shattered. I will run home weeping to Mrs Wu. She will take me in her arms and feed me sticky-sweet dumplings full of honey and give me sips of jasmine tea.

I sleep the night out on the porch.

I dream I am a bird flying out through a window, but my brittle skin is breaking, I'm made of clay not feathers. Something is shattering around me.

When I wake up there are insects crawling over me.

There's a wasp drowned in whisky. All the buttons of my dress are undone. My body aches when I move.

I get up slowly and go inside. It's late. Hal's gone to work.

It's Thursday. Today I'm going to Chinatown with Mrs Wu.

I get washed and dressed and eat breakfast. I look at the Eiffel Tower card, then put it, quickly, into my bag. Then I think, I should write a note for Hal, and stick it on the refrigerator where he'll see it when he goes for his beer. I start, Dear Hal – but then I don't know what to write. I don't know how to tell him. I put down the pen and throw away the scrap of paper.

I look round the house, make sure everything's locked, like he tells me. Then I go to the kitchen door. I'll go out the back way, over the fence.

NAN MACDONALD'S GAMBLE

Hugh McMillan

People used to ask old Nan MacDonald where she got the idea for her roll-up and she used to say 'just a whim. A daft notion with a few pounds that's all.' She didn't dare tell anyone the truth, not even her daughter Ruth, who probably wouldn't have believed it anyway. Nancy had never been one for betting but after she'd retired and she and Jock were trying to live on their pensions she had occasionally looked at the back pages of the *Daily Record* and thought about chancing her arm in one of these accumulator bets, a four-horse Yankee, or a football forecast, or something like that. When she'd worked at McVitie's in Dundee the girls had often, daringly for the times, clubbed together for a flutter, sometimes put a bet on the whole race card, six bets in one. Jock had always frowned on the idea, though, told her it was a mug's game and that she'd be a pound better off at the end of the day if she didn't bother, and so it had always proved. Jock had a bit of a puritanical streak – his father had been a Wee Free. Then Jock had caught Alzheimer's, slowly at first but then with sickening speed and severity and his firm advice was no longer forthcoming. Jock began to talk disjointedly, or not at all for long periods of time, became peevish like a child and spent hours sitting in a chair staring out of the big attic window at the rooftops of Glasgow and the night sky.

They lived in a Kirk House, sheltered accommodation run by the Church of Scotland and though Jock had got so bad that she knew he should be in a Home, Nan did as much as was humanly possible to make his life comfortable and even tried to disguise the severity of the problem so they could stay in the big flat they shared in Royal Circus and had always loved. Exhausted by her daily exertions, she didn't give a thought to betting, she was more concerned with the growing problems of making ends meet and the lack of proper sleep that looking after Jock necessitated. She certainly thought of how great it would be to have a few hundred, or even a few thousands extra to pay for a treat or some of the things that Jock loved, like praline chocolates, or even pay for a nurse part-time, but she reckoned all that was an impossible dream. Then one day Jock had come down from staring out the big window, come down with his strange shuffling walk, and said, matter-of-factly, 'Dundee United to win the Scottish Cup 3–2 from Motherwell after extra time.' This was strange; not only was it decisive and coherent in a way Jock seldom was these days but Nan knew for a fact that the Scottish Cup wasn't even at the First Round Stage. She knew it because she followed football, had done since the days when her Dad used to take her by tram to Dens Park. She always looked out for the results from Dens and Tannadice, hoping, of course that the news from Tannadice was bad.

'What?' she said. 'What did you say, Jock?' But Jock had sat down and was staring milky-eyed at the TV as usual, not seeming to hear or see anything. After a while she'd given up, gone on with her knitting, a wee cardigan she was making for her granddaughter Janet who was a year old.

The next day Ruth had brought the child round while Jock was having a bad day, keeping telephoning his old work telling them he'd be late or not back till Monday week. She took the receiver from his hands for the sixth or seventh time and turned to her daughter.

'He shouldnae be here, Ma,' Ruth had said in a hard voice. 'Yer no'up tae it. It'll kill you.'

Nan shook her head. 'Here we are and here we stay,' she had said cheerily. As she was saying it she remembered her own mother's voice, rallying them all when her Daddy was laid off. Here we are and here we stay.

'Am no having it, Ma,' Ruth had answered, unmoved. She had inherited the same steely resolve, thought Nan, even as she was wishing her daughter would go away and come back some other time when Jock was calmer, watching the TV perhaps.

'Am goint to go to the Social Services, Ma. I am.' Her arms were folded and her wee foot was tapping on the lino. Janet was sitting in her nappie, trying to move her toes to imitate her mother. Nan smiled in spite of everything.

'Och Ruth, things'll be fine. You see if they're not.'

Her daughter fixed her with a look. 'Yer no managing though, are ye? Look at the state o' this place. Ye cannae manage him and a big place like this, can ye?'

Out of the corner of her eye Nan could see Jock reaching for the phone. 'Aye Jock,' she murmured, 'phone for reinforcements.'

That night, after she'd put him to bed, she was sitting in front of the fire with a small whisky and she was half listening to *Sportsnight*, half mulling over what Ruth had said to her, when she heard Dougie Donnelly say something like 'an easy cup win for the men from Tannadice over Second Division Arbroath at Gayfield' and then nearly jumped out of her skin because Jock was suddenly standing at her elbow shouting 'GALWAY GIRL IRISH GRAND NATIONAL AT LEOPARDSTOWN 60–1 WINS BY EIGHT AND A HALF LENGTHS'.

After she'd put him back to bed she rang Ruth's. As she'd hoped, it was her son-in-law Fergus who answered.

'I'm doing a quiz,' she'd said, 'in one of the papers. When's the Irish Grand National?' 'Sometime in May,' he'd answered in a puzzled voice, 'a good bit yet anyway.' 'Thanks very much,' said Nan and quietly but with great determination put down the phone and reached for her pen.

Two days later as she was taking Jock a walk in the park through the fractured sunlight and the wet trees, he stopped her and with great tenderness placed his hand on hers. It was the first time he had intentionally touched her for the best part of a year. She looked into his eyes and it was almost like looking at him again the way it had been walking out with him down the Seagate, him in his big scarf and her in her tartan muffler, the day she'd proposed to him. Jock pulled her head gently to his. 'Jock, Jock,' she whispered, 'Jock, my love.' A tear was trickling down his cheek, though the eyes were unblinking.

'Rodger the Dodger,' he whispered, and his voice was soft and smooth like a young man's. 'Rodger the Dodger in the Greyhound Derby. Comes from nowhere round the last bend.' Nan put her head on his shoulder and wept.

Over the next ten days, with great care and precision, Jock made two more predictions, one when he was on the toilet and the other when he was shuffling round and round the settee in their living room. Plymouth Argyle would win the 4th Division Championship and Tom MacKean the Olympic Gold Medal. 'Are you sure, Jock?' Nan had asked, after a bit of research, 'the Argyle are third bottom just now but I can swallow that nonetheless, but Tom MacKean? Are you sure?' And Jock, as usual, had not answered, just dribbled a little bit and Nan had wiped it away carefully with a napkin.

The day after, it was a Saturday, she had got the Matron of the Block to look after Jock for half an hour while she'd gone for a walk, and had gone into the Ladbrokes on Crow Road.

'What can I do for you, love?' a young man had asked.

She had produced a sheet of writing paper from her handbag. 'Could you quote me odds for these?' she asked. 'I want to put on a six-bet accumulator like we did at McVitie's, the girls and I.'

The man frowned. 'There are only five things here,' he said.

'Indeed,' answered Nan. 'I believe the last and greatest is yet to come.'

It took some time but when Nan hurried home she knew that the odds so far – on the accumulated five bets – were four thousand to one. When she got back she thanked the Matron profusely. 'I didn't realize he was so bad,' the woman had said, 'I really think we'll have to discuss things.' Nan had politely hurried her out of the door, settled Jock for a wee while then opened the third drawer of the bedroom cabinet. She took out a small enamel box and counted out the money she'd scrounged from the pensions and the housekeeping over the last few years. It came to £251.42p. She counted it out again, feeling the folded notes in her fingers, thinking of all the times she'd nearly spent it on a little piece of this, a wee bit of that, and had drawn back. Clever girl, she thought, clever girl. It was what her Ma and Dad had called her when she brought home her first pay packet from the factory, clever wee girl.

Over the next few weeks she waited and Jock had got worse and worse. He'd taken to shouting, disturbing the other residents and had once looked, in his frustration and confusion, as if he was going to hit out, slap her with one of his great paws, but he hadn't, he couldn't. Jock was as gentle as a baby. Mrs Miraglee the Matron had alerted the Social Services and so had the Home Help who Jock had sworn at, and they'd been to Ruth who had given her tuppence-worth, tenpence-worth knowing her, and the outcome of it all was that they had to be assessed, assessment being some fancy euphemism for incarceration and there was no way Jock was going to be locked up, he who had fought the Africa Korps and gone into battle with Nan's letters bound by ribbon in his breast pocket.

'Come on, Jock,' she had said, 'what is it? Tell me: It'll set us free,' but he had been silent, though his head was shaking, the veins in his temple throbbing as though some giant battle was being acted out in his head. Then the day before the final assessment, in the midst of twitching and whimpering, he had rushed upstairs and she had followed and he had looked up through the wide window over the chimneys of the city and had said, calm for a moment, 'Aliens will land on Glasgow Green on Christmas Eve.'

When he was fitfully asleep she had got one of the long-suffering neighbours to pop in and had nipped out, though nipped was not the word as she was so exhausted she could only just drag herself through the puddles. The bookie had to make several phone calls, the manager emerging at last to say, 'We'll give you 50,000–1 on that one.' She'd carefully unrolled the money, the original sum supplemented a bit by the latest pension, had filled in the form and taken her receipt.

Over the next few months when she'd visited old Jock as she did every day, in spite of the fact she had to change buses three times and her own health was not good, she had given him the good news. Galway Girl by a mile, Rodger the Dodger from nowhere, Dundee United in injury time, Plymouth Argyle on goal difference. They'd even watched the TV together as the four Kenyans in front of Tom MacKean had fallen down in the final fifty metres as if swept by an invisible hand from the track. Jock took nothing in. He was fading, really fading, his skin was turning transparent as if one day he was going to disappear. His breath was shallow, his eyes blank or filled with silent panic. The hospital was nice enough but it had few windows, none to rival the one in the attic at home, so on Christmas Eve, while she was pushing Jock in his chair through the grounds she had hurried him to a waiting taxi, got the man to help them up the stairs and had locked the doors and while Mrs Miraglee knocked and knocked she had held him in his old chair, one of the few pieces of furniture still unpacked in preparation for her leaving, and they had both stared at the darkening sky while she stroked his forehead as she used to and they waited, thinking each light in the sky was *the* light, the light of their love, come over the towers of the University and all the grey guttering of Glasgow, to restore them.

CARLA'S FACE

Candia McWilliam

An undertone overlaid the proceedings, escaping through the small crevices between what people said and what they meant. The whole day had taken its toll, from the first unfair bright promise after dawn, until now, when they all sat around with nothing to do after the funeral itself but to drink, or not to. Either option demanded a dedication Carla considered she was short of. She'd come to the island right the way over from Stirling where she'd built up a loyal clientele who appreciated her and the facilities offered by her discreet salon opposite the steakhouse. You'd not get women on an island coming to a person known to be a hairdresser/beautician, not regular enough at any rate to make it worth Carla's while. Twenty-two women on the island, each one prepared to visit a hairdresser maybe the twice in her life – for her own wedding and a daughter's. At the outside, if there were more daughters, up to five times, including baptisms and other people's funerals. So that made a maximum of, say, sixty visits to the hairdresser by each generation. Supposing Carla could expect her working life to last forty years, that averaged out at one-point-five clients per annum, not overwhelming. Topped up, she'd to admit, by doing the hair of the dead. But that was quiet, too; vital, but quiet.

They died at two peaks, the islanders; too young, or very old. The old ones looked prettier, more silvery, less troubled, than the young ones, who as a rule died violently, by drowning or in drink. They got very green as to the complexion when they'd lingered below the water for a good while. The drink made them blue or purple. These were colours you could not massage back to a natural shade unless you caught the body fresh, with the blood vessels suggestible. Carla loved soothing the skin of the dead, it was like putting a quarrel straight for good and all, but the business was slow in a place where there lived no more than a hundred souls, all known to her so well that they seemed like part of herself. As they were. The old ones were the cousins of her grandparents, the middle-aged ones cousins of her parents and the young ones her own cousins, some of them by now parents. On the mainland they fell pregnant as young but were not always as young when they carried a baby the whole way up to the birth. There was no hiding a baby on a piece of land the size of a hill dropped into the sea, dwelt on by more gulls than sheep, more sheep than people and as many herons as children, as many eagles as professional men, and those two eagles soberer.

The doctor was speaking just now, in the front room after the funeral, looking out through the window at the waves that pushed closer as the day advanced. The graveyard was in sight, stones leaning away from the sea and few enough in number to look sociable not military. If rain came suddenly, a family could picnic among the stones for shelter, passing around the salt for the hardboiled eggs. On the stones grew lichens like dried lace and damp velvet. The grave that was newest, around which the men had all stood at the funeral today and thrown earth down on to the coffin in quantities that did nothing to cover its nakedness, that new grave was bright and freshly-made now, with a puffy quilt of mainland-grown flowers high upon it. The flowers would be taken by the rain and the wind even before the rabbits could get them.

Between the two commitments, to take drink or not to, the doctor had taken the high road to heaven and was not drinking. From time to time he went out to his car to remedy this position he had assumed as a man deserving of respect, by taking a nip from the quarter bottle in his glovebox. There were further quarter bottles, to the total of two and a quarter bottles, in places known to the doctor. When it sank below the two bottles in reserve, he became edgy and was a less effective physician. Since there was but the one shop, it was known well what dosage of liquor the doctor prescribed for himself.

So, today, he was not drinking, in contrast to the minister, who held it only right that he, in his position of confidant and comforter of the mourners, should share with them in the loosening and rinsing out of their grief.

'He was a fine specimen,' said the doctor.

'Rare,' said the minister, thinking of the broken heap of flesh and breath that Andrew had been in life. He'd had arms like the sides of feeding sows, loose and pendulous below the one defined strip of lean.

'Rare? That he was. No one like him at all, at all.' The doctor's stern sobriety was catching up with him quicker than the minister's dutiful boozing.

'All God's creatures,' said the minister, seeing an opening to an area where no one could gainsay his superior rights of access, 'are differently wonderful.'

'Differently wonderful,' said the doctor, who, truly sober, would have been turned away by the soap in the words.

'Are you telling me,' asked wee Ian, who had been drinking all the way since Glasgow, which made a train's worth followed by the ferry's worth followed by the welcome from the island followed by last night followed by the freshener before the funeral, the stiffener in the kirkyard and now the serious drinking, 'are you telling me that you came over all the way, Carla MacDougall, just to do Andrew's make-up for his coffin?' If, in life, a man had worn make-up in sight of wee Ian, his voice suggested, he'd've laid him out cold.

'Make-up,' he said. Indeed the word did sound unseemly and dishonest in his mouth. He said it so's you heard what make-up was, thought Carla; a made-up thing, a lie. She didn't think lies were so bad. You might need the odd small one. Wee Ian was too big for the front room, though it was his wife's; he worked on the mainland and came home for a long weekend once a month. He was in quarrying and wanted to get into stone reconstitution. The only work on the island was old-fashioned work, with no future. From time to time wee Ian stretched out his hand for a pork pie and popped it on the end of his tongue like a pill. The acids in his saliva made short work of it before even he reeled it in to the shelter of his teeth. Gratefully his stomach took the liquefied food and dismissed it, needing more soon after.

'Andrew, now; did he look good, according to your estimation, when you'd finished with him?' Ian seemed to be, thought Carla, quite interested in the technicalities, for a man who'd never taken her profession that seriously before. She sipped her wee drink, couldn't mind what it was, she drank that rarely. Anyhow, it warmed her in the head, and she thought kindly of Ian as she spoke to him. He'd been a handsome boy for one summer, and beautiful light on his feet. She'd never had the luck. Now no woman would call him luck if he came her way; all the veins in his face had risen and flowered red under his big hide. Whereas she, who had been a mouse, was, say it herself though she did, transformed since a girl. Getting away from the island had started that. No one in Stirling knew what she had started out with, or why exactly she had each feature, like the people on the island did, on account of knowing every exact last detail of her ma's pregnancy and labour. In a place as small as this everything was explained because there was nothing to do but talk and little but one another to talk about.

'Jesus, Carla, you're different fi how ye was,' said wee Ian. She could not deny it. She'd been a plain kid with legs like pudding pushed in tight to its bag. Her hair had been a mat of turfy brown, and her teeth all over the shop. She'd known nothing of presentation and the art of making the best of herself. Her skin had freckled up like a blotched bird's egg then and she'd no clothes to speak of. And absolutely no poise.

She recrossed her legs and tugged at the jacket of the ensemble she'd ironed this morning on the same kitchen table where the night before she'd worked on the scunnered dead face of Andrew. She ironed at the table on an old yellow blanket so stiff it squeaked under the iron. It had been nice working at that table because of the view down to the churchyard and the flickering advances of the sea, lifting the small blue creel boat that was tied to an iron loop under all the yellow seaweed. She curled a sleek loop of red hair behind her right ear; it was a semi-permanent tint called Unfair Advantage. In her ears shivered silvery sections of what looked like chainmail for fish. These were cool against her neck, calming her when she made herself take another sip, for the conviviality. Her legs began to get the tense feeling they had when she'd held a pose for too long for the Stirling Amateur Photographic Club. She could feel all the tendons twanging for release. But, even though it was just Wee Ian, she decided to give him the full toe-balanced, calves-tensed treatment. As a matter of fact, she could do her exercises at such snatched moments, she'd found, and men never noticed, though women could deliver funny looks. It was pure envy.

Carla had evened out her skin tone for years now by the use of the sunbed in her salon. Honestly, she did not know how other women did without. Her whole skin'd a gorgeous tan, a deep colour, more rose-brown than holiday-brown, she liked to think. She tanned in her undies from modesty, not for health reasons. You did not know when a client might require an impromptu appointment, and readiness was Carla's watchword.

Wee Ian was as uncouth as most of these men, thought

Carla; she could not have borne it if she'd lived here to this day. Not the way she was now, used to the gracious things of life and a certain style.

Carla'd done nail extensions on herself after fixing Andrew's make-up for his coffin. She did not want his family to feel she'd taken no care with her own grooming, like an operative, when they were all family if you thought about it.

'Yes, I will, thanks,' she called to Jessie, who was passing with a plate of ham sandwiches and a bottle, although with her back to Carla. Jessie looked at her in a startled way, and extended and poured. Picking up the sandwich wasn't easy as it was the sort with a big edge on it, crust was it? Nail extensions meet more peaceably around a thinner sandwich. To eat the sandwich at all required two hands, of which only the thumb and forefinger could be used. The nail extensions perforated the bread otherwise, and collected butter and ham in their long copper-coloured arcs. The copper was an echo of the Unfair Advantage. It had been a wee treat to herself on turning forty, the colour change. A shift to the mellower register as a sign she'd no quarrel with anything life might send her way.

Ian was watching her in several directions like a man watching a tank of fish. It was a sign of the way he could not hold his drink, Carla thought. His eyes strayed over her face and body and he looked as if he might cry or be sick.

'Jessie,' he called, 'ye mind Carla?' Ian had only married Jessie from necessity as Carla recalled it. He'd broken all the other hearts his one brief summer of flower, and Jessie was the sensible one of all the girls. Except that she'd married Ian, reflected Carla. 'I do that,' said Jessie. She was slight and had more grey than black hair and a plain old suit in navy wool with sheepdog hairs on it. Not one to set a living room alight, Carla could see.

'Will I get yous a nice cup of tea?' Jessie asked Carla, looking into her painted eyes with clean blue ones.

'How *did* you *guess?*' said Carla, socially, in a great swoop before she finished the rest of her glass, against waste.

As Jessie left, Carla saw how Ian rubbed his wife with his shoulder, quite hard, as though he'd an itch, as she went past with her tray and her dishcloths and her used plates. Flat shoes, Jessie wore, and her face was weathered like spring petals late in the season. Jessie dropped a kiss on to the head of her husband. It was like going unclothed in public, thought Carla. How could a married woman do that?

The doctor came in from outdoors, a healthy flush on him. It was colder than ever out now the stars were starting. Some people with children had taken them home. There was music, the sound of a fiddle from the upstairs room and something on the telly or the radio from elsewhere in the front room. No, it was worse. It was the minister, singing, quite a few of them singing. It was worse even than that. It was religious music, sung quite ordinary-style, as though it had any place in folks' houses. 'Be ye lift up ye everlasting doors, so that the king of glory shall come in. Who is the King of Glory?' They asked the question of each other with their big drunken faces hanging down off their eyebrows. Then they answered the question, nodding, looking pleased as though they had just recalled a name they'd earlier forgotten from an important story. 'The Lord of Hosts and none but He the King of Glory is!' They looked very pleased about that. No one seemed embarrassed at this inappropriate moment to bring God up, when he'd had his way already in the graveyard and at the funeral with the tears being blown off their faces by the wind. Indeed, they were giving this singing their all. It is the way with drunk men, thought Carla.

She took a glass from behind a photoframe with a snap of Ian and Jessie's Rhona holding up a lamb with a face looked like it'd been drinking ink and the black had seeped all into the whirls of wool. The glass was half full; she took the stuff in it down in one and returned the glass carefully behind the now less interesting photo, tucking it thoughtfully in under the support at the back of the frame, so's it wouldn't disrupt Jessie's decor. Such as *that* was. There was another glass needed tidying in this manner, Carla happened to see, just in behind the curtain that had not been drawn. The sea showed only as a crisping pale blur the size it seemed of a hand mirror under the white simple moon. Otherwise the water might have been sky, fallen down to meet the land. She replaced the glass behind the curtain. The creel boat bobbed on the lifted water or floated in the sky, whichever was which. No sound went on as long as the sound of the sea, that was always there. Two hundred yards from Ian and Jessie's house, the graveyard had gone blue and then grey and was now silver.

'If you give her the tea, Jessie,' said the clearly drunken doctor advancing before the brown pot that loomed behind him, 'I'll try to help with the other wee bit problem.'

It was the usual way for Carla. She was just looking about to see who 'her' might be, when she realized it was her own self they were on about. People never let up talking about her. It was why she'd left the island in the first place. No privacy. No time to yourself. No life of your own. No respect, for you surely could not have that in a place where you were too well known.

'Milk, Carla?' asked Jessie, 'or straight?'

'You go on and laugh at me,' said Carla. 'Laugh. I'm soberer than the lot of them. And prettier.' The fat ugly drunken men in the corner looked at her and resumed their indecent singing of the psalms of David in metre.

She felt the familiar powerful helplessness when she gave in to the instinct to do something wrong. As a rule, she did this late at night in the salon, and she would run around talking to her now absent clientele as she did within her head when they were present, answering with her truth instead of their own, anatomizing their faults and explaining why they were right to fear death. Another great advantage of loneliness was the freedom it gave you to meet yourself. And often the self you met was different from the one you'd met before.

'You're tired, Carol dear,' said the doctor.

'You look exhausted yourself, doctor,' said Carla. 'By the same token, if I may so say. And it's Carla. I live in Stirling now.'

'Is that right?' asked the doctor, getting busy with a glass of water and rattling a glittery sheet of what she could have sworn were jumping beans. 'You don't have to change your name when you move house,' he continued. 'I know people who've emigrated down under and they're still called what they were always called.'

'What's that?' asked Carla. She wanted to know the name of someone who had gone all that way, down to Australia. If she'd've done that it wouldn't have been anything as ordinary as Carla she'd've selected.

'The name they were always called. Their first name. The name they had first. I don't know. There are too many to think.'

'You either know no one who has been to Australia, or you are a very drunk man,' said Carla, and she fell to the carpet in a shining heap of orange limbs and pleated aubergine wool, thus avoiding the gelatine-and-insult placebos the doctor had been about to offer her. Her mixed hair, the mauve-red of neepskins and beetroots, lay more successful than the rest of her assembled self, in a rich fan on the carpet. Her poor disgraced faceful of paint had melted under the onslaught of the day.

Jessie began to pour tea for the thirty or so people left in the room. Each time she went back to the kitchen to fill the pot again, she gave Wee Ian a new thing to do. While she poured and milked and sugared the first few teas, Ian carried Carla to the kitchen table, and laid her along it, rolling the tablecloth up against her so that she wouldn't flop on to the plates of biscuits or curl up around the two big trifles Jessie had done in crystal-type bowls for when the last drinkers began to cry and need their pudding, around five in the morning that would be.

While Jessie dished out the second wave of teas, Ian did as she'd told him and went to get cotton wool and glycerine from the bathroom. Carla had that horrible orange skin, he thought, skin that needs watering, it's so parched, dried out to the colour of the sand in Bible lands. She was the colour of certain stones you got in quarries down in England, terrible thirsty stones that lasted less than eight hundred years.

Mind you, he thought, Carla herself must've been thirsty. She was out like a light. As he remembered it, she'd not done this to herself as a girl, when she'd been nothing to look at and never been anywhere but the island. He shook the glycerine in its bottle. It sparkled and shattered like crazy jelly and then pulled itself together till it was back to looking like water.

He was behaving sober but knew as he watched his careful actions from his brain that felt as though it was up on the dresser with the diesel receipts that he was not. He got very good at exacting tasks about a day into a blinder. But, God, he could take it. He was four times the size of the wee orange creature passed out on the kitchen table.

'Undress her,' said Jessie, pouring hot water into the shiny brown teapot that seemed to be spelling letters out of its spout in steam. 'Not right the way down. And fold her suit.'

The aubergine ensemble came away in three pieces. Each time he lifted Carla, he tried not to look at her body. This meant looking at her face, at the unpeeling animal-like false lashes growing off her eyelids, at the runs of mauve and fibrous black that had rained down her cheeks, at the awful shredded moustache of colour that had crept up from her mouth to her nose through the cracks in the orange mask that was like a dry riverbed. When he'd got down to her underthings, he saw she was orange all over except inside the plain flesh-coloured undies that were not the colour of her flesh. Inside them she seemed white as candles. The tiny white hairs grew out of her hard skin the way a pig's did out of a ham. The bottoms of her feet looked nice and soft and ordinary. He covered her with the tablecloth.

'Here's your tea,' said Jessie. 'Now go upstairs and fetch me one of Rhona's magazines. Nothing too way out. I want one with a make-up page. You know, Ian, a step-by-step to teach the wee girls how to put on the war paint.'

Ian had been about to start. He enjoyed the topic of his own daughter and make-up, especially if he'd had a dram. 'Ye'll not leave the house like a hoor!' and so on. He had all the words ready in his head and had heard them said to his sister by his own father. 'What d'ye want to paint your face for, to show it to laddies who've known you unpainted all your life? Eh? Wee hoor? Laddies that're mostly your own folk? Speak out will ye? And don't be insolent!' He knew what to say.

'Say *nothing* Ian,' said his wife. 'And don't wake Rhona. She keeps the magazines on the chair by the bed.'

He came down the stair with a pile of the slippery scented coloured rubbish falling out down between his belly and his forearms. When he got back, Jessie had shut the door from the kitchen into the front room, so he closed it too. On the table under the cloth lay stiff, thin Carla, her face cleaned off by Jessie, who was just wiping it around the forehead with a swab of cotton wool. The white fibre was like snow next to the red-brown skin whose colour was cooked deep in.

'Find me the clearest chart you can. You know the kind of thing. "Getting ready to go out on a date." Something like that. Don't say it's disgusting. It doesn't mean the kids are doing anything. It's practice.'

'Eh?'

'For courting.'

'Rhona?'

'Rhona's fourteen. One day you'll fall off the boat and find she's a big girl. Let her learn. She's safe here, at least. All she does is try out faces. Now, you hold that guide up for me and I'll have a try with the stuff out of Carol's handbag. She'll feel better that way.' Carla's bag contained many pots and sticks and wands, all of them with complicated names that gave no sign of where on the face they were intended for. Jessie worked slowly, without confidence but with the care of a good cakemaker following a new recipe. Layer by layer, as the light for applying colour to a human canvas grew clearer with the rising of the sun, Jessie remade the face of an older Carol into that of a younger, easier, Carla. Ian sat beside the kitchen table and spooned trifle into his mouth, sops of sponge and sweet sherry and custard and dream topping with a delicate adornment of coloured sugar strands falling to his acidic stomach to lie there and counteract with soft bulk the headache that was forming in his head, a not wholly unwelcome reminder that he was alive, that it was a new day, that his brother lay quiet in the earth beyond the house and before the sea, and that two women he had known all his life were close to him in the morning's light, one absorbed in kindness and the other returning to herself.

In the living room beyond the door, those mourners who had not yet left slept in the places where they had at last succumbed. The doctor and minister were away. A familial intimacy carried from body to body. Nothing was ugly. In the creek below the kirkyard the boat lay up on the hard brown sand. The sea was only a white rumour beyond the rocks.

LEAVING ASSYNT

Anne MacLeod

It was breakfast, Sunday morning. Mary turned to Iain;

– You're off, then? she asked.

He nodded.

– See you later.

– No, I won't be here.

– Suit yourself, he said, slinging the rucksack over his shoulder. I'll be off the hill at five. I'll phone.

– I won't be here, she said again.

He shrugged. The front door banged.

Mary drained her coffee, and stood up slowly, carefully. Her back was sore, but she had a lot to do. She left the dishes lying on the breakfast bar, Iain's greasy plate, now empty of bacon and black pudding; her own more modest, sticky with marmalade. If he could ignore the dishes, so could she.

She heard children crying somewhere, she wasn't sure where. It was hard to localize sound on the estate. It could have come from next door, or from across the road. She'd never been able to work it out, and wouldn't learn now.

The box-room was locked, but she knew where to find the key. She strode to the tall-boy by his bed and pulled it from the wall. The floorboard was still loose, the keys and money tightly stuffed in an old sardine tin. It smelled of rotting fish. Mary emptied the tin, left the tall-boy stranded. Packing did not take long.

Her suitcase stood by the front door, with her coat and

umbrella, and the mirror she'd bought in its Mackintosh frame. Iain liked that mirror, but it was hers, she'd always made that clear. He was welcome to the rest, on hire purchase, most of it, except for the video player which they'd rented. The argument last night started over the video. She'd been playing it too loud, too late, so he said. He had to be up at seven, he yelled. The boys were calling at eight. They hoped to fit in three Munros, weather permitting, and he couldn't sleep with that noise, as she fucking well knew.

– For God's sake, Iain! she shouted. Can you think of nothing but bloody hills?

She eased the volume slightly, nonetheless. She still felt obliged to compromise, but this did not mollify Iain, who began the familiar catalogue of her shortcomings. She couldn't be bothered, stared ahead blindly. There was nothing here, nothing to stay for. Iain didn't want the baby.

She sat up all night. Iain came down at four but didn't speak. He stumbled to the bathroom, left the door swinging open. She hated the sound of urine splashing in the lavatory. After all the beer, there was a lot of urine. He flushed the loo noisily, yanked the handle up and down like the lever on a one-armed bandit, then swaggered back as if he'd won the jackpot, smirking. He hadn't washed his hands. Mary shut her eyes, pretended sleep, ignored the stink of urine. Ignored Iain. She was leaving.

At breakfast, she asked him for the key of the box-room, told him she was leaving. He didn't believe her. She'd threatened this before, when he slept with the girl from the corner shop, and later when, despite all he had promised, he organized a day in Inverness with the same woman. He pretended he was hill-walking. Mary knew better. The whole village knew. They made sure she had every detail.

And she knew where he kept the keys, so it didn't really matter that he wouldn't answer when she asked for them. It didn't feel like stealing when she took the money from the tin. Half of it was hers, and the other half she felt she'd earned. There wasn't that much anyway.

Life had been easier when Iain was working. Redundancy left him permanently angry. Impotent. It didn't help that the rest of the village suffered, except the few involved in fishing. Mary kept writing, but poems didn't bring in ready money, and one by one her sidelines faltered. Her grant ran out. Fewer tourists bought her tiny tapestries, woven in tender detail on long winter nights. Her savings were almost gone. A small legacy from her mother was all she had left, and she didn't want to touch that. It was for the baby. That had always been the plan.

Mary sighed, slipped on her coat, strapped the umbrella to the case, and pulled it carefully out of the house, over the step. She slid it along the short path and eased it into the car, aware that every eye in the street would be upon her, screened by scalloped net. She didn't care. She hated scalloped net.

Lifting the mirror, she found a small crack in the left-hand corner. She hadn't seen that before. It was a bad omen, perhaps, something she'd failed to notice in these last unhappy months. She could replace the mirror, but not the frame. She thought of Iain's claim to the mirror, fifty-fifty, he'd said. It belongs to both of us, even if you bought it. Well, he could have the mirror. She sat down in the hall, stripped backing tape from the frame, eased the mirror out. He could have the crack, the seven years of bad or indifferent luck. She could do without it.

She stowed the frame in the car, slipped back to make a final tour. The house was astoundingly small. How had she fitted in? Had she ever fitted in?

With an effort, she refrained from steeping dishes in the

sink. She wasn't coming back. She didn't have to leave the kitchen tidy. She locked the door, left the keys below the mat.

Mary strode towards her waiting car, opened the door, and stooped to enter. Her hand shook as she turned the key, willing the engine to start. It choked and shuddered painfully, but clung to life. There was petrol enough to reach Ullapool, she saw with relief. The pumps here did not function on the Sabbath.

As she swept out of the street, Mary did not look back. Nor did she halt at the Free Church to survey the village. The dipping inlets of the fjord no longer attracted, life was too harsh in this landscape, unmoving, unforgiving. No wonder Iain was hard.

It was March, but winter lingered on the chiselled hills, snow flurries clawed and inland lochs were deep in ice. At times the narrow road disappeared in drifting snow. At others, a cold sun dazzled, even through protective glasses. Mary knew this tortuous way by loch and moor and mountain, but conditions were so bad that she was frightened. If turning had not seemed more dangerous than going on, she might indeed have stopped, but she pressed forward, inch by inch. She would make it. She could do it, if she took her time.

The mountains always panicked her, steep, overbearing; pegs of ancient rock the ice had failed to sweep away, though not a scrap of soil remained on scoured stone. This was giant country, not a land for children.

She was only four months pregnant, and the child hid deep within her, but the wonder and the love for this yet untested human had become the focus of her own existence. They hadn't planned to have a child, not yet. Iain was not ready. He had too much still to do. The uninvited foetus was a tragedy to Iain. Iain wanted an abortion. Mary didn't. Mary wouldn't, and the rows had escalated, sweeping away the softer surface of their partnership, baring unrelenting cores of disparate rock.

Mary wanted this baby more than anything else in life. It wasn't a clump of cells, it was a baby, her baby that she would love and care for, shout at too, if she was honest. Mary wanted the baby more than she wanted Iain, more than she had ever wanted Iain, if she had ever wanted him, which she now doubted. They had become a habit, a perfect combination of would-be-child and would-be-mother. Iain was happy enough if she indulged his every whim, but selfish, he gave little back. The pleasure of serving, that was what Iain offered, like all too many highland men. She didn't need Iain.

What she needed was somewhere quiet and warm to sit and think things through. And a job, she needed a job; she wouldn't say she was pregnant, not yet. It didn't show, and she would need the money. She would start in Inverness. There'd be more chance of a job in Inverness.

The radio fuzzed at Inchnadamph, and Mary realized it had been playing all along, and she hadn't heard a single thing. She flicked a cassette on at random, and flinched at the moan of pipes, a lament, one of Iain's recordings. She sighed. She hated bagpipe music, spare, unyielding; loneliness inherent in the wailing. Iain had tried to interest her in pibroch, ceol mhor. She'd never come to like it, yet today, lost on this bitter road, fighting all the elements, she felt the gracenotes ebb and flow like life itself. Mountains and snow became beautiful, part of a dance you could recognize, but never describe, not adequately, not in words.

These were not her native hills, yet here she was, alive and free, the child within her dancing to mountain music, music of the spheres, overreaching snow and fear. You did not have to climb and conquer hills to understand them. You did not need to live within their shadow to respect them. You did not have to sing their song to dance.

The snow turned to rain in Ullapool, and Mary, peaceful, drew to a halt outside the Ceilidh Place. She would visit the bookshop, she thought, have cappuccino, relax before the next leg of the journey into softer, gentler country. The hills crowded softer here, rounder, green in the distance. Trees grew. There were signs of life. There were streets and people.

As Mary reached for her coat, her eyes were drawn to a couple emerging from the bunkhouse below the road. They kissed in wind and rain, the girl pressed hard against her partner. They might as well be naked, Mary thought. Then the man raised his head and smiled. Mary knew that smile. When she first met Iain, she'd found it irresistible, as this new and unknown female did too.

They broke apart, mounted the hill arm in arm, passing Mary directly. Neither noticed. Iain stopped, pulled the woman to him, fed his obvious erection. She laughed, and placed her free hand in his pocket, fondling, fondling.

The Ceilidh Place swallowed them, while Mary, retching, strove to start the car. She drove as quickly as she could.

She was halfway through Strathkanaird before she realized she was driving north, back into the storm.

THREE TALES

Jane Harris

THE STORY OF BAGPIPES

Once upon a time there lived a great warrior, feared by all who knew of him for his merciless nature and skill in battle. The warrior, let us call him Ahltnagash, was head of a tribe, the existence of which has long since slipped from memory. And perhaps that is how Ahltnagash would have desired it, for he trained his people to be sleakit. They lived in caves along the shores of lochs beneath the grey-blue shadow of an ancient volcano, Stac Pollaidh, painting their skin with dyes made from a leaf that they gathered in the glens, wrestling bears, and calling wolves in from the forests with hypnotic cries, then taming them, or perhaps eating them, depending on their mood and appetite.

Ahltnagash was the most fiersome warrior of them all. His dark hair, when loosed from its metal clasp, tumbled to his waist and it was said that all manner of beasts lived in his curls, and not just insects, for the story went that a mouse had once found shelter there, and a weasel had dived in to hunt it out, then a hungry owl with a weakness for rodents had made its nest and lay in wait somewhere in the thick of Ahltnagash's mane. But this could all have been talk. Ahltnagash's arms were rumoured to be as thick as most men's waists. And it was heard that he'd once offered a fortune in pink river-fish to anyone who could find a tree-trunk in the forest that was thicker than his thigh. And everyone knew that Ahltnagash had the bluest eyes anyone had ever seen. They were bluer than the distant island mountains, bluer than the kyle when the sun shone on the shallows and lit up the coral sands below. They were bluer than the flowers of the forest and the midnight sky in May. And any woman caught in their gaze would freeze and, just as quickly, melt.

But Ahltnagash had little time for women, unless they were warriors, as were most of the females in his tribe. For Ahltnagash lived only for battle, indeed, fighting was something of an obsession with him. So terrified were the leaders of the other tribes, that one year they finally forgot their differences and held a secret meeting in the largest and bleakest glen and hatched a plan to murder the fiersome Ahltnagash.

And so it came about that one night, as Ahltnagash rode alone along a mountain deer track homewards, a band of a hundred men fell upon him with clubs and spears. And though he fought back with the strength of ten bears, they pierced his body in thousands of places and beat him about the head until he was senseless. Then, as they'd planned, they gathered dozens of great stones, tied them with strong ropes about his unconscious body, and cast him into the deepest loch of those regions. Satisfied that he would never again terrorize them, they threw their arms around each other in manly embraces and went straight home for tea, each already planning, now that Ahltnagash was out of the way, how he would do the others out of their goods and land.

Now, as soon as the chill water of the loch hit his body, Ahltnagash regained his senses, and alas, realized he was helpless against the weight of the many great stones dragging him down, down to the bottom of the mirky deeps. And as he fell, struggling with his bonds, he knew he was sure to die and cursed the beards and testicles of the men who had overpowered him. But suddenly, just as a last flurry of air bubbles tickled his cheeks and the dark closed around him, he felt a hand grip his jerkin and swiftly, one by one, pale fingers as slender and sharp as blades shredded the knots that bound him. As the heavy stones tumbled, firm hands grabbed them and propelled them onto the shore, and Ahltnagash was borne up, up out of the darkness and expelled from the loch. He lay, gasping, while gentle hands cleared the weed and water from his eyes. And when he could finally open them, he saw all around him the stones that had weighed him down, cast upon the shores of the loch in a raised beach. And he saw beside him the form of a beautiful woman, dressed in a flowing green gown made of the weeds that floated in the loch, and he knew as soon as he saw her that he'd been saved by a water spirit.

The woman, let us call her Balahuilligh, placed him on a spongy bed of sphagnum moss and built a fire. Then she crushed sweet-smelling herbs and tended his wounds and bruises. After he'd slept, she fed him with wild mushrooms, round berries as red as jewels and savoury morsels of lichen, holding the food to his lips and trickling cool water from the sweet burn down his cheeks. Wherever Balahuilligh moved on land, Ahltnagash noticed that she was followed by a timid and watchful deer which she tempted with scraps from a pouch clasped at her waist. Many days passed before he was well enough to sit up, and during that time Balahuilligh took care of him, disappearing for short periods into the waters of the loch, where she told him she must keep vigil, leaving the deer to watch over him. At dusk, she would lie beside him, stroking her deer's stunted horns, and let Ahltnagash rest his head on her womb, in silence, or sometimes she would tell him wonderful stories about the history of her peaceful people, who were destined to roam the oceans and all the waters of the land, saving those who were drowning. Ahltnagash was enchanted by her beauty and by her stories. And Balahuilligh the water spirit looked deep into his eyes, and they were bluer than shimmering stripes on the great blind fish of the deeps, bluer than the flash from an electric eel's tail, bluer than the heart of the bluest sea anemone. And despite the fact that he was a warrior, and thus forbidden to her, she felt herself melt.

They fell in love.

They spent many weeks together once Ahltnagash was well, walking hand in hand through the silent forest, on warm days swimming in the waters of the loch and in the evenings lying in a clearing on their bed of moss and telling stories. But as time went by, Ahltnagash began to worry about the people of his tribe, and the woman-spirit also became anxious, for here were many lochs and seas to tend, many souls to save from drowning, and she was cursed, for if she failed in her duties, she herself would languish and die.

And so, after much sighing, and resting of heads on each other's bellies, they made an agreement to part, and Ahltnagash made her a promise that he would never pick up a weapon in anger again.

'Let us offer each other a gift,' said Ahltnagash.

'But I have nothing to offer except my love,' said Balahuilligh.

'Then we must make something,' said Ahltnagash, and he turned into the forest to look for the raw materials for his gift. When he emerged into the clearing, Balahuilligh and the deer had gone. He set about making his gift, then waited. At dawn Balahuilligh returned alone with the mists, stepping silently from between the trees. Her face was flushed, her eyes shining. She handed Ahltnagash a set of musical pipes, the like of which he'd never seen.

'These are a token of my love,' she said. 'Take care of them. For I made them from the bones and belly of my deer.' She showed him how to hold and play the pipes, by blowing air into the bag and pressing his fingers to the holes she'd carved in the slender deer bones. The pipes made a beautiful, haunting sound, unlike any he'd ever heard. Balahuilligh taught him a hypnotic, lilting melody and as he played, the notes rising up from the instrument made tears spring to his eyes, and all the beasts of the forest crept close to the clearing and wept. Balahuilligh told him that if ever he wished to see her, he must take his pipes to the top of the highest hill and play the tune, and as soon as she heard, she would come to him.

'But,' she warned, 'you must only use the pipes when you wish to see me, or for some other peaceful purpose. They must never be used in anger, and you must promise never to use them in battle. Otherwise,' she said, hanging her head, 'I cannot say what might happen.'

Of course, Ahltnagash agreed without thinking, for he was so in love, and had already resolved never to fight again. Then he looked sad.

'My gift is no longer of any use,' he said. He held out his hand. In his palm lay a small bell which he'd fashioned from the wood of the forest and metal from his belt. 'It was to hang round the neck of your deer, so you would always know where she was.'

Balahuilligh smiled sadly. But she lifted the bell and fastened it to tinkle around her own neck. 'Now you will be able to hear me come,' she said.

And so they parted and many years passed in peace. Balahuilligh rejoined her sisters and tended the waters, saving drowning souls, and Ahltnagash returned to live in the shadow of Stac Pollaidh, where he discovered that the soil was quite fertile. And he took up farming and the gentle pursuit of fishing and in the evening entertained his people with the beautiful melody of the pipes. He taught them to till the soil and advised them to raise goats. And whenever his longing for Balahuilligh grew unbearable, he would climb to the top of the highest hill and play her the lilting melody, and within minutes, he would hear the tinkling of her bell and she would come to him.

But as the years went by, Ahltnagash became restless. Around him he saw other tribes conquering more land. And before long, he grew jealous and greedy, until one day, he flew into a rage at the thought that one of his old enemies had camped at the foothills of Stac Pollaidh itself. And forgetting his promise to Balahuilligh, he climbed to the top of a hill and taking out his pipes, he blew on them like he'd never done before, blasting out a fiersome call to battle. Angry notes spiralled from the pipes and across the landscape, and his people came running from the fields and down from hills where they'd been tending the goats. Ahltnagash commanded them to dust off their weapons and the tribe marched off across the moors towards the enemy camp, their leader at the head, playing a fiersome tune on his pipes. Clouds gathered, and the sky grew dark, and the sea began to froth and boil. So frightening was the sight of the Ahltnagash tribe, charging on through the lashing rain, so terrifying the wailing of the dreadful instrument clenched in their leader's hands, that the enemy took to their heels and fled even before the tribe had come within a mile of the foothills. Ahltnagash and his warriors picked off a few stragglers, and returned home victorious, the warrior chief at their head, blasting out a rousing march on his pipes above the wailing of the wind and the crashing of the waves on the shores.

For seven days, the storm raged. Once it subsided, and he had washed the dirt and blood of battle from his clothes and skin, Ahltnagash grew lonely and longed to see Balahuilligh. So he took his pipe to the top of the highest hill and played his lilting tune. Notes floated across mountains, over lochs and through forests. He waited to hear the tinkle of her little wooden bell. But no one came. Again, he played, a more haunting tune. Still, she didn't appear. Ahltnagash played on until dusk fell and then he returned home, dragging his feet, desolation filling his soul, for he realized what he had done, that he had lost her for ever.

And far away in the depths of a distant loch, Balahuilligh listened to the sound of the pipes and wept. For not only had she lost her love, but the instrument had been used in anger, and she and all her sisters were now cursed and must turn from saving drowning souls, to tempting men to their deaths in the waters.

And soon, men heard of the power of Ahltnagash's pipes, and of how they made the fiercest enemy fly in terror, and they sent spies to his camp, and made their own copies of the pipes Balahuilligh had fashioned for love from the bones and belly of her deer. The men used them to terrify their enemies in battle, and for every such pipe used in anger, Balahuilligh and her sisters were cursed to take the life of another soul by drowning.

Every day, Ahltnagash would climb a hill and play his lilting tune, but Balahuilligh never came. And Ahltnagash grew bitter and angry. Once again, his only pleasure became battle-blood and conquering land. Before long, he had quelled the mainland tribes and was lord of all the land around him, from the mountains of the north to the rolling hills of the south, from the sandy shores of the east to the sea-lochs of the west. And before long, he cast his eyes further westward, towards the many islands dotting the coast, and resolved to become master of them too.

So he set sail with a hundred of his bravest warriors across the narrow stretch of kyle between the mainland and the nearest island. But as the boat left the shore, the clouds grew dark above their heads, and the sea began to boil and the winds blew them far out across the ocean and huge waves pitched and tossed the boat and finally dashed it against the reef.

And Ahltnagash, weighed down by his weapons, tumbled into the sea, and drifted down, down to the darkest deeps. And as he sank through the salty water, he sensed the weight of many hands with slim sharp fingers upon his shoulders, pushing him further down, down, and he felt a gown of green weeds suffocating him, tangling across his eyes and clogging his throat, and he heard, through rushing of the heavy water, the tinkling of a tiny wooden bell.

THE SPIDER AND THE KING

There was once a fierce, many-limbed creature lived all alone on a great stone plateau, in a world where twilight was infinite, where rain was unknown, where all around were sheer faces of rock and where far beneath the creature's dwelling, lay a huge valley of stone and sand. Food was scarce, light was dim and life was hard and the creature could not remember a time when things were not so. And for a long time, it knew only how to survive. This it did by pumping fine threads from tiny tubes on the undersurface of spinnerets on its stomach. From these silky threads, the creature wove huge nets all over the world, constructions of great beauty, suspended across every plateau, bridging every valley, and even highly ornate ones, tucked in the corners of the sky. This work was one of the creature's only pleasures, and often it took intensive planning, weaving, breaking, folding and reconstructing, to create something of a satisfactory design.

Yet the nets were not only things of beauty. They also had a practical purpose. Occasionally, from a far corner of the world, where things seemed dazzlingly bright, much too bright for investigation, there would begin a faint droning. And the creature would freeze, and try not to get too excited, and wait. And often the droning would fade and die, and it would be left with dripping jaws and aching claw joints and a desperate hunger inside. But sometimes, the sound would grow louder and nearer, and out of the gloom, a fat winged beastie would appear, with a ripe blue body, and tender flesh. With luck, the beastie would blunder straight into one of the sticky nets. The more it struggled, the more entangled it would become. The many-legged creature would abseil down cliffs with the help of silken ropes, climb, slowly but surely up sheer rock-faces, hurry across the floors of valleys, until finally it reached its prey. Whereupon it would bury its claws in the flesh of the struggling captive, sucking out juices and soft internal parts. Then it would mend the net and return to its lair.

And so life went on. The only time the creature knew fear was when, on occasion, giant beasts fluttered into the world, beasts much too big to be caught in the nets and it was only by dint of pressing itself into cracks in the rock that the creature escaped the snap of their sharp, bony mouths and fatal blows from their heavy wings.

Once, while travelling across a far corner of the world, the creature was set upon in the dark and overpowered by another many-limbed beast and in the struggle, felt a sharp, stabbing pain as something pierced its body. The creature lost consciousness for a moment but when it awoke, exhausted, it saw its enemy scurrying away across the valley floor, and in a fury, it launched itself on the beast and devoured every pick with great pleasure, before climbing, exhausted, to a place of safety.

And soon, the creature sensed a great change in its body, a ripeness, and heaviness it had never known before. An important event was about to happen. Without really knowing why, but with infinite care, it began to spin a small sack.

The king had had enough. It had been a bad summer. Successive heavy defeats at the hands of the southern enemy and even by his own countrymen had exhausted him and at the onset of winter, he'd been forced to flee his country and seek shelter. Which was how, he ruminated, kicking at the damp turf with the edge of his boot, he found himself on this godforsaken island, lodged in a household of idiots, surrounded by pedants, jackals and women. And several months of ostracization in such company had led him to complete despair.

He glanced along the boggy headland, where he had come in an attempt to clear his head of choking peat smoke and female gossip, and decided to make for an intriguing crop of moss-covered rock which rose up from the beach to form a craggy headland. The sky, to match his mood, had been growing muddy above the waves. As he trod miserably through bog and mire, his legs felt heavy, and he growled as the first drops of rain spattered his cheeks.

Soon, he glanced up at the headland, checking his progress. Deep hollows in the rock surface promised caves and the thought cheered him slightly. He'd always liked caves. Even as a boy he'd found comfort in the still, dark air of a cave in the rolling hills behind his family home. It was there, alone, that he'd first discovered his manhood, and such was the joy and deep pleasure of the find that for weeks he returned there, often many times in the course of one day, to renew its acquaintance. He found that the pleasure increased if he availed himself of some soft, delicate garment belonging to his mother. This, he would sniff and stroke gently against his cheek with the left hand while the right was occupied elsewhere. And afterwards, he'd feel rested, his mind clear of confusion. Even now, he marvelled at the energy that gripped his loins in these private moments, the bitter tang of his milky seed, and the renewed purpose the activity gave him.

Just the thing, him in the state he was in.

And with a sudden burst of energy, the king hurried on.

Eventually, the creature completed the fine decorative stitching on its sack. Its body had swollen greatly and it felt weak and heavy. But it knew the work was not yet finished. Before long, pain gathered in a tight band around its abdomen. Waves of agony, like hot knives, ripped through its belly. It writhed in terror, gripped with a desire only to die, every fibre straining to be rid of the load that tore its flesh in two. The torture was eternal, sending the creature in and out of a stupor. And just at the moment when it felt it could no longer bear the torment, something gave way and a creamy froth of translucent eggs burst from its belly and, gently, the creature eased the seething mass into the safety of the sack and stitched up the opening.

Nearly there, panted the king. He splashed through a small burn, and clambered up its bank. His boots sank into the last stretch of sodden moss below the rocky outcrop. He'd already picked the cave from a distance, the middle one, with an overhanging shelf at its entrance.

Nearly there, thought the creature. Now to find somewhere no intruder will follow. And it considered all the corners of the world, determining a secure hiding place for the sack. High above, the rock changed form and split into many packed layers and crevices. There was one particularly deep fissure, right at the brighter edge of the world, where the eggs could nestle undisturbed for as long as necessary. Picking up the strings of the pouch, it began to climb.

Hellfire! offered the king, as he cracked his skull on the low opening to the cave. He stooped for a moment, rubbing his brow, bestowing upon all humanity, and in particular the Welsh, a swift volley of oaths and imprecations. Then he crouched and peered into the shadows. As his eyes adjusted, he saw that the cave was a shallow structure, with high, uneven walls, spattered with bird dung. But the air inside was warm and dry and the floor comfortable and sandy.

Oh, apposite, said the king, and he scrambled in on all fours.

Hellfire! thought the creature, as it lost its footing and tumbled backwards, clutching the pouch. It sprawled, winded, for a moment. When it recovered, it saw with terror a huge hairy giant of many colours, larger than any ever seen, crawling across the floor of the world. The creature froze, afraid to make a move. But the giant, which had only four legs, seemed ignorant of the surroundings, and stretched itself out, as if for sleep. So the creature made some hasty repairs to the sack, and with renewed determination, recommenced its ascent.

Pox! muttered the king. Having made himself comfortable, he had conjured his most usual images, to no avail. Perhaps the bang on his head had affected his other parts. This was worrying. He tried again, summoning a veiled maiden who danced before him, twitching up her skirts to reveal her ankles. Nothing. He urged into the picture another maiden, more amply endowed than the first, and had them press their bosoms to him. Still nothing. He set the maidens upon each another to lap at their parts, but neither this image nor the introduction of a slavering hound, which pinned each damsel in turn to the floor, caused a stir. He wished, all too late, that he'd lifted some frivolous feminine garment from whatever blasted chamber in the blasted household where he blasted lodged. Some fragrant wee thing, like the snatched fripperies, embroidered with fine silken threads, that belonged to his mother. Deciding a change of tack was necessary, he fell upon the image of a young boy, no more than sixteen, who murmured his name, and adding a breathy 'master', turned on his stomach and offered up his sweet, spicy buttock cleft for a lingering kiss. But it was no good. All that should be turgid, was flabby as pulverized mutton;

strain and buck, lay limp in his palm like a withered rabbit's ear.

Pox! he groaned and rested his hand.

The creature took a second tummel, crushing a leg, and paused to survey the damage. The leg shivered, limp and useless. It would drag the creature down. In a fury, it turned on itself and severed limb from body with a swift flash of cutting parts. Trembling with pain and exhaustion, it looked to where hairy four-legs lay. The giant shifted, and uttered a low sound. Perhaps he too had been injured, and was nursing his wounds. Ensuring no harm had come to the pouch in the accident, the creature limped off again, resigning itself to a more circuitous, but less hazardous climb, with only one deep gorge to be crossed.

The king lay on the floor, humming, and stroked his limp parts abstractedly. It had definitely been a bad year. Defeat, exile and now, the potency of an inebriate eunuch. He gave up. With a sigh, he glanced towards the roof of the cave and noticed a shaft of sunlight cutting through the gloaming.

The creature crawled along a rock shelf and paused at the edge of the deep gorge. The light here was blinding. Each renewed effort had drained it of energy, and it realized that this climb was a journey towards the very threshold of death. But first, it must cross the gorge. Easier said than done, for it would have to fire out a strong thread, out and up, and then climb across the gap to reach the higher ledge on the other side. Ensuring the pouch was safely fastened, it gathered all its remaining strength, and shot out, out and up, a sticky, silvery rope, which caught and danced in a shaft of sunlight.

* * *

The king gasped, for out of nowhere appeared a shining silken thread.

Slowly, inch by inch, the creature crawled along and up the thread, clutching at the pouch to make sure it wouldn't fall. And slowly, inch by inch, it reached the other side.

Mither! whispered the king, alone on the sandy floor. He'd closed his eyes the instant he saw the silken thread for it had roused an image that troubled him, and he tried to push it aside. It was a memory of his mother, pressing her finger to his mouth, then unfastening, one by one, the clasps of her robe. A single silken thread hung loose from the ornately embroidered bodice as she pushed it aside to reveal her pale, heavy breasts.

The king groaned, and something stirred and twitched in his hand. He was picturing his ten-year-old self, gazing in wonder at the flesh emerging from his mother's garment, remembering it had always been as if he was seeing it for the first time. Still smiling, she gave her almost imperceptible nod of permission. And slowly, he bent his head and fastened his lips about her nipple. As he lapped and suckled, his mother sighed, and closed her eyes, stroking the hair at the back of his neck. And he reached out his small hand to her loose garment, patting her softly.

Success! thought the creature. With a titanic effort, it hauled the egg sack over the threshold of the crevice and stored it tenderly in the darkest nook, where it would be safe from even the sharpest and longest bony mouth. And having thus ensured the birth of its babies, the creature lay down right beside the pouch and drifted towards death, happy in the knowledge that when the ravenous babes burst forth, they'd feast upon the body of their mother, nourishing themselves with her blood, in preparation for the rigours of the grim life to come.

* * *

The king chuckled. He felt loose, clear-headed and buoyant, as if the spaces between his bones were filled with air. He scooped up a gobbet of his seed with his fingers and smeared it across his lips. To think he'd almost given up hope of tasting this rich and salty dew.

It just showed you.

He fastened himself in all the necessary places, and rolled over on to his hands and knees, feeling a little shaky. He rested there a moment, considering the deserted cave. There was, on reflection, something a little eerie about it. The overhanging layers of rock, the mirky crevices. No creature in its right mind would spend longer than necessary in such a place, he thought. Thus, he nodded sagely to himself, its desertion. Moreover, the mire he'd lumbered through on his approach would deter all but the most foolhardy. Shivering slightly in his damp duds, he reflected that no mincing sassenach cavalry could make way effectively across such boggy ground.

Of course! he cried, shuffling to the cave-mouth, anxious to be away from the place, with a dripping mutton-leg before him and a glass of ale at his elbow, for he'd just had an idea.

THE STORY OF TARTAN

Many years ago, there was a princess who could speak only the truth. Her father, the king, was troubled by this, as the land he ruled was a land of lies. The problem began in early childhood, when the princess would look around her as they travelled on horseback through the mountains and glens and say naive things, like: Why Father, those people have only turnips to eat! or, Why is that poor woman carrying such a heavy load of peat? Luckily for the king, no one but he seemed to understand what his daughter said, and at her every comment, his courtiers would merely nod and remark: Jings, what an ugly hag you are (meaning My, what a pretty chick! Remember this was a land of lies) and: She'll be gey lucky to find a husband (meaning: Ah, the time will come when many a heart will be broken by those dark eyes like forest pools). The princess was confused, but did not give up hope. One day, she thought, more of them will truly hear my words, and the people will come to understand me. The king managed to keep control over his subjects by entertaining them with a constant supply of beer, the occasional border skirmish and frequent public executions. But as time went on and the girl grew to be a beautiful young woman, she became even more vocal, and spoke the truth on many embarrassing occasions. But Father, she'd say, why do you make treaties with our sworn enemies in the south? and, Father, it is surely not right that the Chancellor should drink so much wine and beat his wife across the back and legs with a great leather belt. The princess so liked the sound of these truths, that she repeated them many times. And as the years passed, it became distressingly obvious that people were actually beginning to hear and understand what the princess said, and, worse, to speak the truth themselves, for now they would say, Ah, how beautiful she is. And maybe she has a point.

The king became very worried, for his subjects were beginning to doubt his ability to rule and despite extra beer and a flurry of disembowellings, he heard disturbing tales of truth rallies in the low lands and honesty meetings in the high lands and even in the castle itself where he'd gathered a faithful court of the most renowned fibbers in all the world, there were murmurings of discontent. He summoned his Chancellor, the greatest liar of them all, to ask advice. The Chancellor frowned, because he was very happy, and said:

Your highness, it would be absolutely inadvisable to cut out your daughter's tongue.

And thus, the matter was decided. The king summoned his daughter and told her not to stick her tongue out, whereupon, being, despite her incorrigible honesty, an obedient child, she poked out her tongue, and quick as a flash, the king cut it off.

For a time, the kingdom returned to a healthy state of deceit and the king was very happy. The princess kept to her room and seemed to have lost both the desire to tell the truth and her appetite. But the princess was determined, as well as pious, and little did the king know that with the help of a wise woman who'd been cast out of the village, his daughter was learning to read and write. The wise woman would steal into the castle at midnight and from then until dawn, she would teach the princess new words, by showing her them on pieces of rice-paper, which the princess would then eat, for though she had no tongue, she still had her teeth. The lessons began with short, easily digestible words, like 'cat', 'sat', 'mat', which the princess devoured without even pausing to wipe her lips, and within weeks she'd progressed to a steady and more extravagant diet of words and phrases, including 'censorship', 'self-perpetuating oligarchy' and 'meretricious'. At last, after months of word-meals, when the princess couldn't force another piece of rice-paper past her lips, she and the wise woman knew it was time. They took paper and pens and the wise woman watched while the princess scratched out her first simple message of truth to the people. The princess so admired the words on the page that she repeated them many times, to drive the message home. Then, like the wind, the wise woman ran from glen to glen, distributing the princess's words. At first, the people were puzzled, unable to see the truth written on the pages clutched in the wise woman's hands. Besides, hardly any of them could read. And those who could thought, well, after all, ken, these scribblings are only the crazed philosophy of a dumb princess. But the king's daughter did not give up hope. One day, she thought, more of them will be able to read and make true sense of my words and the people will finally come to understand me. And as the weeks went by, and her messages passed from hand to hand, from the cities of the south to the mountains of the north, from the sands of the east coast to the mists of the western isles, and as more people learned to read, they became curious to understand her words and some even began to believe what they read in the papers. But alas, once again, there was a whisper in the king's ear, and he learned of his daughter's midnight activities. Once again, he summoned the Chancellor, who postponed beating his wife, and rushed to his master's side, wiping the wine from his lips. The king relayed his problem and the Chancellor frowned, for he was very happy, and said:

Your highness, it would be a great shame indeed to kill this wise woman and to chop off your daughter's right hand so that she could no longer hold a pen.

And so, the matter was decided. The wise woman was hunted down in the forest and murdered and the king himself summoned his daughter and chopped off her right hand.

Once again, the kingdom returned to a state of complete falsehood and the king was very happy and felt quite safe, for he not only cut off his daughter's hand, but ordered her to be locked in one of the castle towers. Years passed with no event of consequence. The princess, after moping for some time, regained her appetite, though she seemed to require nothing but a diet of fruits, mosses, seaweeds and vegetables. Paper and pens were banned from the castle, but the king allowed his daughter some wool and a loom, which she could pedal with her feet and feed with her remaining hand. A harmless domestic task, thought the king, but little did he know that the princess had not given up hope. In her tower, she boiled vats of the fruits, moss, seaweed and vegetables and dyed reams of wool into many subtle and different colours. She hung hanks of moss green from the rafters, draped rosehip red around her couch, stowed deep blackberry blue beneath her bed and tucked delicate buttercup yellow away in tissues in the closet, so that its brilliance wouldn't fade. Over the months, as she dyed and dried the wools, she conceived in her head a code of colours, so that when the fibres were woven together in designs of stripes and checks of varying width and hue, each pattern would contain a simple repeated message of truth. When she had enough coloured wool, she began to weave, her one remaining hand feeding fibres into the loom, her little feet pedalling furiously. She produced many designs, each using a different pattern of stripes and checks, each with a simple message of truth woven into the plaid. She worked day and night, making ream upon ream of the beautiful, coded cloth, and, with the help of the wise woman's daughter (whose birth was in fact the cause of her expulsion from the village in the first place), began smuggling the cloths out of the castle. The princess knew that at first, the people would not understand her messages. Indeed, the wise woman's daughter brought back terrible tales of how the people had seized on the cloths, stunned by their beauty and in their confusion and desire to be surrounded by subtle colours had made the fabric into all manner of tasteless things: lap-rugs, footstools, coats for wee dogs and daft tammys. Some of the men had lost the place altogether and were draping the cloths around themselves to make exotic skirts. Eventually, whole industries were set up around copying the designs and producing similar cloth. But the princess carried on weaving, piling the cloths around her room and smuggling them out of the castle at night. It will take time, she thought. But one day the people will be able to read the messages that are woven into the cloth and they will finally come to understand me.

A STORY OF FOLDING AND UNFOLDING

Ali Smith

My father sits on the bed in the bedroom at the back of their house, one hand just brushing on the raised ridges of the candlewick cover over the continental quilt, the other holding a pair of women's pants coloured a very light pink. The light is on in the room at four o'clock in the afternoon.

The room smells clear and airy, of something like talcum powder. There are fitted wardrobes that, if opened, reveal clothes neatly arranged with shoes jigsawed into pairs in the dark at the bottom. There are fitted cupboards, this one full of presents given by friends and children, some placed on one side waiting for use, some stored on the other to be recycled usefully into presents for friends and other relatives. In another there are books of photographs, albums over forty years since the first one. Next to this cupboard there is a mirror, round which photographs of children are stuck, slipped in at the corners in the little gap between the mirror and its rim. There are bottles of perfume on the dressing table in front of the mirror, and a pair of glasses, and leather gloves with the shapes of hands still in them. In one drawer are boxes of jewellery, little plastic boxes that say *Silvercraft* on the tops, with necklaces, brooches, rings nestling inside them on cotton wool strips; these boxes are, just in case, hidden under a magazine called *Annabel* dated New Year

1977. On the front of the magazine the year's horoscopes are promised.

Two bedside tables stand on either side of the double bed on which my father is sitting. One has a clock-radio and a still-tidied store of crime fiction and fishing books, the other has three small pillboxes that, when you open them, have separate compartments for different tablets. Beside these are medicine bottles and pill bottles made of plastic, different sizes arranged beside each other like the architectural model of some complicated building. Each table has its own lamp, and the one with the plastic bottles also has an electric blanket regulator next to the lamp.

In the chest of drawers two drawers hang open, one hangs lower than the other. In the middle one are brushes and combs, and a collection of lipsticks. This drawer smells pleasant, waxy and thick of make-up. The room has the air and the smell of someone who's just left, throwing the last lip-print paper tissue crushed into a ball into the tin wastepaper bin, her movement through the room displacing the settled air like a light breeze in humid weather, but it's winter, and the big light is on, the room is stark, and my father is sitting on the bed looking at his feet or the floor.

The pants resting in his hand are smooth, you can still see the crease from their having been ironed. In the chest of drawers, in the open drawer next to the one filled with lipsticks and brushes, there is women's underwear, and round my father on the bed is spread more, more pairs of Marks and Spencer's cotton ladies' briefs, smooth cotton coloured in pastels, blues and pinks, peach colours, in little haphazard spilling piles, clean, soft from having been worn and washed. My father's fingers are large and rough, the seams of his fingers look dark against the slightness of the pair of pants he holds; he is holding them as if he doesn't even know they're there. He is looking at his feet. The pants lie gently round him, colouring the room so that he looks out of place, some country swain from a Thomas Hardy novel wooing someone he has no chance of having on a hillside of meadow flowers, offering one his clumsy hand has pulled up, not knowing the words to say it with.

In the open drawer are larger, longer pairs of white pants, made to offer more support to stomachs, made of a material that shines when the electric light catches it. My father looks up from the floor to the drawer, and turns to look at us, standing in the doorframe of the room. Then he looks around him at the scattered contents of the first drawer he's picked to unpack. 'What,' he says. 'What am I supposed to do with all of this?'

*

Twenty-five, after the war, after having pretended to be old enough to enlist in the navy. After his bombed boat with the drowned bodies in it is taken into harbour in Canada, and they saw into the metal side of it and the bloated bodies gush out with the water; after recovering from his arms mysteriously stopping working, all the muscles refusing to respond. Just before his mother dies of cancer and just after the nightmares about the planes coming over start recurring, one of the electricians is larking about with his apprentice mate in the women's dormitory of the WAF station while the women are all elsewhere working. The electricians are wiring some lights up in the places men don't usually get into, and are high with excitement, high as boys at being let loose in with the beds and the imagined smells of women. The room is hardly exciting, it's a drab room filled with the air of punctuality. The beds are identical, identically made, sheet folded over blanket and pillow tucked under, regular and neat, tightly packed; each bed has a wooden chair and a knee-high locker next to it, and there is nobody supervising the men because today the electrician is in charge.

The lights have to be wired with cable which must be fitted next to the ceiling all the way along above one row of beds, and the electrician is teaching his apprentice how to fix cable tidily so it won't be noticed and so nothing can be hooked on to it to bring it down. He's holding the ladder steady while his apprentice nails the thin cable up along the top edge of the wall, where the wall meets the ceiling.

The ladder is positioned next to one of the first of the lockers in the row, and as his apprentice hammers, his head squashed sideways against the ceiling to do so, the electrician notices that the door of the locker isn't properly shut and so he gingerly coaxes it open with his shoe. The locker door clanks alarmingly loud, the apprentice shakes on the ladder, and the electrician steadies him and halts the door's swing with his foot, at the same time he checks behind him to see that nobody is coming into the dormitory. The two men grin at each other in delight.

Pictures are stuck all over the inside of the locker door; the electrician recognizes a picture of Bogart sitting on the other side of a desk from Bacall, and shouts up to the apprentice, 'This one likes hers ugly, mate!' On the shelves of the locker clothes are crammed; the electrician reaches in and, winking at his friend, runs his hand over the front of a hard-starched uniform shirt. From the top shelf he pulls a pair of greyed-white women's pants, and as his apprentice watches laughing he holds them up to his nose, raising his eyebrows and closing his eyes in mock intoxication, then leaving the pants covering his face and looking up blindly in the direction of the apprentice, he sings through them, 'Le – t me put my arms about you, I – don't want to live without you.'

'Watch the ladder then!' says his friend, laughing.

The electrician folds them back up, places them on top of the others, shuts the door and holds the ladder steady as the apprentice climbs down. The next locker along has clothes stuffed in any which way, and several pictures of Sinatra taped on to the inside door. 'Not so good,' says the electrician, 'though she's got better taste.' In this locker clean clothes have been mixed with dirty laundry, as he soon discovers when he plays the pants game again with some well-soiled pair. 'Serves you right,' says the apprentice, though it's a game he wants to play too, so with one eye on the door in case of interruptions, they work their way through an examination of the dirty and clean underwear, and move on to the next locker and the next, giving marks out of ten for the smell and the state of the contents.

But then the apprentice comes to one locker that's stuck, he can't open it with his fingers because the handle's off its door and the door's firmly wedged shut. There's a small hole in the metal where the handle was, however, and the electrician rummages in his overalls' chest pocket and takes out his small screwdriver and, inserting it into the little screw-hole, jerks the door open. It swings back. A light scent escapes.

'Oh,' the apprentice breathes.

'That's the best. That's the winner,' says the electrician, shaking his head. The few clothes in this locker are remarkable, not grey but white, and smooth, arranged and unrumpled, folded with talent. The underwear on the top shelf is thin and white. The electrician reaches in and feels his hand touch something silken. He pulls gently and a petticoat disarranges itself, coming away in his hand and knocking the underwear out of harmony as he takes it out and it falls away from his hand like liquid, like light. The two men watch it as it hangs, moving, unearthly and lovely. The electrician is struck by guilt, and by delicacy.

'How in hell's name are you going to fold it up again?' asks the apprentice. The electrician memorizes the name above the bed of this locker. Later in the week he will ask her out and find her as lovely as her underwear to him, and a little later still he will tell her about his mother dying, and sitting in the pub one night he'll show her his mother's wedding ring in its wooden box with the velvet inside. She'll say 'Oh yes, it's a very pretty ring,' and as she says it someone at the next table will see the scene, misread it and shout out, 'They're getting engaged! They're getting engaged!' and all of the people round them in the small pub will smile and point and jog the shoulders and arms of the couple looking at each other in laughing alarm and embarrassment, and the people at the back will try to see what's going on, to catch a glimpse of the ring, the couple, anything of the moments and materials of which love gets made.

SLAB CITY, APRIL 12TH

Hal Duncan

The angel walked into Slab City off the Jornada del Muerto, the journey of the dead man which runs north from Kern's Gate, El Paso, through a dry plain of natron and uranium, salt, sand and dust, and the moment I saw him I knew he was an angel, because, although I was only thirteen at the time and had never seen one of *them* before, one of what Finnan called the unkin, I recognized right away what I had been taught to look out for, the particular kind of mark.

Nearly everybody has some kind of mark, Finnan told me – doesn't have to be physical, although sometimes people wear their mark in their eyes or on their skin for everyone to see, like a thousand-yard-stare or a knife-scar or tattoo. You get it for your own reason, if you ever get it at all; maybe you get it the first time you fuck, maybe the first time you kill, either way it's your own special mark, a secret name carved into your soul at that precise moment when you suddenly, instantly realize: I know what I am.

Anyone who doesn't have their mark yet won't get what I'm talking about; first time Finnan told me, I thought it was bullshit and said so in my foulmouthed tomboy terminology. But since then Finnan had been teaching me to read those secret names and by the time the angel came to trailer-town I could damn near *smell* him on the dead, desert air, even before he came into sight over the low brow of the Jesus Hill.

He was black; at first I thought it was just shadow, but

the sun was due east, still rising, and he was coming in from the south, so he wasn't in silhouette. He stopped at the top of the hill for a while and stood under one arm of the large wooden cross like a man waiting to be hanged calmly scanning his audience, and though the air was shimmering around him I could suddenly see him in perfect focus, his black leather clothes, his black leather skin, his dreadlocks and goatee, his deep hooded eyes. He was carrying what looked like a small but thick leatherbound book in one hand. As dogs, chained to their owners' trailers here and there, barked at the dawn, and somebody, somewhere, played *Crawling King Snake* on a tinny radio, I heard him clearly as he whispered to the wind: '*Finnan*.'

'Never saw anyone *walk* into Slab City before,' said a friendly voice behind me.

'Morning, Mac,' I said. 'Maybe . . . uh, maybe his car broke down . . . or something.'

I was pretty sure that wasn't even near the truth, but I didn't want to start on the subject of unkin with Mac. Mac was a fusion of old-style Christian evangelist and acid-crazed flower-child who never quite made it into the ministry, just a bit too eccentric for any orthodox faith to handle. Instead, he took to his vocation in his own, individual way. He was painting a hill.

He'd started his mission before I was born, before my parents even started their semi-nomadic lifestyle. For as long as anyone could remember, in fact, he'd been painting one side of the low hill that marked the southern boundary of Slab City, decorating it inch by inch in whites and pinks and corn-yellows and sky-blues, with giant hearts and massive flowers. Originally he'd just freshened up the paintwork as often as he could afford it, but as time went on the thing took up more and more hillside and more and more paint, so that Mac found it hard to keep up with the wear and tear of New Mexico weather. Then someone suggested using clay as well and the Jesus Hill took on a whole new dimension. By the time our family arrived to spend our first winter in Slab City, it had become a permanent adobe sculpture, a landmark-sized masterpiece of Christian kitsch.

I remember watching it growing larger still throughout the warm winters of my childhood, its bible slogans in six-foot letters proclaiming love to the world and salvation for all. Despite my neo-pagan upbringing I always found it a welcome sight to return to this in the fall, after a summer spent around the cool Great Lakes up in Canada, and I was always sort of sad to leave it in the spring as we followed the other mobile families escaping from the coming heat of the Mojave summer. Between May and September, Slab City belonged only to the real desert-rats, non-mobiles like Mac or Finnan who, it was generally accepted, had long since fried what was left of their brains.

'Hey, that's right,' I said. 'Mom picked up some paint over in Santa Fe; some guy she was doing hackwork for had it lying around and she said to ask if you could use it.'

'Sure could,' said Mac. 'What colour is it?'

'Eggshell . . . puke yellow, perfect for the hill.' Mac laughed. 'I'll bring it over before we head off. Maybe you can have a big "Jesus Loves You" done for when we get back. Real tasteful, like.'

'So cynical, so young,' said Mac. 'In trash lies truth, remember. The Good Lord loves a glow-in-the-dark madonna much as he loves the biggest cathedral – hell, more so, if it means more to one of his lost sheep.'

'Baa,' I said. You didn't argue theology with Mac; he was too nice a guy to take away his sense of Grand Purpose In The Simple Act. He was nuts, yes, but fifty per cent of trailer-park society as a whole, and about seventy-five per cent of Slab City in particular, was at very least eccentric if not outright certifiable. My own dad was trying to map Atlantis using regressive hypnosis to 'access the mental database of his prime incarnation's experience'. Our neighbour at the moment, Mr Willis, thought we should all be buying up NASA leftovers and trying to colonize Mars as autonomous collectives. He already had his own spacesuit. Up in the parks around Lake Superior you got a lot of people who were real 'tolerant' of this sort of weirdness, but I hated their patronizing attitudes. Sure, I thought Mac and Mr Willis were lunatics but I respected them for that and, in the same way I hated to be treated like a little girl, I hated the way some of the middle-class mobiles talked down to people I considered my friends.

'Hey,' said Mac. 'He's coming down.'

The rasta angel started slowly down Jesus Hill, climbing round 'LOVE' and over the Sacred Bleeding Heart, cracking 'CONSIDER THE LILIES' under his feet and scuffing dirt on 'THE LIGHT OF THE WORLD'. Mac and I waited at the foot of the hill for him to arrive, me standing in the open, trying to look bored by kicking at the dry grasses under my feet, Mac leaning out the heart-shaped window of his junk-augmented schoolbus-cum-shack, scratching at his grey stubble. The black guy jumped the last five feet or so down the hill and landed damn near in my face.

'Can I bother one of you for a little water?' he asked, looking at Mac, then shifted his gaze to me. The bastard was fucking tall. 'My . . . um . . . car broke down on the highway other side of the hill there, and this desert air's given me one mother of a thirst.'

'I'll get you a bottle,' said Mac. 'I could offer you a beer, if you want one.'

'No, thanks, but water'll be just great.' The heart-shaped wooden shutter snapped closed as Mac disappeared. The angel was still looking straight at me.

'What's your name, little one?'

'Phreedom,' I said, 'but spelled PH instead of F.'

'Is it?' He smiled. 'Tell me, Phreedom, do you know of

anyone around here good at fixing things . . . cars, that is.'

Finnan.

'You mean like a repairman? A mechanic or something?' I said.

'Exactly.'

Don't lie to an angel, I thought.

'What kind of car is it?'

'Here's your water,' said Mac, stepping out of his open front door and handing a bottle of mineral water to the stranger. 'What's up?'

'I was just asking Phreedom here if she knew anyone might be able to fix my car.'

'You want Finnan,' said Mac. 'The guy's some kind of a wizard. Electrical, mechanical, you name it – if it's broke he can fix it. Slab's over that way, all corrugated iron and old rubber tyres, you can't miss it. Phree'll take you, won't you, Phree? Her and Finnan are great buddies. You're not doing anything just now, are you, Phree?' I looked from one to the other then down at my feet.

'Guess not,' I said.

'So, how come you're up and about while everyone else is still in bed?' asked the angel. He was walking about two paces behind me as I led him the short distance to Finnan's slab.

'Just heading out to gather some peyote buttons for Finnan,' I said. 'You get better mojo if you collect them at dawn, he told me.'

'I imagine he's told you a lot of things.'

'I like your coat,' I said. It was long and black, with a high, turned-up collar, the leather scuffed and dusty like he'd walked around the world in it. 'It looks good and warm for the cold, desert nights.'

'I wouldn't know,' he said. 'I'm never usually this far from civilization . . . no offence.'

'None taken.' Slab City *was* pretty primitive. When trailer-parks first took off in the Home-of-the-Future 1950s a lot of white-collar families wanted trailers and campers for second homes. By the last decades of the last century, these recreational vehicles were the only thing a lot of shit-poor people could afford as a *first* home. So you got some trailer-parks which were like holiday camps, with leisure facilities and every amenity you could name – just drive up, rent your slab and plug into the water, electricity and disposal pipes, or, better still, get a valet to do it while you take the kids for their tennis lesson. Other places were cheaper and nastier, with less and less amenities. Slab City was really just a flat piece of dirt where people started to park one day. With no charges and no power or water, its denizens were pretty much confined to the self-sufficient or the financially desperate.

'So what kind of car was it you said you had, again?' I asked the angel.

'A red one,' he said. 'Tell me about this Finnan.'

'I don't know much about him.'

'Mac said you were his friend.'

'He doesn't talk a lot.'

'Perhaps he's got something to hide.'

'Finnan doesn't have anything to hide.'

'We *all* have something to hide.'

'So what are *you* hiding?' The black guy stopped and I turned, shoved my hands in the pockets of my oversize bike jacket – a handmedown from my brother – and stood there, trying to stare down an angel.

'I imagine your friend Finnan would call it my . . . "mark",' he said. I looked away, at the dog lying sprawled out on the makeshift porch of a nearby trailer-home. Gazing over at us, without lifting its head, it wagged its tail, thumping it lazily on the wooden planking. I looked back at the angel.

'You're not doing a very good job of it,' I said, and he laughed, the air wavering around him, dust swirling in barely perceptible vortices and currents. He raised a hand like he was playing with the breeze. Way off in the distance: a high hollow note like the coda of a song played on a flute carved out of bone.

'Don't try to teach a birdman how to fly, hatchling.'

'"Birdman"?'

'What does Finnan call us – angels, gods?'

'Unkin.'

He looked at me like I'd eaten his grandmother, pushed past me and started straight for Finnan's slab – as if he'd known the way all along. I hurried after him.

'I thought you said your friend didn't talk much.' His voice was clipped.

'He never told me what it means.'

'Ignorance is bliss.'

'Bullshit,' I said. The angel glanced back at me and the dog we'd just passed started to howl.

'Did he think we wouldn't gather you as well?' asked the angel.

'I don't know what you're talking about.'

'Then your friend Finnan didn't tell you everything. Ask him sometime what it's like to walk the Road of All Dust. Ask him what he paid to cross the River of All Souls.'

'Hey, all I know is what he taught me about mojo, about voudon and santeria, which is nothing you can't learn in books. And all I know about you unkin is that some people let the mojo take them over, carve it into their own souls till they think they're some sort of fucking superior race, some kind of "living manifestation of divinity", and sure, they've got power, but they're so fucking full of themselves, so fucking self-righteous, so fucking . . .' I lost the word I was looking for and shook my head in disgust.

'There are righteous unkin and there are fallen unkin,'

said the black man, 'and there are fools like Finnan who think they can stay neutral, who think they can hide from their duty in the middle of nowhere and pray it never finds them.'

'And that's your job, right, recruitment officer for the war in heaven? Hunting down AWOLs and deserters? You going to press-gang him or shoot him at dawn?'

'I've come to gather him,' said the angel. 'I've come to gather your good friend Finnan.'

And Finnan's slab came into view ahead.

The place had the look of an old sepia photograph, with its sand-scoured chrome and rusted steel and everything all dusty faded brown. The old Airstream trailer stood high up on red brick piles and girder stilts, and formed the centre of a large structure of retrofitted salvage. Canvas, corrugated iron and even old car hoods formed the walls and roofs of annexes built around and under the main living area, which was accessed by an old rusting ladder.

Round the back of this industrial gothic folly, rubber tyres had been piled up to form three walls of an open garage-workshop area, roofed with obsolete twelve-foot solar panels and linked to the Airstream by wires and cables. In front of the main construction, the sandblasted shells of two dead automobiles stood like two stone lions at the steps of some grand City Hall. All around, the place was littered with electrical and mechanical equipment, old and new, broken and fixed, with computers, TVs and satellite dishes, with stripped-down washing machines and motorbikes built up from spare parts.

Finnan's slab was a junkyard in its own right and Finnan was the junkmaster, the man who could take a broken food-processor, a frigidaire, an electric boiler and a bus-engine, and rebuild them into a single unit that turned raw sewage into fresh water, fertilizer and sterile non-toxic dust. Right now, Finnan was standing in his dead-car gateway, waiting for us patiently with his staff in his hand and a cigarette in his mouth.

He looked about eighteen but he claimed to be in his late twenties and there was nobody who knew for sure. The clothes he wore seemed always the same, the same white button-neck T-shirts, the same sandstone-coloured chinos and the same scuffed desert hiking boots, everything always smudged with the same black engine oil and grease that slicked back his dirty blond hair. He was short and skinny, but with muscles that looked like they were made of steel cable, every fibre of them showing under the taut skin of his arms, shifting as he moved them as he worked on whatever his latest project was.

At the moment, you could see the tension in those arms, the knotted muscles and wire veins, as one hand took the cigarette from his mouth and flicked it away, while the other gripped the iron railing that functioned as the shaft of his staff. A TV aerial was fixed at the top of the railing, pointing downwards, its crossbars hung with chains and charms, wound round with barbed wire and crowned by a plastic doll's head. Finnan held the thing with white knuckles like it was his only connection to sanity.

'Well . . . good morning, reality,' he said. 'Let's go inside and talk.'

'There's nothing to talk about,' said the angel. He and Finnan were sitting at the Formica top of the little dinner table in Finnan's Airstream, one drinking bottled water, the other bottled beer. I was nosing round the fridge, looking for a Coke, but watching them all the time out of the corner of my eye, and listening intently to everything they said. 'Your name is in the book,' said the angel.

The angel's leatherbound 'book' – actually a tenth-generation palmtop with slick packaging – was sitting up on the table in front of him, open and switched on. Scrolling over the screen, row upon row, was a sequence composed of four different glyphs arranged in seemingly random order. As I watched, the scrolling gradually accelerated until the screen became just a grey blur.

'Then the book is wrong,' said Finnan. 'I was never named. I was never marked.'

'But you were *called*, birdman. We need your answer.'

'You can't take me without my true name. You've got no hold over me, and you sit here at my table by *my* invitation.' Finnan lit another cigarette and took a draw.

'You *will* be gathered,' said the black guy.

'Not by you.'

'Then by the others.'

'Not by them.'

I picked up Finnan's lighter from the table and started playing with it.

'When *they* come for you they'll be less . . . diplomatic than I am,' said the angel.

'And I'll be less hospitable,' said Finnan.

'They'll rape your little apprentice here and drag you down into hell by your greasy matted hair,' the angel said. I blinked and flicked the lighter open, sparked it.

'Don't underestimate the girl,' said Finnan. 'She can look after herself.'

'A chicken-bone cross around her neck is going to save her from hellhounds?'

I fingered the charm-necklace that Finnan had made for me. Finnan blew smoke in the angel's face.

'You know . . . birdman . . . your organization will never beat the opposition, and they'll never beat you, because underneath the bullshit you're exactly the same thing.'

'You never did understand us, Finnan. The point of the struggle is not to "beat the opposition" as you put it, but to separate the . . . chaff from the grain . . . and the good seed from the bad seed, and if it means burning the world to dust and fire, well, the most fertile fields have come from ashes.'

'You bastards are inhuman.'

'We're *more* than human, boy. Their little rules of ... etiquette don't apply to us. We don't *need* to be judged; we judge ourselves.'

'You mean that isn't a scorebook you're keeping? Measuring the credits and debits of good and evil? Balancing the accounts of Light and Dark? Like it's not an inventory of souls saved and a register of souls damned?'

'This is a record of all known true names and callings,' said the angel.

'It's the little black book of your master's conquests.'

'This is a book of unkin,' the angel said.

'I've *never* been named,' hissed Finnan.

'But you've been *called*. And I'm calling you now, Finnan. I'm calling you out and it doesn't really matter to us whether I leave with your heart or with your head; all that matters to us is that you make the choice.'

'Is this some kind of fucking *dare*? Wake up, birdman, the gangs are dead – the Annunaki, the Athenatoi, they're all long gone – but you zombies are still looking for the Last Big Rumble in the Sky? Wake up.' Finnan flicked ash on the linoleum floor. I fidgeted with the alphabet magnets on the fridge door.

The angel sat silently for a moment, then punched a few buttons on his palmtop while Finnan took another draw on his cigarette and a swig of his beer. He looked across at me, then at Finnan, then out the window at his side.

'My name is in this book as well, you know,' said the black man. The scrolling had stopped now and the screen was flashing up matrix after matrix of those four glyphs repeated. 'Would you like to know my true name, Finnan, or should I tell the girl so she can call on me when the demons –'

'Neither of us want to know your name,' said Finnan.

'What is it – Rumpelstiltskin?' I said, and immediately felt stupid.

'It's –'

'I won't join you and I won't fight you,' snapped Finnan. 'I won't be named, numbered, called, gathered, saved or damned.'

'– Metatron,' said the angel, and it hurt. He said it real quiet, but I could feel the resonance deep in my skull and it was like a thousand dog-whistles had been blown in each of my ears. For a second – for less than that, for a fraction of a second – I felt like the sound was carrying a living information into everything in the trailer, myself included; that by speaking that single stupid-sounding word the angel had stamped his name into me and into everything around me. For that fraction of a second this seemed totally natural and logical, then the world stopped ringing and I leaned back against the fridge, looking at Finnan to see if this new development was good or bad. It was bad.

Finnan's anger flickered through his body, in the wire vein in his forehead, in the cables of his tensed neck muscles, in the twitching of his arms and clenched fists. His eyes, though, were as calm as ever, cool ice-blue and never blinking.

'Nice of you to introduce yourself,' he said.

'You *invited* me in. It's only polite,' said the angel.

'Polite, sure, but there's no need to be so . . . formal.'

'I always think courtesy is the basis of any good working relationship.'

'We have no working relationship. We never will.'

'It's also important to "know thine enemy".'

'What makes you think we're enemies? I ask you into my home. I offer you hospitality –'

'And in gratitude, in return, I give you my name; I'm in your debt,' the angel said.

'You don't owe me a thing.'

'But I *have* to repay your hospitality. If you refuse me that then you offend me, and if you offend me then you're my enemy. Which is it?'

'I release you of your debt. I take back my hospitality. Get out of my home.'

I noticed that some of the magnetic letters on the fridge had arranged themselves to spell out a word – M-E-T-A-T-R-O-N. It looked like some inane comic-book superhero's name, spelled out in all its pompousness. It looked harmless.

'You're expelling me?' asked the angel.

'I'm requesting that you leave.'

'Just say the word and I'm gone.'

'Please,' snarled Finnan.

'Not that word, boy. You know what I mean.'

'I know what you mean, you arrogant fucker,' I said.

Finnan shook his head. 'Don't even think of it, Phree. I taught you how to read the marks, but the name would just be a word in your mouth . . . and it's a word they'd damn you with.'

'Let the little girl try, birdman. Let the hatchling chirp her first angel-call.'

'Don't patronize me, you bastard,' I said.

'Leave her out of this!' said Finnan, half-rising from his seat. 'Get the fuck out of my house, now.' He bowed his head. 'I command you in your own name, I command you twice, and I command you for the third time –'

'Metatron,' I said.

The empty bottle in the angel's hand shattered, and the shards themselves shattered, and sand rained across the Formica table-top.

'Metatron,' I said, again for the first time, time echoing itself.

The world was screaming in my face, a golden, burning sound of fire and rust. The angel was white and Finnan was green and my own hand was crimson as I raised it to try and stop the song from shaking my whole existence apart.

'Metatron.' I thought I was going to be saying that one word for the rest of my life, forever in that one moment, living, reliving the reverberations. The air was liquid in front of me, its intricate flow tracing sigils and symbols, all instantly understood, all woven into a single living word, that name. I reached into the deepest part of the mark carved into the world inside Finnan's Airstream, and, with thumb and forefinger, I twisted it at its heart.

The angel threw back his head and laughed, and wept.

Finnan stubbed out his cigarette on the table-top.

The world became normal . . . almost.

'I'll be leaving now,' said the angel, picking up his palmtop, switching it off and closing it as he rose from his seat. 'The choice has been made for you, Finnan, and young Phreedom's bought you a little more time.'

'Maybe I'll do the same for her some day.'

'I don't think you'll have to. She's a fighter, that one; she's made her choice already and she's not even named yet.'

'My parents called me Phreedom,' I said. 'That's all the name I need.'

'My father named me Enoch,' said the angel, 'but when you walk with God you soon find those human names too small a fit. Phreedom is what they call you, yes, but is it really who you are . . . *what* you are?'

'As long as I'm alive,' said Finnan, 'it will be.'

'You'll protect her, birdman? You damned her to hell the day you taught her that the gods were real. And when the Desolate One gathers her in his arms she'll probably thank you for it as she rips out your heart.'

'Get out of here,' I said. 'Get the fuck out of here.' He pushed past me to the door and opened it, but stopped at the threshold as he turned to go down the ladder. He flicked his hand in a sort of John Wayne salute.

'Be seeing you,' he said.

* * *

'How long has Finnan been here?' I asked Mac as I put the last tin of eggshell-yellow emulsion down on the ground at the foot of the Jesus Hill. Mac grinned and shrugged.

'Longer than me,' he said. 'And I been here near forty years.'

'So how old is he?'

Mac shrugged, and laughed this time. He pulled the baseball cap off his head and scratched at his scalp. 'Looks to me like he's about nineteen,' he said. 'But I reckon he must be over a hundred.' As Mac replaced his cap, he grinned at me with a carefully cultivated innocence. 'But, hell, my memory isn't what it used to be. Who knows, maybe Finnan only got here yesterday.'

'You know what Finnan is, don't you?'

'No. No, I'm just another old drugfucked hippy hermit; I don't push my trip on Finnan, and he doesn't push his trip on me. If someday he comes up to me and tells me, hey, I know where the fountain of youth is, I can take you back to the garden, man, well, maybe I'll follow him and maybe I'll just stay here and paint my hill. I figure you got to make your own way through; you can't walk another person's journey.'

'So you never asked him where he came from or anything?'

'I didn't ever think he *wanted* to be asked.'

'Are you sure about this?' asked Finnan.

Evening was falling and I lay in his arms in his bed in his trailer in his world. The last echoes of the black angel's true name were fading now, but I could still feel the call, the song of all lands, in the rhythm of Finnan's breath, in the beat of his heart, and in my own breath and my own bloodstream. I touched his thigh and life quivered.

'Nothing I've ever done ever felt so right,' I said. 'I want you to be the one who names me, and I want *this* to be the . . . the sacrament.'

'I could go to jail for this in Texas,' he said, smiling gently.

'We're unkin,' I said. 'Their rules aren't our –'

He put a finger to my lips. 'No they, no us, just you and me, okay?'

'Okay.'

We stayed there for a while in silence, not doing anything. Then Finnan slid his hand down to my cunt.

'What does it feel like to you,' I said, 'the call, I mean?'

'It's like a million tiny wires firing charges through my flesh, down into my bones. Sometimes it's just a low buzz, other times I feel like I'm burning in the fucking electric chair.'

'With me it's like a song, like everything is resonating around me, inside me.'

'"Everything is broken up, and dances",' he said.

'That's it exactly.'

'I envy you.'

I turned over to lie on my back, looking out the west-facing window, where the red and golden sunset seemed almost artificial in its numinous washes of light, like the painted backdrop of some 1950s Technicolor and Cinemascope movie – it all seemed so staged.

'How long do you think I've got,' I said, 'before they come for me?'

'Not long,' he said. 'I think they're gearing up for a final showdown. The gatherers will be scattering across the face of the earth right now, hunting down, one by one, every last draft-dodger and deserter, every last free unkin. They want me, and they'll want you.'

'We don't have to join their stupid war. There has to be a third choice.'

'There is,' said Finnan. 'I can feel it in the call, like the power is pulling me apart, everybody wants a piece of me, the matriarchs, the patriarchs, the Light, the Dark. But there's something else in there, something hidden and secret. I don't know what or who it is, but I know that it's there and I know that it's *free.*'

'I can hear it,' I said, 'like something echoed from the other side of the world. If we could find it –'

'I've been looking for centuries. It doesn't want to be found.'

'We have to try.'

'Nothing else we *can* do.'

He rolled over so he was on top of me, and rested his head on my shoulder, kissing my neck as he fingered my clit.

'I'm ready,' I said. 'I want to know my name.'

And his other hand pressed down through me and curled electric fingers round my heart, reading me, writing me, fusing sacred and profane, in grace and obscenity, and he leaned close to me and he whispered it in my ear.

The next day I left with my family for the north, and I knew already that I was never going to see Finnan again. When we returned in the fall to that trailer-city in the New Mexico desert, Mac was still working on his Jesus Hill but Finnan's castle of junk was uninhabited and the air was empty of his sepia lifelight and steely soulscent. I tried looking around inside the Airstream for any clues to why he'd left or where he went, but all there was was a half-empty pack of cigarettes, making it look like he'd left in a hurry. It was too depressing to stick around long enough for a thorough search. Before I left, though, I rearranged the alphabet letters on the fridge door so they spelled out the word PHREEDOM, then took off my chicken-bone necklace, the santerian charm to ward off bad mojo, and placed it gently down on the Formica table-top. By that time I no longer needed it.

THE PAPER

Gordon Legge

Yet again, the hoity-toitys had beaten him to it.

Sandy went over to the rack and got himself a copy of *The Sunday Times Magazine*.

He sat near them this week. Just two tables away. Close enough maybe to get on their nerves.

'In the name of God!'

The two women looked over.

The Sunday Times Magazine was doing a famine special. Page after page of starving weans. Sandy hadn't realized.

He liked the reaction, though. He kept an eye on them as he turned the page. 'Tch,' he said, 'that no terrible. Break your flaming heart, so it would.'

They never reacted. Sandy gave up and looked at the page he'd turned over to.

'Christ almighty!'

This time the two women did look over.

The photo was of three weans. Sandy'd never seen the like.

'No real,' he mumbled to himself, 'just no real.'

The young thing over at the desk was watching him. Her that went in for them big, thick woolly tights with the wee flimsy skirts that you'd have struggled to get a decent sneeze out of.

She was giving him a look.

Sandy gave her a look back.

You could get away with looking when you were old,

giving them the once-over. To them you were just a crabbit old git stuck with your crabbit old thoughts.

The young thing got up. She walked over to the store room. She had boots on. Cherry reds. She was a bonny lass all right. Sexy. She entered the store room and Sandy turned his attention back to his magazine.

'Jesus God!'

And there had been him thinking all manner of thoughts when next thing, staring him right in the face, was a poor lass as naked as the day she was born. Just skin and bone.

'Excuse me. Are you all right?'

It was her with the boots.

Sandy shook his head. 'Just these pictures,' he said, 'mean, hen, what can you say?'

Sandy'd got out of jail with that one, answering a question with a question.

Her with the boots looked at the picture. She was leaning over him. She had on enough jewellery to sink the *Titanic* but her wee black vest might as well have been Marmite.

And there was that poor lass in the photo.

Her with the boots said 'O-kay' as if she'd been thinking about it. Then she said, 'As long as you're sure you're all right.'

Sandy pointed to the poor lass in the picture.

Her with the boots put her hand on his shoulder. 'I know,' she said. 'But could you keep it quiet, please?'

Sandy just acted the dafty. 'Mean, God love them, but can you no see they're only weans? Couldn't harm a soul even if they wanted to.'

Her with the boots put her hand on his shoulder again – they were awfy into touching, these young folk – then she put her finger to her lips and winked at him.

As she headed back to her desk a great big woman with a right torn-face came in. Bold as you like, she marched right up to the two hoity-toitys.

'Excuse me,' she said, 'but do you think I could possibly bother you to have a wee look? Just that I want to check and see if my niece's photo's in. I mean you don't want to go out and buy it if it's not in, you know.'

The woman looked through the paper.

Sandy was raging. This was his job. This had always been his job. He was the one that got the paper on the Thursday afternoon. He was first on. He'd always been first on.

'No,' said the woman, 'can't see it. She did say, right enough, mind you, that it would most likely be next week's. Still, you don't want to miss it, do you? I mean . . .'

Would you listen to it? Talk about hoity-toity. And talk about tight-fisted, if Lady Muck here wasn't willing to part with a few bob for the paper then what hope was there for these poor buggers that had to feed themselves off scraps.

Lady Muck got the jacket off and sat herself down beside the hoity-toitys, yapping away.

That was that then. They'd made a boo-boo on that one – this was a strict no-yapping zone. There were signs up. No flaming yapping.

Being a card-carrying user of the premises, Sandy felt duty-bound to draw to their attention the error of their ways.

Sandy went ahead and cleared his throat.

'Ach-hemm! . . . Oh shit!'

The contents of Sandy's throat, a dollop of phlegm the size of a two-bob bit, had flown across the room and found a home for itself on the spine of Cassell's English-French French-English dictionary.

Her with the boots was attending to somebody but Sandy could tell she was watching him all the same.

Lady Muck and the hoity-toitys were giving him the if looks could kill treatment.

Sandy reset his teeth.

He wasn't going to clean it. No way was he going to clean

it. No way. No way was it his fault. Damned if it was his fault. It was the flaming hoity-toitys. It was their fault. It was them as was to blame. If it hadn't been for them none of this would have happened in the first place.

Her with the boots was on the phone.

Oh no – that would mean Mavis on the warpath.

Sandy laughed to himself. Mavis on the warpath, that was a joke. Mavis was one of them nice folk – and Sandy hated nice folk. You never knew where you stood with nice folk. You were that busy being nice to them and they were that busy being nice to you that you forgot what the hell it was you were all supposed to be so worked up about in the first place.

The squelch of sticky slippers announced the arrival of Mavis.

Mavis stopped at the desk. Mavis was talking to her with the boots. Her with the boots was pointing at Sandy.

Sandy was praying she wouldn't come over.

This was a new one of his, this praying lark. Not that he was turning all holy-holy or anything like that, just that these days he spent half his time wondering what atheists did when they were told their plane was about to kiss the mountain.

Her with the boots and Mavis were still at it. Mavis was doing the talking. Her with the boots was doing the nodding. Mavis started wagging her finger. Her with the boots kept nodding.

Mavis went back through and Sandy allowed himself a sigh of relief.

They hadn't seen it. Sandy was convinced they hadn't seen it.

It was then that Sandy noticed that the blob on the spine of Cassell's English-French French-English dictionary hadn't moved.

Sandy looked at it.

Then something really weird happened – the blob looked back.

Sandy took off his reading specs and put on his seeing specs.

It did, too, the thing was staring at him. It was the exact shape and size of an eye.

Sandy got himself up and started heading across for a better look. When he reached halfway, though, he decided it would be best to kill the two birds with the one stone and went back for *The Sunday Times Magazine*.

In close-up, the blob on the spine of Cassell's English-French French-English dictionary not only managed to retain its optical illusion but actually looked even more realistic.

Sandy took off his seeing specs and put on his reading specs.

It had a kind of milky consistency and suspended at its centre there was a dark brown dollop that gave the impression of being a pupil. Sandy had half a notion to take it round and show it to the doctor.

Sandy removed the book from the shelf. He held it close to him, then he held it at arm's length. Then he held it out to his left, then he held it out to his right. It was amazing. Whichever way he held the book the eye continued to stare at him.

Sandy was fair tickled. He raised the book above his head so that the eye was looking down on him.

At this point, though, the forces of gravity intervened and brought an end to the short-lived bond between the blob and the spine.

The new bond, between the blob and the right lens of Sandy's reading specs, got off to a stormy start when a full-scale flinch caused Sandy first to recoil, then to bang into a chair and finally to exclaim something about 'Jesus!'

Her with the boots was watching him.

Lady Muck and the hoity-toitys were watching him.

Sandy thought about what he was doing. In one hand he was holding a copy of Cassell's English-French French-English dictionary above his head. In his other hand he was holding a copy of *The Sunday Times Magazine*, rolled up as if he was about to strike out at something.

The folks probably thought he looked a wee bit startled.

Sandy could live with that. As long as they didn't know he'd gobbed on his specs then Sandy could live with the folks thinking he looked a wee bit startled.

First things first. Sandy replaced the copy of Cassell's French-English English-French dictionary. He made like he was studying the shelves until the coast was clear then he quickly wiped the spine of the book with the sleeve of his jacket.

Sandy then headed back to his table. He kept his back to Lady Muck and the hoity-toitys so that they wouldn't see what he'd done to his reading specs. He also had to incline his head at such an angle so as the blob wouldn't slide off.

Sandy had it all figured out, though.

He would just act as if he was holding back a sneeze. And if Lady Muck and the hoity-toitys had their wits about them, they would realize the reason he was facing in the opposite direction to which he was going was so that in the case of any mishap he wouldn't be sneezing in their direction.

Everything worked out fine. Sandy made it. He'd banged into two tables and three chairs along the way but Sandy made it back to the safety of his seat. All he had to do now was switch specs and return *The Sunday Times Magazine* to the rack and get something else out.

Sandy took off his reading specs and put on his seeing specs then walked over to the rack.

There was a problem, though. Sandy's seeing specs couldn't make out the titles. It was all a blur. Sandy told himself that didn't matter, that wasn't important, all he had to do was put back *The Sunday Times Magazine*, take out a copy of something else and get back to his seat.

Sandy picked up a copy of what he thought was the *Radio Times* and returned to his table.

It was all over. He'd done it. Sandy sat himself down, took his hankie out his pocket and cleaned his reading specs.

The sense of relief Sandy felt once his specs were clean, positioned and primed for perusing was somewhat tempered, though, when that which lay before him came into focus.

'Dang and flaming blast it!'

Auto Parts, flaming *Auto Parts*. Of all the things he could've picked up, why did it have to be flaming *Auto Parts*?

'Really!'

Sandy looked up. It was Lady Muck that had spoken.

Sandy glowered at her.

Lady Muck glowered back.

Sandy had to concede she was good at the glowering. Obviously put in a lot of practice over the years. Right evil-looking and all. Sandy pitied the poor bloke that had to go home to that of an evening. If she started anything, Sandy decided he would go for the shins. There was nobody as liked being booted in the shins.

Out of the corner of his eye Sandy could see that her with the boots was on the phone again.

Oh God, that was it this time. Sandy was going to have to go a few rounds with Mavis. He was going to have to try and understand Mavis, and at the same time try and be polite to Mavis. He'd rather have faced one of Lady Muck's right hooks.

The sticky slippers squelched past the desk with barely a nod to her with the boots and homed in on Sandy.

'Well,' said Mavis, 'it seems there's been a wee bit of a bother. Now I was wondering if maybe you could begin to explain . . .'

Mavis was amazing. The poor wee woman was so shy and nervous that she swallowed the whole time she was talking.

Sandy thought about it. It had to be sore doing that. It was like forcing yourself to hiccup. Surely to God you could choke yourself going through all that carry-on.

Mavis had stopped talking. She was bright red in the face and swallowing thirteen to the dozen.

Sandy hadn't listened to a word she'd said, all he'd been doing had been staring her in the throat.

Jesus, the poor woman must've thought he was going to sink his gnashers into her!

'Aye, well, eh,' Sandy moved about in his seat, 'got a wee touch of the cold you see.'

'Well,' said Mavis, 'should you maybe not be back in your bed with a hot drink and a couple of aspirin?'

Sandy sniffed. That would do. She'd walked into that one. Cue the violins. 'Oh, it's a right cold house, my house, hen. The only heat you'll ever get out of that place is the day you take a match to it.'

Mavis fell for it. She was struggling to hold back the waterworks.

'It's rare and warm in here, mind,' continued Sandy, 'I just like to come in and have a look through my paper.' Sandy indicated the copy of *Auto Parts*. 'It does you good to get out and about and mixing with folk.'

The trouble with the waterworks was that the waterworks were contagious, and as soon as the first tear rounded on Mavis's eyelash, Sandy felt himself going and all. If Mavis didn't sling her hook soon the pair of them were going to end up looking like a right pair of Jessies.

'Well,' whispered Mavis, 'if you could just try and keep it quiet then please or, well, you know. There's other people to think of.'

Mavis went away and left him. The squelch of her slippers seemed faster than usual and Sandy wouldn't have been surprised if she was heading up to the staff room for a good greet.

Sandy got back to his magazine.

Auto Parts, flaming *Auto Parts*, what did he have to go and pick that up for?

There was nothing else for it. Sandy got himself up and took the magazine back over to the rack. He had a fly look over at Lady Muck and the hoity-toitys just to see how far through they'd got.

District Round-Up! They were only as far as District flaming Round-Up. Good God, what were they trying to do, memorize the thing?

This was getting bad. Sandy picked up a copy of the *Radio Times* and returned to his seat.

Drastic situations called for drastic measures. It was time for the lethal weapon.

Sandy was going to let rip.

One . . . two . . . three . . .

But it wouldn't come. Nothing happened. Sandy sat there, really straining, really trying, but nothing happened.

He tried again. Clenching everything. Then a really good shove and . . .

Talk about blood from a stone.

Nothing.

All that jumping about must've played havoc with his insides. There was nothing there. Not a puff.

Sandy gave it one last go.

It was then that he noticed that Lady Muck and the hoity-toitys were up out their seats and ready for the off.

At last, at flaming last.

One of the hoity-toitys came over to Sandy. 'Are you feeling all right?' she said.

'Aye,' said Sandy. 'Doing away. This you off, is it?'

The hoity-toity looked at the other two before saying, 'Yes, need to get back and start getting the tea on.'

'Good,' said Sandy, 'good. Turned out nice, though, eh?'

'Aye,' said the hoity-toity, 'it's brightened up a wee bit. Pity about the rain, mind you. Listen, are you sure you've not got any pains or anything, in your arms or thereabouts?'

Pains, thought Sandy, pains in the arms? What was she on about? What, did she think he was having a heart- . . . ?

'No,' said Sandy, 'no, no pains. No, I'm all right. Fit as a fiddle.' Sandy gave a wee upper body jig. 'Keeping fine yourself, aye?'

'Come on, Rita,' said the other hoity-toity, 'we best be getting a move on.'

As soon as they were out of sight, Sandy went over to get a look at the paper.

He had a wee laugh to himself. The daft thing had gone and thought he was having a heart-attack. He'd have to remember that one.

Sandy sat himself down. He was still laughing to himself as he opened the paper up at births, marriages and deaths, looking to see if there were any decent funerals worth going to.

THE MURDERER

Iain Crichton Smith

At the time she was in Toronto on holiday with her sister, there was a murderer loose in the city: he had killed three women, all blondes and all in their thirties or forties.

She was boiling with rage and rancour in those days, for she had just left Hector. 'I'm not going to marry for a while yet. I haven't seen enough of the world,' he had said: and they had been 'going together' for years. They were both lecturers at S_____ University: and she had been feeling particularly insecure that afternoon. Of course she was not beautiful, she was in fact rather mousy, spectacled, with soft brown hair. He on the other hand was quite handsome, physically fit, energetic, always in a hurry: often trying to catch up with deadlines, taking on too much.

She had finally told him to leave her flat, for she had her dignity. She had thrown his jogging shoes out after him on to the landing. And all the time she was boiling with anger, at him and at everybody. It even affected her teaching, made her short-tempered, so that she was glad when the term was over.

And then Sylvia invited her out to Toronto, and she accepted, not because she liked Sylvia all that much, but because she didn't know what to do in the months ahead of her. She of course had a passport, for she and Hector had been to France twice: and she had enough money.

Sylvia greeted her with extravagant warmth. During the

phone call, Rosemary had told her what had happened, and had been apparently light-hearted about it.

'I never liked him anyway,' Sylvia said, for she had met him some years before. 'He didn't seem to me to be very trustworthy.' Did that mean he had made a pass at Sylvia, Rosemary wondered.

Sylvia had met her at the airport and as she drove confidently to the flat she pointed out some sights to her, but Rosemary wasn't particularly interested.

'I'm taking the weekend off,' said Sylvia, 'but after that I shall be working and I'll see you in the evenings.'

Sylvia was divorced but had a boyfriend called Norman, who was a doctor: she herself worked as a secretary. She looked well: her hair was yellow in the yellow lights.

That first night of course in the luxurious flat they talked for hours. Sylvia had cooked quiche and they had a bottle of wine, and Rosemary admired her sister's collection of dolls. The flat was larger than she had expected, with plenty of glass-topped little tables, and leather seats, pictures and photographs, a fine white fireplace, and lights scattered about the room.

'Norman is on duty this weekend,' Sylvia said, 'but we'll all have dinner together some night next week.' During the dinner Norman phoned and asked to be remembered kindly to Rosemary.

Sylvia was almost as lovely as ever, with those striking facial planes, blue eyes, and slim figure.

'I was sorry to hear about . . . things,' she said carefully, pouring out more wine. 'But then, if I remember correctly, he was always selfish and left everything to the last minute.'

Rosemary drank rather a lot of wine, and became slightly tipsy. 'To hell with him,' she said.

Sylvia thought her sister was looking rather pale, and it was odd to see her drinking so much, and to hear her swearing. She wore jeans, which did not suit her, and a black blouse which made her appear meagre. Also her eyes were red-rimmed as if she hadn't been sleeping too well.

Rosemary was quite drunk when she went to bed.

On the Saturday Sylvia took her to see the Niagara Falls, picking up a newspaper on the way.

They stopped for lunch at the Oban Inn, and then continued on their journey. At that time of year, of course, there was a large number of visitors at the Falls, which made a continuous thunderous noise.

'I wouldn't like to live here,' said Rosemary, who was wearing a brown costume which suited her.

'I'm sure they get used to it,' said Sylvia, manoeuvring her car expertly into one of the few parking spaces available. Rosemary couldn't drive.

Her sister told Rosemary of a family who had drifted in a boat, at night while they were sleeping, towards the Falls and had wakened up to hear that ominous din around them.

'What happened?' said Rosemary.

'They were okay.'

They took the lift down to the basement from which they could see the Falls close to. They had been given yellow oilskins, and stood watching the water in fascination, as the drops hit their faces. The noise was tremendous and the power unbelievable.

Later, in the café, Rosemary opened the newspaper which she had taken with her from the car. She is as studious as she ever was, thought Sylvia, she needs to read. It had been like that in their childhood too.

Rosemary noticed the story about the slayings in Toronto. One blonde had been killed while parking her car, the other two had been slain in their flats. They had all been strangled.

'Aren't you frightened?' she said to Sylvia. 'You're blonde and you live alone in your flat.'

'I have a chain and a peephole,' said Sylvia. 'I'm sure

they'll catch him soon.' Actually Rosemary had been to the cinema once since Hector left her (it was ages since she had gone to the cinema) and she had seen *The Silence of the Lambs*: it had both fascinated and repelled her. Of course from any critical point of view it was crap.

After their coffee they went into a shop where they had a look at some Eskimo and Red Indian stuff, but they didn't buy anything.

'Toronto is usually very law-abiding,' said Sylvia, as she drove back. 'It is unusual to have these kinds of murders.'

'I suppose it's very cold in winter.'

'Very. Norman and I have thought of leaving and heading south but we can't decide exactly where to settle.'

So she had seen Niagara Falls. They had been impressive all right but one could do without seeing them. Still, their raw power had excited her. You could be broken like a matchstick in all that weight of water.

Sylvia drove fast but carefully: she was always more daring than me, Rosemary thought. That came of having no imagination, always believing that the road would be there. When they were young, Sylvia never thought that a branch would break: Rosemary always did.

And when Sylvia had married that insurance man and they had emigrated to Canada, that also had been decisive. She herself had never liked him: he had a big shaggy body, and an insensitive mind. A vulgar person, she had always thought. A quick sharp mind had however taken him to San Francisco and out of Sylvia's life.

'He was such a liar,' Sylvia had told her. 'Tremendously clever and slick but a born liar. I've never met anyone who could hold his drink like him, and one moment he could be charming and the next vicious. I'm sure he's doing very well in San Francisco.'

Rosemary had not kept much in touch with her sister at that time: she had quite a lot to do, she had to start a course on the Romantic poets. In fact she had found it hard to believe that anyone could leave Sylvia: surely it would always be the other way round.

That night after her visit to Niagara Falls she slept quite well.

The following day, which was a Sunday, they went to the Tower and saw Toronto spread below them. Rosemary could even make out their tiny car in the parking lot. They also visited a market, sat in a park, and finally in the evening went to an Italian restaurant. She didn't think that Toronto was the kind of city in which such murders would occur; it was pleasant and open and leisurely, and had many fine buildings. Sylvia insisted on paying for the meal, though it was quite expensive.

In the flat, Sylvia showed her how everything in the kitchen worked, and gave her a key if, as was highly probable, she wanted to explore Toronto the following day.

'The Underground is excellent,' she told her, 'and cleaner than the London one. I shall be leaving at eight-thirty, but you don't need to get up then.'

When she got up, Rosemary put out some orange juice and made herself a cup of coffee. The house was very quiet and very tidy. It seemed to her that nothing murderous could happen in a place like this. On the road outside the flat she could see cars and some fallen blossoms.

She had another look at Sylvia's dolls. They didn't seem to be very expensive but very varied. There was one of an Eskimo fisherman, one of an Indian woman who was sitting cross-legged in a tinselly green robe. There was an Irish one, of an old woman carrying a creel of peats, a number of flamboyant Spanish ones, some porcelain Chinese-looking ones, and many others.

In the flat Rosemary felt quite relaxed. She had brought some books with her, one about Coleridge, one about Keats and one about Wordsworth, and she could easily sit there and read them. But in fact she read Sunday papers – huge weighty assemblages – and searched for information about the murders.

A psychologist said that the murderer might be quiet enough to talk to, even insignificant. His compulsion to kill blondes probably had something to do with some blonde who had jilted him or perhaps insulted him, or had taunted him about his manhood. Because he strangled his victims, clues were thin on the ground. For instance, he need never have blood on his clothes. The psychologist gave the opinion that he was almost certainly unmarried.

After she had read about the murders she thought that she would go out. It seemed ridiculous that she should come all the way to Toronto only to read about Wordsworth. So she left the flat, locking the door carefully behind her and putting the key in her purse.

The first thing she discovered was that Toronto was a paradise for shoppers. She had never seen so many shops: she could walk endlessly from one shopping precinct to another, and the shops were all so new, but also pricey. The place was a dizzying cornucopia of luxurious goods, though she couldn't find any bookshops: they must be in the area outside the malls.

Once she felt very insecure and panic-stricken. She was sitting at a table outside a restaurant, having a coffee, when a man sat down opposite her. He was wearing a blue track suit, had reddish hair and reminded her of Hector.

'Do you mind if I sit here?' he asked, and took out a newspaper and began to read.

She could hardly speak but drank her coffee carefully, though the shopping mall was spinning around her.

This is ridiculous, she said to herself, quite absurd. She went to the Ladies and washed her face while saying to herself, What's wrong with you? Don't be so silly.

After a while she was all right again, though she thought

she had seen enough shops to last her a lifetime. She found Toronto people very friendly, for once when she couldn't find the entrance to the Underground a middle-aged lady from the city took her there. She seemed to have walked for miles.

As a matter of fact she couldn't understand why she had quarrelled with Hector. But it was certainly to do with his untidiness, the way in which in spite of repeated tellings he had always strewn his jogging clothes and shoes all over the floor. He wasn't, she was sure, seeing any other women. She had grown tired of picking his stuff up every day. Why couldn't he understand, why couldn't an intelligent person understand that she was exhausted by his untidiness, why couldn't he do something about it, why couldn't he put his stuff away neatly, as she did? Obviously it was because he didn't really listen to her, thought her demands trivial and unreasonable. He was kind enough, and free with his money, but he never listened to her. She began to think of him as a sloppy boy, and couldn't have any respect for him.

After he left she had in fact fainted. Then when she came to she had felt the most dreadful anger and rage. She would never speak to him again. The trouble was that she would have to meet him at the University when she went back, unless she managed to get a job in another university, which was not easy, in fact, practically speaking, impossible.

The following day she decided to stay in the house and read. First of all, she spent some time sitting in the room where the dolls were, and imagining that certain couples were married to each other. The young boy in the naval suit was the husband of one of the Spanish dolls: and the flat-faced doll was married to the white-faced clown.

Then she read about Wordsworth.

Once she thought she had left the door open. She was frightened and ran to it but found that it was securely locked.

When the paper dropped through the letter-box she read about the murders, but there were no new developments. She imagined the murderer as young, well-dressed, and with coppery hair. Some blonde must have jilted him, she thought, agreeing with the psychologist, and now he was taking his revenge. She thought that he must be possessed by an insatiate rage. Wordsworth was allaying her own.

When she had tired of Wordsworth she went around the flat, looking at photographs. There were ones of her mother and father, who had been proud of her academic career but had, she always thought, preferred Sylvia to her. She could understand that, as Sylvia was much prettier and also more affectionate than she was. They had warned Sylvia against her insurance agent but not Rosemary against Hector. In fact, they had liked Hector and sometimes her father had played chess with him.

She tried to think why Hector wouldn't marry her. Was it because he felt she nagged too much? In fact she couldn't help herself about that. Or was it that he found her ugly or boring? Another thing that she hadn't liked was his dilatoriness. He would, after leaving assignments till late, work like a demon and then stay in his bed all weekend, exhausted.

The phone rang suddenly and surprisingly, but it was only a woman reminding Sylvia of a tennis match.

When Sylvia came home that evening Rosemary didn't tell her that she had spent the whole day reading in the flat. It seemed silly, and wasteful. Norman, Sylvia's friend, was an attractively pleasant straightforward man, who brought each of them a big bouquet of flowers. Rosemary found him a very natural relaxed person who clearly loved her sister. He too was divorced and had three children, who were now teenagers and away from home. He came from Scotland, like themselves, and having been on a holiday as a youth in Toronto had liked the city so much that he had come back and settled there.

'His patients love him,' said Sylvia, 'they are always giving him presents.'

'Yes,' he said, 'I was given a complete set of Sir Walter Scott by an old man. You might tell me some time if it's worth anything.'

She didn't know what he thought of her. She drank a great deal of wine but didn't eat very much.

She said that she liked Toronto, and that there were a large number of shops. 'I suppose you'll be looking for bookshops,' he said. 'I'll give you some addresses,' which he did. 'Incidentally, did you know that the biggest bookshop in the world is in Toronto?' he remarked.

She gave Sylvia the message which she had received on the phone, and then Norman and her sister talked about tennis, which they apparently played a lot. Did she play? No, she said, she had never played: her only hobby was reading.

She noticed Norman studying her seriously a few times. Perhaps he thought there was something wrong with her health. Doctors could tell a great deal by simply looking at you. She made sure that he didn't see her hands trembling, and for the most part kept them in her lap.

These two had their own world. They would allow her into it for a short while, but then they would grow tired of her. They would try to think of things they could amuse her with, however, and indeed that night Norman and Sylvia took her on a tour of Toronto after they had had their dinner.

'That's the red light district,' he said at one point, grinning. He and Sylvia were planning a holiday in Greece. They had been to South America often and of course to the United States.

'In fact,' Norman remarked, 'we might leave Toronto. It's very cold in the winter. Florida would be an alternative.'

They were really very kind to her, perhaps kinder than she would have been to them in similar circumstances. Neither of them mentioned Hector: Norman had obviously been warned by Sylvia in advance. Rosemary wasn't by any means a gifted conversationalist and found it a strain to be with them. She also felt a failure, since she had nothing hopeful to say about herself.

Toronto was indeed a large city and at night very bright and busy. There were many young people about, some of them laughing and horseplaying.

She mentioned the murders, and Norman said, 'Of course I'm not a psychiatrist, but I agree with what they've been saying. He would, I imagine, be very commonplace and quiet on the surface. He will be very difficult to catch,' he continued. 'You mustn't imagine that Toronto is another New York. It is usually very peaceful here, and the commonest headlines are about the language question, and Quebec.'

That night, Rosemary had a terrible dream. She had left the door of the flat open deliberately and the murderer had come in. Kill me, she had said to him, but he had contemptuously pushed her aside. You're too ugly, he said, and I only go for blondes. So he had gone in search of Sylvia instead. He wore a track suit and looked as if he had been out jogging. When he went in search of Sylvia she sat down and read about Wordsworth. She woke up sweating and for a while didn't know where she was.

It was quite soothing to be reading Wordsworth in a flat which was much more comfortable than her own, but on the other hand it seemed a waste of a holiday. One day a man came to the door trying to sell insurance and she took the chain off and let him in. She thought he might be the murderer and watched him carefully, but he seemed to be a genuine insurance agent. He told her that business was declining as housewives wouldn't open their doors to him, as they were frightened.

'Blondes aren't taking much insurance out at the moment,'

he said, grinning, 'but of course you're not blonde. You're safe enough. Perhaps they should dye their hair.'

After he had gone she decided to go out and buy a blonde wig. It was quite expensive, but she was happy walking about the flat wearing it as if she owned the luxurious rooms with the leather seats. Sometimes she sat idly crossing and recrossing her legs, imagining that she was a prostitute. She practised speaking to herself in a husky voice. Perhaps if she had been blonde she might have kept Hector. She felt restless and didn't want to read about Wordsworth. She remembered from her childhood an incident when Sylvia had torn a few pages from a book that she herself had been reading, and she had been very angry about it. Sylvia had remained much more confident than her, and had a very pleasant thoughtful boyfriend who would eventually take her away from the cold to Florida, while she herself had to return to the university and see Hector every day.

She imagined that Norman was the naval doll and she herself one of the flamboyant Spanish ones. They would marry and live happily ever after.

One morning, on impulse, she phoned the hospital where Norman worked and told him that she wasn't feeling well. She made her voice sound panic-stricken, as if she were having a nervous breakdown. She rambled on incoherently about the murderer being at the door.

'Hang on,' Norman said, sounding very calm and strong, 'can you come to the hospital?'

No, she couldn't go, she felt breathless, she had never been like this before.

Finally, he said that he would drive over immediately.

When he arrived she was wearing her blonde wig, and a short black skirt. She crossed and recrossed her legs as she told him that she felt unreal, shaken, very frightened. He stared at her blonde wig in amazement.

'Have you phoned Sylvia?' he asked.

No, no, Sylvia wouldn't be able to help. She told him a story about how once during her childhood she was bleeding from a wound in her leg and Sylvia had simply laughed and laughed.

'I can't believe that,' he said. 'What exactly is wrong?' She talked about the murderer in an intense rambling way: maybe he would kill Sylvia and then . . . All the time however he kept glancing at his watch and seemed extremely uncomfortable. He made her coffee and sat there, almost silently. Eventually the room began to become calm, and she felt as if they were man and wife.

'Where did you and Sylvia meet?' she asked him. He said it was at a tennis club. At times she would put her hand to her eyes, and say, 'This will probably pass. I can't describe to you how I felt.'

'Will you be all right if I leave now?' he said.

'Yes,' she answered, 'and don't, please don't tell Sylvia. She will think I'm crazy. Will you have another cup of coffee?'

'No, no,' he said, 'I have to get back. Are you sure you don't want to phone Sylvia?'

'No, I'd rather not. She'll think I'm pretending. I know her.'

He was unsure about leaving her, she could see that. What was all that about a murderer and an insurance man? Of course he didn't really love Sylvia, but only her yellow hair. He hadn't as yet realized her utter emptiness, that she was simply a pretty blonde doll.

When Sylvia came home from work Rosemary told her that Norman had called.

'What on earth? I thought he was working.'

'I gave him a cup of coffee.'

She didn't tell her sister about the wig which she had hidden at the bottom of her case.

I am an evil woman, she thought, but I can't help myself.

I wish to smash up this flat, she thought, like a murderer. She smiled and smiled at Sylvia, but really hated her. She was nothing better than a doll; she had no brains at all, she knew nothing about Wordsworth.

She felt Sylvia's antagonism and was pleased about it. She suggested that Sylvia should phone Norman, but Sylvia refused to. The phone indeed rang a few times but her sister didn't answer.

Suddenly she said to Rosemary, 'You don't really like Toronto, do you?'

'What makes you think that?'

'I just know that you don't. You don't like me either.'

Rosemary smiled and felt superior.

Sylvia brooded and said, 'You're trying to separate Norman and me. Why else would he come here for a coffee in the middle of the day? I'm not surprised Hector left you. I suggest you go home if you can get a change of plane. Look at you. You're supposed to be on holiday here and all you do is sit in the apartment and read. Don't think Norman is interested in your sort of life.'

I should really put her out of here, thought Rosemary, I should put on my wig and push her out of here so that the murderer can get her. I've always hated her and she's always hated me. There's no disguising that.

'I'm sorry you feel like that,' she said. 'I'll go to the airport and see if I can book an earlier flight.'

'You do that.'

That night when Sylvia had gone to bed (there had been strained silences) Rosemary slipped out of the flat wearing her blonde wig. She walked about the streets as if to find the murderer and to say to him, Please kill me. She wasn't at all frightened as the streets progressively emptied. She felt wide awake and clear-headed, as if she could see for miles and miles.

Not every woman would do what I am doing, she thought,

they would be too frightened. But though she passed many men who were drunk and muttering to themselves, she remained inviolate. No one tried to attack her and even if they had she would have been invincible. Perhaps they thought that she was a prostitute.

Eventually she went back to the flat and slipped into her bed, and slept well.

At breakfast-time Sylvia was penitent.

'Forget what I said last night,' she said. 'I had a bad day.'

'No, you were quite right,' said Rosemary. 'I shall try to book a flight back for tomorrow. I'm sure there will be no problem. I feel confident.'

'I had a rotten day at the office,' said Sylvia, 'that was all it was.'

'Actually it doesn't matter,' said Rosemary. 'I should never have come. Canada is not my sort of place. For one thing I don't play tennis.'

She did manage to get a seat on the plane, after she had said that she must go home as her mother was dying. She put on her blonde wig, looked suitably distressed, and told the young man at the desk that she had just learned the news about her mother. Her performance was brilliant, she thought. She should have been an actress.

'It was a heart attack. My mother lived on her own.' The Canadians were very sympathetic and considerate. She dabbed at her eyes now and again.

The day she left she bought a newspaper as she waited in the lounge in her blonde wig. The murderer had been caught. He had attacked another woman who was in fact a policewoman in disguise. It turned out that a blonde had actually jilted him years before. He worked in a garage, had a lisp, and was, according to the newspaper, very quiet.

So that's it, thought Rosemary, as she boarded the plane. Goodbye, Toronto. To the astonishment of the woman sitting next to her she took off her wig and put it in her handbag. For a good part of the time she read her book about Wordsworth. She felt quite relaxed, as if all her anger had left her.

As a matter of fact, she mused, I was right to be bothered about his untidiness. He was of course purely selfish, and why should I tolerate it? She sat back in her seat, glad to be leaving Canada, and continued her reading.

THE UNLOCKED DOOR

Stuart David

I

Often, at night, Stanley Garret would take a train out of the city, to a little harbour town he knew well. And as he walked past the loading bays there, where crates and cases were being lowered down to packs of night workers, the foremen would sometimes take note of his tattered clothes and his idle state as he approached.

'No work here, not tonight,' they would shout apologetically when he got close enough to hear. Then they would stare after him, puzzled, as he walked on without question; calling back to them over his shoulder,

'It certainly looks that way.'

It wasn't work Stanley went out there to look for. He already had work. But he was sure there was something else that someone, somewhere had forgotten to give him. So when he had passed all the loading bays he would sit down on the harbour wall, with his feet hanging down towards the water, and he would speculate about what it was.

It wasn't money, he was all but sure of that. And it wasn't love either. It was something more along the lines of an opening of some kind, a way in. Something he could use to perhaps *win* love and money, and whatever else there may be, but something he could use to win them by his own hand.

He had no particular talents that he was aware of, no special abilities. The most precious thing in his possession was a cheap old wedding band which had once belonged to his grandfather, and which hung a bit loosely even on his middle finger. But he was sure that something more was coming to him, and that when it came it would come from out there on the water, so he waited. He waited each night until all the lights in the anchored ships had been turned out, then he walked once more to the station and let the train return him to his city.

By day Stanley worked in the city square. It was a dusty place; an area of powdery white gravel dotted here and there with statues of city fathers, and surrounded by historic buildings. It swarmed constantly with tourists, and, off to one side of the square, a line of horse-drawn carts permanently waited to give them short tours of the historic city.

Stanley worked on the other side, at a stand which sold coffee and postcards, and all day long he could feel the dry dust settling in the roots of his hair and at the back of his throat. He lived only for his night visits to the harbour town, where the gusts of salt wind cleansed him of that dusty feeling, and where eventually, he was certain, the spell which had placed him in such a lowly place would be lifted, by a kiss from the lips of fortune.

But years passed, and one night Stanley sat out on the harbour wall, wondering how long he had been coming there. He watched the lights of the anchored ships reflecting on the black water, and he was so absorbed in his thoughts that for a while he didn't notice there was someone sitting beside him. He became aware of their presence only gradually, first noticing the click of a heel which wasn't his own against the harbour wall, then looking across and seeing a second pair of shoes suspended above the river beside his own. He turned around momentarily, still deeply absorbed in his thoughts, and his companion flashed him a quick and greedy smile, missing one front tooth.

'Resting?' the man asked Stanley quietly, in an attempt

to pull him out of his contemplation, and Stanley began to look at him more carefully, noticing the strange bend in his nose and the small crate on his knee.

'What?' he asked.

Having caught Stanley's attention the man didn't bother to repeat the question. Instead he cut directly to the subject he'd been meaning to ease into.

'Here,' he said invitingly, and shuffled himself closer to Stanley. 'Take a look in here.'

He removed the lid from the crate and Stanley looked inside without much interest.

'Have you ever seen anything like that in your life before?' the man asked.

Stanley, who was unable to see anything much at all in the darkness, said he hadn't, and the stranger put both hands into the crate and pulled out the contents.

'What the hell are *they*?' Stanley asked, suddenly attentive.

'Little monkeys. Squirrel monkeys,' the man said.

'They look like little men. Little men with yellow legs.'

'Well,' the man grinned, showing the space between his teeth again. 'This one here's a little man, but this one here's a little lady.'

He indicated to Stanley to lift the empty crate from his knees, and sat one monkey on each leg, taking a handful of figs from his pocket to feed them with.

'I came in on a boat which had these on board,' he said. 'All they eat are figs.'

Both monkeys had white markings around their eyes in the shape of little mannequin's masks, so that they looked like tiny bandits or highwaymen. Stanley's interest in them began to grow and the man offered him one to hold.

'That one's the little man,' he said. 'This other one can be a bit mischievous at times, but the little man's no trouble. Hold him tight now.'

Stanley held the monkey in the crook of his arm and, when he had grown confident of it, he asked about where they came from.

'From Brazil,' the stranger told him. 'There are people there; they . . . I'll tell you an interesting story. There are thousands of monkeys like this in the forests there, and people . . . they get them drunk. They cover bunches of fruit with alcohol. Then they catch them when they can't think straight, and afterwards they teach them to do things. You can teach them to do anything, any kind of trick at all. Have you ever wanted to be rich?'

'How big do they get?' Stanley asked, sidestepping the question.

'They're fully grown now. This is as big as they get. And all they eat are figs. So . . .' He fingered his gum where the missing tooth should have been and turned to Stanley. 'So how about I sell them to you?' he said.

Stanley looked down at the monkey he was holding and then, reluctantly, handed it back. His gaze drifted out on to the water and he shook his head.

'I've got no money,' he said.

The man looked disappointed and reached for the empty crate. He lowered the monkeys back into it and, in a dejected way, replaced the lid.

'Don't you have anything else?' he asked Stanley. 'How about the ring? Is that gold?'

Stanley held his hand out and looked at the ill-fitting wedding band. It slipped easily off his middle finger and he held it in his flattened palm.

'I think it is,' he said.

'Give me a closer look.'

The man turned it over in his fingers a few times, until he seemed satisfied. Then he pulled his feet up onto the harbour wall and tapped the lid of the crate.

'They're all yours,' he said.

And as he walked away he put Stanley's ring into his pocket.

II

For Stanley, that was the end of the coffee stand. The very next morning he quit for ever, and with that done he went out into the city's back alleyways, looking for discarded things he could make into props for the monkeys' tricks. He carried armfuls of wire and wood and plastic back to his hot rooms in a crumbling building, and when he had what he thought was enough he set about turning it all into miniature tight-ropes and swings, hoops and stilts and little carts.

From the crate the monkeys had crossed the ocean in he made a working seesaw, and from some wire and wood he'd found he made two large cages to hold them in at night. Then, when everything was complete, he began upon a strict regime.

From nine o'clock every morning until ten o'clock each night he sat with the monkeys at a table in his room, concentrating on one prop at a time, working to subdue the female monkey's mischievousness and to bring the male out of his complacency. With the windows and the door thrown open, and his tattered shirtsleeves rolled up to his elbows, he sweated and coaxed and praised, rewarding the smallest signs of improvement with a fig and a cry of approval.

Sometimes when ten o'clock came round, if the monkeys still had some energy left, he would attach their leashes to their little collars and take them out for a short walk. But for days at a time that short walk was all he saw of the outside world. He became oblivious to everything but training the monkeys, forgetting some days to feed himself, and thinking only: Here comes the way into the world at last. Here comes the unlocked door.

Soon, without him being aware of it, three weeks had gone by. And so engrossed had he become in his work he was also unaware that a young face had begun to appear in his open doorway from time to time. It had first appeared there during the second week, and as it became more and more mesmerized by the tiny monkeys, it appeared more regularly, sometimes standing and watching for an hour at a time when Stanley was at his most absorbed. It belonged to a little girl who also lived in the building, and most of the time she was exceptionally careful not to be seen by Stanley, in case he should forbid her to watch in future.

But one day, as she stood there, Stanley suddenly pushed his chair out from the table and threw his exhausted head down upon his folded arms. She waited in a state of quiet excitement for a few minutes, to make sure he didn't move. Then, emboldened by the certainty that he was asleep, she tiptoed into the room, and crept silently up to the table.

An awkward urchin with dirt on her forehead and chin, wearing boy's boots and a faded dress, she stood in amazement, watching the monkeys picking at Stanley's hair with their tiny hands. She longed to reach out and touch one of their tails, and she was trying to gather the courage to do so when Stanley lazily extended a hand to push them away from his hair. At that her heart leapt almost up into her throat, and gripped suddenly by a fear of being discovered, she decided at once to disclose herself.

'Are you all right, Mr Garret?' she asked quietly.

Stanley sat bolt upright, shocked for a moment by the idea that one of his monkeys had spoken. And he was so relieved when he saw the girl standing there that it didn't even cross his mind to apprehend her.

'I live a few doors along,' she said timidly, and Stanley, who was quite sure he'd never seen her before, nodded.

'*Are* you all right?' she asked him again.

'I'm tired,' Stanley replied. 'Just tired.'

He pointed at the monkeys and the girl finally gathered courage enough to reach out and touch one of their tails.

'They've worn me out,' Stanley told her. 'I've worked solidly for three weeks on trying to teach them tricks, but . . .'

He lifted the female and placed her on the seesaw to illustrate his point. She sat there obediently enough while he placed the male at the opposite end, but as soon as the male was settled the female climbed out of her seat and began to chew it, while the male sat on his as motionless as if he had been asleep.

'You see what I mean?' Stanley said.

But the girl was so fascinated by the monkeys that she didn't even notice their non-compliance.

'What are their names?' she asked instead.

Stanley shrugged without much interest and lifted the female on to a swing. Almost immediately it dropped down into the position of a quadruped and strutted around on the table top.

'They don't have any names?' the girl asked indignantly. 'No wonder they won't do tricks.' She bent down towards the male sitting on the seesaw and peered into his white bandit's mask. 'My name's Angela Arlon,' she said to it. 'I'll call you Shilling.'

'Shilling?'

'Yes. Now, what about the other one?'

'You're the expert.'

'Okay then, what about Triplet?'

'Triplet? Why?'

But Angela was already lost in moving Shilling and Triplet around amongst the props. She held up hoops for them to step through, and tried placing them one at a time on the delicate little tightrope. However much she called them by their new names made absolutely no difference though. She had no more success in getting them to cooperate than Stanley had managed when they were unchristened.

'It's pointless,' he told her. 'They can't do anything. Here, give them a fig.'

He passed her the bag and she gave them one each.

'Can we take them out for a walk?' she asked. 'On their leashes?'

'You take them out,' Stanley said. 'I've had enough of them. I need some sleep.'

Angela's face broke into a grin and she wiped her nose all the way across her cheek.

'How far can I take them?' she asked.

Stanley handed her the leashes and shut his eyes.

'Take them as far away as possible,' he said. 'Just as far away as possible.'

Before he lay down to sleep he didn't even bother to close the door. There was no longer anything in his room that anyone could possibly want to steal, excepting maybe the props he had built, and he half hoped someone *would* come and take those away. As he lay sweating on his bed he thought of the only thing he'd ever had worth stealing; his grandfather's ill-fitting ring. And dwelling upon the loss he'd made by trading it, he fell unhappily asleep.

The afternoon was all but over, and the room had begun at last to cool, when he awoke again. He put a hand on his tight brow before opening his eyes, to try and massage away the pain that had gathered there. And as he pulled gently at the muscles something suddenly landed with a force upon his stomach. He recoiled in panic, but when he opened his eyes he found it was only Triplet. Angela Arlon stood above him, holding Shilling in the crook of her arm, and excitement burned behind the dirt on her face.

Stanley brushed Triplet down on to the floor and slowly

dragged himself up until his back was propped against the wall.

'I was hoping you wouldn't bring them back,' he said.

But Angela's excitement was such that his weariness had no effect upon her. She put Shilling on the floor beside Triplet and sat down between them.

'They showed me the trick they can do,' she said.

Stanley eased himself away from the wall and looked down at the monkeys on the floor. Shilling was staring off into nowhere while Triplet hyperactively picked at the threadbare carpet.

'Tell me about it,' he said half-heartedly.

'Well . . . I walked a long way with them. I was waiting on them growing tired, but they just kept walking. People stared at us a bit in the streets, but I didn't mind.'

'Tell me about their trick though.'

'Well, I took them into the city square, and we had a rest on one of the benches there. I sat on a bench with them on my knees, and after a while some tourists came and sat beside me and started asking about them. Asking if they were mine and things.'

'You should have found out if they wanted to buy them.'

'And then they asked if they could have a photograph taken with them. So I let them, and soon there were lots of tourists all asking the same. And some of them gave me money.'

At that Stanley began to be infected with Angela's excitement. He reached out to pick up the monkeys, getting only Shilling, as Triplet dodged his hand and ran off to jump up on to the table.

'Some of them gave you money?' he asked enthusiastically.

Angela Arlon put a hand into the pocket of her raggedy dress and pulled out some notes and coins, and Stanley laughed.

'I knew they must be able to do one trick or another,' he said.

'What you really need is a camera,' Angela told him hurriedly. 'One that spits the photograph out the front as soon as you take it. Then you can charge everyone the same amount to have their picture taken with the monkeys. It's easier than teaching them to walk a tightrope.'

Stanley returned Shilling to the floor and smiled sadly.

'It's perfect,' he said. 'But I won't ever have the money to buy a camera.'

Angela held out the money from the pocket of her dress again.

'This is a start,' she said. 'And you can borrow the rest. Sometimes my father borrows money. I hear him talking about it with my mother. We'll find out where he borrows it from and you can do the same.'

Stanley began to massage his forehead again, having forgotten for a while about the pain there. Then he stood up and gave his hands a single clap, causing Angela to jump at the noise.

'All right,' he said. 'That's exactly what we'll do.'

He chased playfully after Triplet, finally catching her underneath the table. Then he scooped up Shilling from where he sat motionless on the floor, exactly where he had been left.

'Would you like to help me to begin with?' Stanley asked Angela. 'Since the tourists seem to like you?'

She smiled eagerly and wiped her nose on her arm.

'But there's one more thing the monkeys need,' she said. 'They need nice clothes. My mother knitted some clothes for my doll which would fit them perfectly.'

III

Thereby Stanley returned once more to the dusty city square. And in a very short space of time he and Angela had become an almost permanent fixture there. They stood each day at the base of a bronzed city father, Angela wearing her tattered old dress and holding Shilling and Triplet tightly, Stanley wearing his brand-new camera and shouting to every tourist that passed to have their photograph taken with the squirrel monkeys.

'Help the girl have a proper meal tonight,' he cried persuasively, and the tourists flocked to them.

They became such a popular novelty that Stanley had soon repaid what he borrowed to buy the camera. And once that debt was cleared he allowed Angela and himself one afternoon off, so that they could go and buy Angela a new dress and new shoes.

Near the square there was a shop where Angela had often stood and gazed in the window, when she and Stanley were on their way home from a day's work. Inside there was a dress which she had always dreamed of wearing, and when she tried it on that afternoon both Stanley and the shop assistants agreed that it had probably been made for her. But after they had bought it Stanley insisted that she continued to wear her old clothes whenever they stood beneath the bronzed father.

'It wouldn't do for me to be shouting "Help the girl eat a proper meal tonight" if you stood looking like you were born into royalty,' he said.

So she wore it only in the evenings, when their work was over for the day.

They arrived home at about six o'clock most nights, and Angela would change into her dress and shoes to eat dinner with her parents. Then she would go down and sit on the entrance steps with Stanley, watching Triplet chasing around in the courtyard after spiders and insects, while Shilling sat contentedly somewhere close by.

The courtyard was surrounded by three buildings; the one which Stanley and Angela lived in, the one which faced it, and the one which joined those two buildings together at the bottom end. It was a peaceful place while everyone else was indoors eating their meal, and Stanley usually ate his own dinner out of a can down there, forking it into his mouth as he told Angela about how close they were to becoming wealthy, and about all the delicious and extravagant foods they would be able to eat when they finally got there.

Then, when the first signs of life began to return to the court, they would take the monkeys back upstairs and wash the day's dust out of their coats, bathing them in a little bath Angela had made from an ice-cream tub. Afterwards they dried them both with a few blasts of hot air from a hairdryer, which Triplet seemed to enjoy above every other event in the day. She jumped up and down on all fours, peeping and chirping wildly, while the hot air blew back her tiny ears. And when that was over Stanley always put both monkeys into their cages and dropped a blanket over the bars, to encourage them to sleep.

'It's only birds you can fool like that,' Angela regularly told him, as Triplet continued to chirp now and then from beneath the blanket.

'I know, but it doesn't matter,' Stanley replied. 'It saves me having to look at them any longer than I have to.'

As soon as Angela went home Stanley would turn out his light, and most nights, as he lay on the bed, the chirping would continue for a while. It was always Triplet's chirping, never Shilling's, and Stanley would fall asleep to the sound of it, drifting off into the promise of a wide open future.

And so things went on, until one evening, near the end of summer, Angela mentioned that she would be going back to school soon.

'School?' Stanley asked in surprise.

'Yes.'

'I hadn't thought of that before. Have you only been on holiday all this time?'

'Summer holiday.'

Stanley leant forward on the step and stirred his fork around in the empty can.

'Do you think we'll be so popular without you?' he asked.

Angela wiped her nose and remained silent for a while.

'I can still work with you at weekends,' she said in the end.

Just then Triplet caught both their attentions, running in a crazy zig-zag after something too small for either of them to be able to see. They laughed together as they watched her, but they laughed a little sadly, and Angela brushed some stones off the step with her fingers.

'I can still help you with them at night too,' she said. 'Can't I?'

Stanley nodded and had begun to speak when he was interrupted by a sudden disturbance in the courtyard. Both he and Angela jumped, thrown for a moment by the erratic chirpings and peepings and yelpings. Then Stanley ran out into the courtyard with Angela close behind him.

Provoked by Triplet's crazy zig-zagging, a passing dog had charged through the archway at the top end of the courtyard and made straight for her. It was a few seconds before she noticed what was coming and, agile as she was, the dog got close enough to snap at her before she was out of its way. But the second time it came at her she was fully alerted, and scrambled up a drainpipe on the side of one of the buildings, until she was safely out of its reach. The dog turned in confusion then, looking for something else to exhaust its excitement upon, when its gaze fell upon Shilling. Determined not to be outrun this time it charged at him twice as fast, not knowing that if it had swaggered up to him as idly as a prospective mate Shilling still wouldn't have moved out of the way.

By the time Stanley reached the dog it had trapped Shilling's entire body in its jaws, and Stanley lashed out at it, kicking its underside so hard that Shilling fell out on to the ground when the dog opened its mouth to yelp. Then it ran off through the archway, while Stanley swore after it and Angela dropped down to pick up Shilling.

When Stanley was sure the dog had gone he put a hand on his forehead and began to massage his brow, and he knelt down in the court beside Angela.

'He's dead,' Angela said plainly. 'His neck's broken.'

Stanley looked at the little monkey lying loosely across her palms and she held it out to him. Gently he took it from her and she stood up.

'I'll go and try to coax Triplet down,' she said.

As she stood by the drainpipe and called persuasively to Triplet, Stanley took a rag from his pocket and wrapped it around Shilling's body. He folded it tightly and watched while Triplet came down warily into Angela Arlon's arms. Then he walked off towards the entrance steps, to pick up his fork and his empty can.

There was a patch of blood spreading out across Angela's dress when she reached the steps, from a gash the dog's teeth had left on Triplet's side. Stanley handed her his can and took the monkey from her, to prevent it from spoiling her dress completely, and they quickly climbed the stairs.

In Stanley's room they cleaned and bound Triplet's wound, and after the bleeding had stopped Angela dried her off with the hairdryer. The monkey took very little delight in the hot gusts of air though. She tipped her head back only slightly and stood there without enthusiasm. And as soon as they placed her in her cage she settled quietly down to sleep.

Stanley dropped a blanket over the cage and stood for a while by the window, looking out into the courtyard. He'd left Shilling wrapped in his rag on the table, and as he stood there Angela noticed the bundle and took an uncertain step towards it. She hesitantly lifted a corner of the rag, then, gathering her courage, she removed it completely and lifted Shilling's body into the ice-cream tub. She washed him down, watching the water turn red and dirty, and afterwards she dried him off with the hairdryer one last time. When his coat was dry she picked up his woollen suit, which Stanley had removed and left folded on the table before taking him down to the court, and she dressed him up in it to hide the rips and tears in his body.

She was crying when Stanley finally turned back into the room. She was sitting on a chair with Shilling on her knee, dropping tears down on to his little white bandit's mask, and Stanley crossed the room to stand beside her.

'Come on, Angela,' he said. 'Come on. He doesn't look all that different to how he always looked.'

Angela coughed and wiped her tears across her dirty face. Stanley put a hand on her shoulder and took Shilling from her. He wrapped him in a rag again and put him on the table.

'It wasn't a big step for him,' he said.

Angela looked at the blood on her dress and got up from her chair. Then she wiped her eyes again and walked towards the door. She stood by it for a moment after pulling it open, and before she left she said,

'I'm sorry about school, Stanley.'

IV

In time Triplet's gash scarred and healed, and in time Stanley returned with her to the square. As the years passed they became so well known there that they began to appear in the city guide book for tourists, along with the horse-drawn cart rides. But they were never quite so popular again as when there had been four of them.

Most weekends Angela still went with them, and things usually picked up temporarily then, but only ever to subside again when the weekdays returned. And gradually Stanley watched as the handle of the unlocked door began to retreat beyond the extent of his reach.

Triplet had begun to grow old. Grey patches appeared in her coat and she no longer struggled in the arms of customers. At night in the courtyard she would sit, more often than not, between Stanley and Angela on the steps, rather than chasing around wildly in the court. And the hairdryer never really regained its appeal for her. But sometimes, at night, Stanley and Angela would treat her to a trip out to the little harbour town, and all three of them would sit on the harbour wall there, letting the salt wind cleanse them of the city's dust.

Angela liked to hear Stanley talk about how he'd often come out there to wait for something when he was younger, and she loved to picture the man with the crooked nose and the missing tooth settling down beside Stanley on the harbour wall.

'Is that why you still come out here now?' she asked him. 'To wait for something else?'

But Stanley was no longer waiting for anything. What he'd once been expecting had already come, and it hadn't come to much, and now it was starting to go away again.

'I didn't start out with enough to bargain with,' he said. 'That was all.'

One night, as they sat there, Angela stared into Triplet's sad little eyes and smoothed her tiny ears back.

'Just think, Stanley,' she said. 'Just think of how many photographs of Triplet there must be throughout the world. If everyone who had one taken took it home she must have travelled to almost every country on the globe.'

Stanley smiled at the idea. 'She'd travelled a long way before she even came to us,' he said. 'When I bought her with that ring she'd just come all the way from South America in a crate.'

They looked out on to the water and the light of a ship appeared on the horizon. It moved towards them, getting a little brighter, and Angela turned to Stanley with a smile.

'Here it comes,' she whispered. 'Here comes your ship.'

Stanley laughed as the ship got steadily closer and the light grew steadily brighter. Then, when they could just begin to make out a hint of the ship's outline, it slowly turned and began moving parallel to the horizon. And gradually, as the outline faded, the light grew dimmer and more distant, until it disappeared altogether over the horizon again.

Stanley laughed appreciatively. 'That certainly was my ship,' he said. 'In fact, that was my song.'

Angela looked at him a little puzzled, as he got to his feet and brushed the back of his trousers with his hands.

'Your what?' she asked.

He winked at her and clipped the leash on to Triplet's collar.

As they walked back to the station Stanley glanced at Angela Arlon's cheap old clothes and her worn-down shoes, remembering momentarily her expensive dress; remembering how quickly they'd been able to afford it, and then how quickly she'd grown out of it. But before he could say anything to her about it his thoughts were interrupted by Triplet straining unexpectedly on the leash, as she ran on ahead of them with a short burst of energy. And by the time the leash had gone slack again, and Triplet had fallen back into step at his heel, he no longer cared to diminish the poignancy of the moment, by putting any of it into words.

BEADY EYES

John Cunningham

It was cosy, domestic; windy March outside. We showed the slippers to people who dropped in and they laughed at her wearing them. As soon as she got home she plunked her feet straight in. She'd seen them at the Barras and took them on account of the guy's patter, she already had a pair. We'd be back around the same time. I walked home from my work unless the weather was bad and on the way bought things for our tea from the Italian shop. I went along the Clyde's dark water smelling of the sea and stopped to watch the birds near the bridge, out in the middle; one dived and brought up bits of weed or God knows what and pretended to eat them as far as I knew, and the other stood on a beam sticking up from the water, always about the same place, the remains of some old framework shifted by the tides and currents – stood on it ignoring his mate and held out his black wings bent at the elbows. Skart, said our upstairs neighbour, the old man from Skye, when I told him, skart drying his wings. After the river I went along St Vincent Street and Dumbarton Road, the lighted windows, the dentures-fixed-while-you-wait shop whose sets of snappers glowed in dim pink light; and might buy herring at the van because they're good for you, good and cheap; then with bags of food I'd go up Hyndland Street glancing in the windows. Sunglasses, half-price, winter. The street rose into clear air. I was reluctant to arrive but keen to be home, to open the second half of the day, touch and talk. We didn't say much on weekday mornings.

She wasn't interested in skarts and couldn't take the bones in the herring. We were soon out of our clothes and in each other's arms on the floor in front of the gas fire. On the windy evenings of that long wait for the warm weather we might go for a drink in a wine bar, down a long flight of steps arm in arm in our anoraks, close, bodies familiar, steps dropping slow, step by step, warm where we touched. I thought us a pair of horses, companions in the shafts.

Or domestic stuff. I liked our clothes turning together at the Laundrette. She said it was boring, smelly and a waste of time but we went together, that's what you did. We showed the student that we were together, the student on the evening shift who said one night when sweeping fluff from under the driers, Do you know what this is – human skin. I wanted to know if it was true. She said he was making it up. I liked her frowning in the Laundrette and her wanting to save for a washing machine although I thought we had all we needed. We'd go home and share the ironing.

The slippers were furry animals with a short tail at the heel for pulling them on. And at the toe a face made of brown acrylic fur like the rest. The cheeks and ears were darker brown, they had a blob for the nose and glass eyes. They'd be all the rage for a month I thought, in various people's homes, then be thrown in the back of a cupboard.

I'd asked for a morning off – the gas man coming – and was fitting tiles round our bathroom mirror. We'd chosen blue and white mosaic tiles. I hoped she'd like them that evening. I placed them in an arch round the mirror, timing myself, expecting to be finished at midday. The radio was going, bathroom full of light, venetian blind up; tree in the back green motionless, pale green leaves bursting from its buds, and it was warm, spring at last, and I had a free morning during the week. I went whistling through the hall full of coats and junk to make a cup of coffee, whistling along with the radio and no thought in my mind, the perfect state, the perfect moment, existing, that was all. A slipper sat on the edge of the doormat, in the middle, by itself, tail to the door – it was watching me with beady eyes. Things rushed through my head and became one: that she'd put it on purpose to watch me – to tell me she was watching, even when she wasn't here. A discovery not a thought, her spy watching when she's not here. And I stepped back. I knew then it was a permanent state, being watched, beady eyes or not. The brightness of the eyes reminded me of hers but with an expression or scary lack of one I hadn't seen in her, part of her character I hadn't seen, hadn't considered, deliberately ignored. They gave her away. The mug tilted in my hand. Coffee dripped on to my shoe.

The tiles could be unfinished yet. Or someone else has done them . . . or she's finished them herself.

I couldn't step over the animal to reach the door but grabbed it by the tail and flung it against the skirting as if it would twist and bite my hand. With its mate they'd have been only slippers, a pair of slippers from the Barras. Having seen what I had, I fled.

In Edinburgh my room has a view over scoured rooftops to Arthur's Seat, the Forth and the Fife hills; the room, bedroom with an armchair, is in the house of Mrs Muir, a forty-ish lady whose husband is not here. When I open my door I see the giant cheese-plant that flourishes in her airy hall; its branches with knobbly joints snake along the cornices and colonize the ceiling. She gets up on a pair of steps to dust the leaves. There was a limp avocado in the Glasgow kitchen. There are plants all through this house including the kitchen we share, tactfully. She goes out a lot. When she'll be cooking for herself or friends I've learned to know, she tells me by the way she walks daintily across the hall and pauses thoughtfully . . . the message passes and I'll say I'm going for a beer tomorrow night. I'm amazed. A woman I would have laughed at, and here I'm respecting Eileen's wishes, that's her name, and enjoying it. I'm sure she has said more than once in chat though I don't remember the occasion that she needs her own space – not, as someone else would have said, I want you out from under my feet. But I'm a different person here and her phrases are wonderful to me. I cooperate with the give and take, the way of life, I'm the lodger. We get on together. Weird.

I go for a beer with a couple of friends in the Canny Man and also across the road to the flash place with wall-to-wall women, as they say; it means there are single women. Go on, they say but I don't – the notion that I would betray Eileen.

On Sunday evenings she stands outside my door and calls: Have you any washing, Neil? I hand it to her in the bag she gave me. The washing machine is off the kitchen in what's called the scullery. There's no room to stand back and see the clothes whirling and I haven't gone in there and looked. Does she put our stuff in together? Has she red, black and lilac pants?

I told her my parents live in Airdrie and she doesn't know I saw a blink of distaste cross her face or if she does, hasn't let on. She'll be ten years younger than Mum yet she's a different generation; and a different nationality.

I've told her that I lived alone in a bedsit in Glasgow. That I came to Edinburgh for a change and might think of buying a flat whereupon she brings details of what she thinks I can afford; what she has gathered about me. I know nothing of her except she's always lived in Edinburgh and has no children. Nothing of the husband who may be dead but I don't think so. I've seen his photo but that doesn't mean one thing or the other.

If Eileen wants her space and I don't fancy a beer I usually stay in my room and look out the window. There's the queer lump of Arthur's Seat. A foreign land, I wish I had binoculars. Can't settle to read.

I've been here three months. I take the early bus, 7.15, and notice the same people in their cars on the same stretch of road each day. By the time we get to the M8 I'm seeing the poppies on the roadside in a haze of sleep and the droning, cosy vibration of the bus. Before it makes its halfway stop at Harthill we pass a place where they're landscaping mounds of earth into pyramids. They'll be covered with grass and bushes probably. The bare earth's almost completely shaped now and a digger is perched on the slope doing the final smoothing with its delicate arm.

It changes about here, at Harthill, a slight difference but no special place, like a border crossing, it changes here in the frontierland, the no-man's-land of undulating central plateau. We cross an invisible ridge about Harthill, other than the crest of the road. Everyone in the bus must feel it, more or less; they slump back in their seats for the second half – we've crossed over. I can't help thinking somehow that the trouble they're having in Shotts prison must be connected with the situation, the poor guys being affected, perhaps dragging over the nerve each time they cross their cell, doing time in this twitchy no-man's-land. We go up the hill to Kirk o' Shotts. Over to the right black mounds and nothing much, to the left kirk, graveyard, fields and wood but – the bus angles down and there are the towerblocks and spread of Glasgow.

I walk five minutes to the office. Some evenings, many evenings, leaving feels a wrong direction and commuting an illusion, a road to dreams.

But from high ground before Harthill, Arthur's Seat sticks up like an island on the horizon. It's a real hill that during the day has been a memory, a painting of another country. Soon the city in miniature shows twenty miles away: the castle and the crags and Arthur's Seat, the tiny needles of church spires. The bus hurries towards the real suburbs of the romantic city.

I'm fixing a shelf in her kitchen and feel her looking at me. She goes on looking, suddenly without a mask, after I look back. Her little bare feet in leather sandals will step towards me.

. . . one of these evenings she'll ask me along on her walk and we'll be in a sheltered nook of the golf course looking over the city, the two of us, then a pause, the long hesitation there's nothing else like . . .

The curtains in her sunny kitchen stir in a flower-scented breeze, no kebab and diesel, and Eileen smiles at her sandals and up at me again. She has gears I haven't engaged, and could get through the box at racing speed. If I touch her as I want to, tip of my finger on her arm, everything will change and won't go away; perhaps finally come down on this side.

And I'll go down to Claudio's and buy things for our supper . . .

There's a blue spot from when she painted the ceiling, on the white basin, in her bathroom, and I'm staring at it and it's absolutely here.

I don't believe Glasgow, but the bus will go through the looking-glass tomorrow.

I could walk along the Clyde, up Hyndland Street, to the Laundrette, down the steps . . .

Edinburgh, Edinburgh, the white gulls. There's one on the chimney stack shifting its feet, turning cold eyes and yellow beak to the wind.

ST ANDREW'S DAY

Mark Fleming

They crept on all fours, Devlin squinting through the nippy smoke from the roll-up poked between his lips, Kareen grim-faced and imagining they were soldiers in Bosnia. Until she burst out giggling again.

'Wrap it!' Devlin hissed through teeth that might well have been gripping an invisible knife instead.

'It's just the way your arse is wriggling . . . Makes me want to give each cheek a huge chowie! Just as well it's not been raining, too. Your new Versaces and that, likes? Eh, Dev? Your knees'd be fucked! Heh! Imagine if there was puddles? The two of us trying to duck in here all hunched up like that . . . What was his name? That American comedian? From the old days . . . The glasses and moustache? The cigar and that. They were brothers or something, I think. Eh, Dev?'

'Sssh, Kareen, fuck's sake! I'm just asking you to zip it for five fucking minutes. Right, sweetheart?'

Kareen watched him flick the expired smoke off into the darkness.

'They Regal King Sizes you're smoking the night smell funny.'

'Kareen . . .'

Devlin stopped; he lay stretched out by a van's bonnet. Kareen squirmed alongside.

Seven cars were arranged ahead of them, waiting in the cold for owners supping beyond the arc of light from the pub windows.

Devlin stared past Kareen. He tried to picture this car park in daylight. His memory conjured a large concrete square, similar to the concrete squares all over the city where there had once been green squares. The pub was a large pillbox with glass; condensation had crept over the windows to keep the concrete square masked. The shifting figures inside seemed like apparitions.

Kareen saw what Devlin was watching. 'That's like my telly when it needs tuned.'

He turned to her. The light was catching her profile, her small hooked nose and her blonde bob that night-time had turned to silver. His eyes dwelled on her cleavage. He saw how it trembled with her weight on her elbows. He murmured: 'I think you need tuned in half the fucking time. You Muirhouse bam!'

Kareen's whisper carried across the car park. 'I'm not from Muirhouse, you. I was born in Lancs. As you well know. Bet I'm the first Lancastrian you've humped. Apart from Tanya off Corrie that is, in your dreams.'

'Never denied the bam bit.' He shook his head at her, then more vigorously, eyes screwed shut. 'Quite a fucking wicked hit, man. That skunk. Fuck your astroturf . . . It's much better being on grass, ken?'

Kareen nodded. 'Uh-huh. Magic. Here! You listened to that tape I gave you yet? The last mix that Hectic done on the radio?'

Devlin looked at her, faced the pub again. He had tensed. A silhouette was moving just inside the doorway, tugging at a cigarette.

'Mind that song "Grim up North"?' she went on. 'Couple of year ago, it came out. The boy reels off the names of all these northern towns, likes. Manchester and Crewe and Rochdale and that. Oldham, too . . .'

'Naw, Kareen. Christ . . .'

'That's why I liked that one. Hectic's "Grim up North

Embra". Sound mix it is, by the way, Dev. Wait till you hear it. Specially if you're ripped, likes.'

'Aye. DJ Hectic. You know all about that cunt, eh, Kaz? Let the cat out the bag on that score, you did, sweetheart. When I got you pished in Slammers that morning.'

'Not exactly a state fucking secret, Devlin.'

'Moving to the Hectic beat . . .'

'Hah.'

'Bonking to the Hectic beat . . .'

'Fuck off.'

They remained frozen by the van wheels, like two accident victims. Until Kareen's jaws got going again, up, down, sideways, smacking her gum.

'Get fucking back inside, you. Fucking bugging my happiness, this cunt.'

'Heh . . . What's this cunt about, Devlin?'

'Ssh. Don't know. Just watch, sweetheart. Keep your eyes well peeled.'

The man was hunching his shoulders, tossing his cigarette to the deck, grinding it in. Then another man emerged from the shadows. They started arguing. This was obviously a continuation of what had begun inside; it escalated.

Devlin and Kareen gaped at the action, mesmerized. Presently another person stepped into view. This third man was drunk and his slurs were aimed at the man who'd been smoking. He poked his finger towards the smoker's chest. The smoker brushed the finger aside, but it came back, then back again. The smoker wafted it off like a midgey.

Then the less drunk of the two facing the smoker grew bored with this display. His bunched right hand crashed into the smoker's face.

'Aaah!' the smoker growled, his head whiplashing sideways.

'Oyah!' Kareen whispered from where they were lurking.

The smoker and the hitter performed a tentative and elaborate squaring-up, like a matador practising in a mirror. The drunk kept his thumb raised at the hitter whilst staggering on the spot as if he'd been hit himself.

But the smoker had only been taken by surprise. His reaction came all at once. His limbs flayed at the two bodies ahead of him, the drunk crumpling when the first hook connected, the hitter cowering, attempting to block the rain of blows, screaming: 'No, son! No, son! Christ, no! Enough.'

More shapes tumbled from within.

'Deek this lot, Kaz. It's the fucking Wild West. Like the films . . . I swear John Wayne'll steam through the lot of these cunts any minute. Sounds like a fucking wedding reception.'

Devlin couldn't believe their luck. A shrill woman's voice added to the masculine battle cries, yelps of pain and the dull smacks of skin against bony skin: 'I'll fucking chib you, John! Touch your father once more and I'll fucking chib you, d'you hear?'

Devlin gave Kareen's backside a quick pat. 'Let's do it.'

They heaved themselves to their feet, keeping their backs arched. Devlin began to weave through the cars. Kareen held back, continuing to spectate, listening to Devlin's soft curses at wheel locks or blinking alarms. Eventually he called to her: 'Kaz . . . Kareen. Quick!'

She whipped round to see him giving the okay sign. He'd stopped by the driver's door of the car furthest from the pub battle. He held his left hand out to her, beckoning.

'All clear, eh?' he whispered, looking over the light shining across the curve of the car's roof.

'Aye,' Kareen replied. She sprinted on tip-toe, ducking down at the car. She began jigging her body, bobbing on her trainers. She murmured lyrics that were floating through her mind, snippets of Hectic straddling his deck amongst the light sabres and sweet clouds of dry ice at *Pure*: 'Gonna take you to the limit, take you to the top, baby baby baby, gonna never gonna stop. You know it's grim up Granton when the horneys they crawl, but I'm sorted, I'm mental, life's one fucking ball . . .'

'Kaz!'

She shut up but her jaws persisted with the gum. She gazed at Devlin hovering by the car door to gape through the window.

'Watch you don't disturb some Tory cunt shagging a tart, likes, Dev!' She fired a glance back towards the melee.

Then another tune implanted in her brain, a punk chorus that an older cousin used to bawl out. She gave a muted version under her breath. 'Yeh yeh, Industrial Estate. Yeh yeh, Industrial Estate. Yeh yeh . . .'

'Kaz. This is fucking serious shit, you wee radge. Don't fucking know about you but this is pure freaking me out, man! The fucking state I'm in, likes. Pure fucking wasted, likes. It's bad enough facing your old dear when I'm as fucking ripped as this. But twoccing some cunt's wheels, ken? Fucking serious shit. Plus those fucking clowns over there'll have the horneys down on this place fucking . . .'

'Devlin. You know the pigs never show till they've given whatever stushie there is a good twenty minutes to cool off.'

Devlin nodded, rubbed his palms up and down his jeans.

She nodded too, mumbled: 'Casualty?'

'Right, Tape.'

Kareen dug into the pockets of her jacket. She brought out the thick brown reel and pressed it into Devlin's gloved hand. Then she hunched over him, eyes darting between the pub's exit and the approach from the main road.

'That's it, sweetheart. Just keep on keeping shottie.'

Once Devlin's criss-crossed pattern was achieved, Kareen backed off and watched Devlin take a step back. He stood with his arms outstretched, glanced once towards the pub, then flashed his steel toe-capped boots towards an orange lamp-post behind them. The dull gleam spread smiles across their faces.

Then his expression twisted, the smile vanishing into an almost constipated grimace. Snatching his breath in he moved each black hand outwards, making a hypnotic motion with his outstretched fingers.

Kareen's heart flipped once when Devlin's leg lashed for the door, his body perfectly angled. His tae-kwon-do kick struck the window dead centre. There was a muffled splintering.

Devlin repeated the trained movement. His mind had turned that square of glass into Wallace Mercer's belly. He cracked right to the rib cage a third time, a fourth. Then his left foot ceased balancing him and he tumbled back on to the car park.

'Dev!' Kareen's stare checked the drunken violence, then went back to his collapsed frame. She shoved her hands over her mouth and doubled up at the sight of him on his arse. 'The state of you, Dev. Fucking . . . Van Damme on drugs. Jean-Claude Van Devlin. Ha-hah!'

Devlin sprang up. He rubbed at his backside. Marching over to the car he fisted the window until it had fallen inside. He poked around for the handle, heaved the door open. He tugged the destroyed pane out and to one side, then jumped in. 'Fucking hate that bit, ken? That fucking Rotty last week. Must've thought its dreams'd come true and a huge fucking human shish kebab had just poked into its owner's car . . .'

Kareen grinned. She'd spent part of a passion-crammed fifteen minutes that afternoon giving his wounds post-coital caresses, in her single bed, whilst her mother got messages. The previous weekend's snarling guard-dog had not drawn blood but there were still nasty gouge marks on his 'KAZ' and 'YLT' Indian-Inked flesh. She had laughed most of all at his new Stone Island top losing its right sleeve.

He was crouching inside. Hand reaching again, he said: 'Torch.'

'I've forgot it, Dev. Sorry, man!'

He snapped his fingers once. She lifted out the small black cylinder and handed it over, peering back at the pub. Various bodies were being restrained. Three people kept the smoker arm-locked; he was firing verbal insults at the woman who had now folded into hysterical greeting.

'The evils of legal drugs, Devlin.' She could make out that someone had selected Two Unlimited on the jukebox.

'Not that fucking gash again,' she murmured. She turned to the beam of light beneath the dashboard where Devlin would be clawing into the car like a surgeon. She found herself joining in with part of the song's chorus. A voice inside the pub followed suit.

Before the Dutch pop duo had completed their work, Dev had completed his and a grand and a half's worth of motor transport changed ownership.

As he wired the engine into life Kareen bent double into a stupid walk, round through the headlights, towards the pub, then turning sharply for the passenger side.

'Fuck's sake . . . Heh! Groucho Marx, Kareen! That's who you were trying to think of. That was fucking nipping me, that!'

He added a triumphant yelp like a movie Indian clutching a fresh scalp. He leaned over and wrenched Kareen's door open.

The two youths caught one last glimpse of the smoker wriggling free of his guards to lunge at the female. She produced something from inside her jacket. Devlin stomped on the accelerator before they could see what she'd drawn and whether she'd managed to use it.

Christine stubbed out her cigarette as she watched the camera on *News at Ten* panning the debris inside a Bosnian house. She pressed the mute button. Then she got up and stepped along the hall to glare at the debris of her daughter's bedroom again.

The quilt remained discarded. A trail of clothing led to the Caterpillar boots, their labelled tongues sticking out at her as a reminder of the amount that she had had to fork out for them after weeks of huffs and tantrums that had verged on method acting.

She was angry at the state that the bedroom had been left in, at her daughter having been out all day and at knowing that she could expect a phone call at any time which would state: 'Staying at Debbie's, Ma. Her Ma says it's okay.' Click.

She knew that it was absurd but she also felt angry that Kareen was out there somewhere without these boots.

Before switching the room back into blackness she shuddered. These crumpled bed covers and strewn clothing had made her picture that farmhouse after having been ransacked by Serb militia, not much older than Kareen, inflamed by cheap vodka.

Once she returned to the settee she fired the remote control at the screen. The activated volume introduced men seated around a conference table. Little flags and nameplates were poised next to jugs of water before them. Each one was poised for his turn to speak earnestly into microphones. Cameramen jostled in the background like crash spectators.

A man with wild grey hair took the floor, the caption giving him a Transylvanian Count's name. He represented the Bosnian Serbs. He started to wag his finger at the world.

Christine sighed and checked the time on the video's digital display.

Kareen staggered out of the doorway, sniggering as she managed to tip several chips down on to the pavement at her feet. Devlin made a lunge at the contents of her newspaper parcel. She laughed even more as she pulled them out of his reach with a customary, 'Fuck off you.'

Devlin halted by the front door of the car, watching Kareen sway over to the passenger side.

Kareen heaved her side open and landed on to the seat, jolting the car.

'Watch my suspension, Kaz!' He scowled as he ducked in.

Kareen leaned over and tugged his hood back from his head. She ran her slender purple-tipped fingers down his stubble, stroking. Then she shouted into his ear: '*Your* suspension?! That's one of your more beautiful beauties, Devlin, you cunt! Just like all they pairs of 501s you used to wear in your drainpipe days when I first met you were *your* jeans. No fucking receipts, though, but. Neither had those radges you used to buy them off. Car fucking boot sales outside Gladstone's after closing time, eh?'

Devlin gave her another look, poking a finger into his earhole, drawing it free so that his hand could toy with the large gold hoop dangling from its lobe. 'Kaz. You're bammy as fuck, by the way. I'm just speaking at my normal forty-five, ken? But you! You're at fucking seventy-eight! Where's my fucking smokes, by the way?'

He patted each pocket, coughed and spat through the window frame.

Kareen was laughing in-between mouthfuls. She watched Devlin checking the floor below the dashboard. Whilst his head was bowed she dug into her jeans and tugged the fags from where she had hidden them after pickpocketing him in the chippie. She placed the packet on the dashboard behind the steering wheel. She nudged him.

He scowled over at her. Then he noticed. 'Right before my fucking yacks the whole time, eh? That'll be shining fucking bright!'

Kareen nodded, gulping her food down. 'Well crash the ash then!'

'One thing at a time, Kaz. Christ. Finish your scran, at least. Time to hit the yellow brick . . .'

Kareen chewed a handful of greasy chips as Devlin got the purring engine back into gear. She lunged towards his frowning eyebrows and smothered his lips with her own, her tongue darting across his teeth, probing the gaps.

Devlin used his own tongue to ward hers off, giving her a noisily smacking kiss. 'You taste of salt and sauce, daftie.'

'You taste . . . all nicotiney. Here, d'you want another one of my chips?'

'Nah, sweetheart. I'll just get this fucker shifted again, Kaz. Fucking . . . It's fucking cold enough the night without having any glass in my fucking window, ken?'

The car jumped forward. Swinging the wheel round towards the main road Devlin dug his left arm to and fro, climbing up the gears.

Kareen eased back into her seat, stamping her left trainer out on to the dashboard as she finished the last mouthful of her food. Crushing the papers into a ball, she peered out the window for a while, now chewing the gum that she had kept poked between teeth and cheek until she had finished her chips. She unwound the lever until the window came down to halfway. She bowled her wrapper out towards the verge flashing past, then grabbed at the handle again, twisting it back.

'Sound motor this, Devlin. She can't half move, eh? A pure gem, she is. I don't know where you get so much bottle. Big fish like this, likes, right down to the tiddlers. The tiddler fucks and that. I mean. Take the other night. When was it, Dev? A week past Tuesday or that? Nah, Monday? Aye, Monday. 'Cause I'd wanted to see my home team on Sky, you know? Oldham.'

'You going to cast up me tipping that yuppie cunt's drink over?'

Kareen nodded slowly. 'Oldham against the bastard Gooners. I was feeling shit at the time, coming down from the weekend and that and watching the Latics getting fucked again by those southern scum was making it really fucking shit. You just wanted to slag Ian Wright for being such a posing bastard. Just cause he can afford to walk into shops and actually take his gear over to the bird at the till and not have to do the fucking Linford Christies along Rose Street Precinct, eh Dev?'

'You casting up the Friday afternoon before the old Hibees done the business against the Tims? Going radge on the Parkhead terraces with my Kickers after doing nought to fucking twenty out the fucking Schuh changing room. Those bastard shoes got scuffed to fuck, too. Parkhead's a bigger fucking tip than that fucking Gorgie slum, eh sweetheart? These weedjie cunts. They're fucking scoobied about looking cool, like, Kaz. You can see them through the fucking segregation fence. The closest they've got to Casuals're a couple of gadges who've stookied some cunts at a golf course and robbed their fucking Pringle jerseys. Thereafter it's a sea of green scarves, Irish flags and blond-streaked hair.'

'Just imagine all their pairs of white towelling socks, Dev? Slip-on shoes and Poundies trainers.'

'Exactly. Parkhead and fucking Ibrox're the only two grounds you still get young cunts in Snorkel jackets. I swear it, Kareen.'

'What? Those fucking hideous anorak things? With the furry hoods?'

'That's the ones, Kaz. I blame the soap-dodger dress sense on all that fucking Buckfast and solvent abuse. And the Tims call their ground Paradise, too. And what about that fucking Rod Stewart song that was on your radio last night? Fucking

. . . Can't mind what it's called, but he goes on about Celtic, Rod Stewart.'

'Another fucking Londoner bastard, he is. What's he like with his tartan scarves?'

'You're Celtic and you're Man United, cunt was singing to one of his birds. Well, Kareen, my sweetheart. You're Hibs and you're Man City.'

'City fuck all, pal. I'm a Latic, likes. I was telling you about the Oldham game. And you being a game cunt, likes. Last Monday, likes? They might've been gubbed by Arsenal and heading back up the M1 with fuck all but thanks to my loving boyfriend I was on the last number six with a fucking score in my sky rocket that I'd never had when Wright was doing his fancy patter. You cunt! Just watching you going up the bar and tipping that half-pint down that snobby bastard's Pringle jacket, flapping over the cunt with a bar towel, then fucking off to the toilet with the bar towel wrapped around the boy's wallet and fucking off out the fire exit . . . I'm telling you, Old Fagin would've been proud of you. That goes for all the Crewe Crew!'

'Old who?'

'Oh, nothing. It's the musical I was telling you about. That we're supposed to be doing at school the now. I'm a pickpocket. In Victorian times. The Artful Dodger, likes?'

'Never did like musicals, Kaz. Quadrophenia was all right. That video we seen up at Gabby's on Tuesday.' He paused, checked his wing mirror. 'Christ, this fucking van's almost right up our arse. Fucking cowboys. Shouldn't be allowed on the road half the cunts . . . Sorry, Kaz. You were on about the Artful Dodger? That's that well dodgy pub near Wester Hailes, is it not?' He was grinning at her.

'Ha ha, Devlin. I've drunk in the Dodger before. When I went out with Mark Hunter just after last Christmas. I liked it. Used to go there all the time. Even after I chucked him same night he got himself barred.'

'What? You bevvying all the time? Last Christmas? All of fourteen you must've been.'

'I've always been tall for my age, though. Long legs. Long blonde hair. A low-cut lycra T-shirt that shows me off to cunts. What's it you say? Two good handfuls, Devlin, you cunt? That's what the barmen see first, likes. Then they ask theirselves do I want to worry about the off chance the CID might show up or do I give blondey the benefit of the fucking doubt and get in a good night's fucking oggling? You only get asked for ID if you get tipsy on two halfs of cider and can't stop giggling and drop your bottle or fucking boak without bothering your arse to get to the bogs. Like Carri-Anne's capers the other night.'

Devlin was hooked on his stoned impression of the scene ahead, the white lines drilling underneath, the bright shapes that the headlamp beams were carving out of the darkness.

Kareen was getting her own impressions; the orange streetlights blinking over Devlin's face. She thought that it was like a mask on a stage, a slow strobe light catching the features. She watched this for a while, riveted. The gaping window frame had been tossing his hair out of place so he'd pulled his hood over. Now she was thinking that he looked like one of those daft old-time pilots.

'All you need's a white scarf and you could be that Biggles cunt, Dev.'

'Eh?'

'Nought. Thinking aloud, just, likes.' She could still smell their last spliff, the glorious sweetly pungent skunk that they had smoked after driving out by Port Seton to the Forth; watching the white of the waves endlessly curling over, their new car dwarfed by the power station. Her mouth was dry from that grass; her tongue had gone numb. She felt that she had to continue talking to keep it exercised. Then she thought that there was so much to say anyway.

'What the fuck you going to do with this motor?'

'Do with it, Kaz? I thought we could take her out to Cramond, ken? Out to the sea again . . .'

They cruised past Portobello police station. He glanced into his wing mirror, easing their speed down for one gear change.

'Cramond?'

'Aye, Kaz. The sky'll be pure clear as a bell out there the night. I'll point out Orion with his belt up in the sky, arms up in the air giving it lald as I crank the volume up to max. I'll skin up and we'll just stare at the lights on the Forth, ken? Reflected in the water. Like a painting. The lights from Kirkcaldy or whatever the fuck's on the other side. You can try another one of your radge handstands. See if the picture looks the same. Ha ha.'

'Like that painting we seen in that shop window down from Avalanche that I said was upside fucking down? Fucking price tag would've robbed you inside out!'

Kareen shut up. Her lips kept on with their relentless smacking at her gum. After they'd made the next amber lights she poked into her mouth and tugged a portion of the gum out to toy with in her fingers. She stopped this when she noticed that her fingertips were giving the once-mint gum a nicotine tinge.

'Gross,' she murmured.

'What's that, daftie?'

'I was just thinking, Dev. These cunts that try nicotine-flavoured chuddie or they daft fucking patches, man. I mean. What the fuck? The way I see it is. One out of every four smokers die from smoking. Lose one of their fucking lungs at least, likes? That's what they said on the telly the other night, likes. Some cunt in a fucking white overcoat. If you're still hooked when you're forty-odds then either your next pack's got your name on it or it hasn't. If you're one of the three who don't get cancer you could get ran over, or get bayoneted, or catch the virus or live on to be like my Na-Na who thinks she's one of the fucking Royal family. Ha! That's gospel, by the way, Dev. Did I not tell you? I have to curtsy now when I go up to visit her in her home. If you're a member of the Royal family where's your fucking yuppie lover hiding I say to her. Where's the swarm of fucking *News of the World* photographers outside this fucking sheltered scheme, Na-Na?'

She halted, chewed some more, stared out the windscreen.

'Joppa!' Kareen announced a street-sign that had just whipped in and out of sight. 'What a daft fucking name, eh? Joppa . . . Joppa. Sounds like a martial art, eh? Karate. Kendo. Judo. Joppa. Seen Van Damme's Joppa video? Taught me a few tricks, I'll tell you. These Hearts Boys from over Saughton Mains were outside the chippie pure getting wide so I said to the cunts okay then square-goes now you HIV cases and the cunts kicked off but I fucking banjoed the radges with this move I learnt off that tape last week and that, you know?'

'Steady, Kaz. You know you've not shut up for a second since we left Port fucking Seton. Not even to draw breath. What, have you got gills or something? Don't tell me you turn into a mermaid at midnight? That's why you like chilling out near the sea, eh?'

'I talk when I'm happy, you know? Like a dog wags his tail, I fucking wag my tongue. And when I'm out my face it fucking wags like fucko, Devo!'

And here she picked up on the DJ mix currently blaring out of the speakers. She wriggled her body, elbowed Devlin. 'Here . . .'

'What? And fucking sit still. You're putting us off, man. All these fucking double parked clowns, man.'

'Dev, baby. Once we hit Ferry Road, which'll be sooner rather than later the way you drive, likes, I'm going to duck when we go past Drylaw Road, right? I'm supposed to be grounded. Since my Ma came back early from the Doocot and found you raking about in the kitchen with just your scants on, man!'

Devlin lifted one hand from the wheel as he burst out laughing. He unzipped his jacket's top pocket. 'Here, Kaz. Might as well drop this the now. Only a quarter, but what the fuck. Enough for that wee buzz.'

'Sound, Devlin.' She reached out for the tiny corner of paper, then watched him producing a cassette from a lower pocket.

She swallowed, then asked: 'What's this shite you're hitting us with?'

'Shite fuck all, you. This is one I snaffled at that car boot sale over at Duddingston, ken? At that school.'

'Snaffled? From a car boot sale, Dev? What about that pride you love to go on about, likes? Probably would've cost you ten pee or something.'

'Just stick the fucker in so's I can get give it a listen, Kareen. I never fucking coughed up for it cause I don't even know if I'll like it.'

'Who is it, like?' She squinted as its cover in the gloom.

'Happy Mondays. An early yin, like. Squirrel and G-Man or some fucking shite. From about ten year ago, like.'

'Ten year ago? I would've been at Primary, still. Didn't even know where Edinburgh was, probably, likes.'

'Aw. Sweet. Imagine you being sweet, Kaz?'

'Fuck off. And don't you dare mention those fucking horrible photos my Ma's got pinned up.'

'Wouldn't fucking dream of it. I've bad enough bruises on my arm from being attacked by that fucking Rottweiler. Fucking . . . Just stick the Mondays in, eh? Let's see if Shaun Ryder's singing was just as fucking chronic in they days.'

'In a fucking minute, man. I love this bit coming up. When fucking Prodigy comes in. Here it is . . . I'll take your brain to another dimension! I'll take your brain to another dimension!'

'Aye. If you don't stop distracting me I'll take us both into another dimension. That starts six feet fucking under!'

Christine hovered by the phone, bottle in hand. She slugged the last of the 20/20 and grimaced when the fortified strawberry-flavoured drink bit into the back of her throat. Her hand reached to the receiver, snatching it up.

As the other end purr-purred away she stared at the carpet, trying to keep its pattern in focus. She'd had her usual three bottles of liquor, the 20/20, the fruit-flavoured brain-cell obliterator and was therefore drunk, or sixty-sixtied as she liked to describe it. The carpet went all blurred again.

Her thoughts were drifting everywhere so she was surprised to hear her voice on the other side of the room, sounding slurred, shaky, amidst a frantic squealing of feedback, like the music she'd heard on the radio when tracking through the dials to uncover Radio Forth that had sounded like The Who when they were finishing a song and smashing up their instruments at the same time, this noise having been described as Sonic Youth to which she'd murmured: 'Sonic Youth? Chronic Youth.'

Christine was steaming and trying to hold an earnest conversation with Andy on the Radio Forth Open Line. Once she'd followed his request to switch off her radio, she began to ramble about her daughter and her daughter's boyfriend.

'. . . And how am I on this first day of Christmas, you said, Andy? Well . . . Well I'll tell you . . . I'm a bit tiddly the night, but . . . But my problem is my daughter's boyfriend. He's the problem. And it's driving me up the bloody walls and that. Pat. Pat Devlin, in case he might be listening to this. He's got my wee baby out there. Thing is, Andy. He came to pick her up two . . . three weeks ago in a red car, a Volvo. The next again week it was a blue . . . Cavalier. What's it the papers call it? Joy riding? Can't be much joy having some hooligan steal your car for . . . for kicks, likes,

Andy, eh? I mean . . . My girl's not even old enough to be doing what they do in the back of a car, let alone a stolen car. You know, Andy? And she's so wrapped up in him . . . Her wee face . . . She'll be scowling at the telly and not speaking to me one minute, then he'll phone up and it's like she's schizophrenic or something the way her face lights up soon as she hears from him . . . Christ, Andy, I think she might've fallen in love. Can you believe it? In love at fifteen! And when she's explaining to me where she's been when she's not got in till God knows what time it sounds like she's been brainwashed . . . As if this Devlin's a cult leader or something, likes. Occult leader, more likes. He's got this wee devil tattooed on the back of his hand, you know? And the way he says "Cheers Christine, doll" when he's leaving messages, if Kareen's not back from the school or at the shops for me or on the odd occasion she still sees one of her own pals, likes. The way he says that . . . Sets my teeth on edge, Andy . . . That's the way Kareen's dad used to say things. He'll be saying the same things to his Filipino girlfriend, likes. Met her in a restaurant, the bastard, but that's another story. Sorry for swearing on your radio programme, Andy. You should hear the radio station they pair listen to, plays that dance music all night long, that rave stuff. 'Cause it's a pirate job and they don't have a licence the DJs can eff and blind it . . . Kareen . . . What if she falls pregnant, Andy? I mean . . . I don't know what I mean . . .'

Without waiting to hear Andy's words of conciliation she hung up. The pattern below had become garish as a seventies disco floor. There was a single cigarette lying in the middle of the carpet. She couldn't remember the tantrum that had involved throwing it there. She plucked it up.

She went back to her chair, checking that there were still fags in the packet, ensuring that she would have one to wake up to with the alarm in the morning. This was as much a morning ritual as cleaning her teeth.

She switched off the TV. Confronted by the living room's silence she suddenly burst out crying. Tears began to stream and she made sounds as if she was being strangled by the silver necklace which she was tugging between her fingers.

Her jewellery snapped. One hand mopping at her cheeks she threw it towards the TV screen. It lashed across the surface. Static crackled, then it was gone, falling somewhere in the carpet's thick pile.

She sobbed and looked towards the mantelpiece where Kareen posed in various fashion phases. Her swimming eyes rested on Kareen in 1st-Year colours and herself, a Manchester Zoo polar bear a white shape behind bars in the background. She stepped closer to the photograph. She felt caged herself. She stared at this blurred scene. Kareen, herself, occupying two-thirds of the frame up to the frayed edge where she had torn the third person away.

But there was a noise from Kareen's bedroom. She checked the time on the video: 00.40.

Hurrying along the hall she felt for the light switch, anticipating Kareen's blonde curls suddenly twitching to life as the face they masked said: 'I've been in bed for hours, mum. You were dozing on the settee.'

The room remained as it had been during *News at Ten*. Except that a poster had fallen from the wall to drape over the pillow. Christine went over to it and turned it to face upwards.

She looked at the five young men posing there. It said: 'Inspiral Carpets. Cool as f**k.' She aimed a fist at the baldy one nearest the legend. 'How cool as fuck's that, son?' The force of her blow tore his cheek wide open.

Earlier in the week Kareen had went on and on about how she couldn't wait for Thursday's *EastEnders*, how that black bam was going to react on finding his bird in bed with a bird. Christine considered the coldness of the silent TV, the rectangle of glass where Kareen would berate the Mitchell brothers, laugh at Reg Holdsworth, shriek whenever Brad Willis strode on screen with his surf-board.

By the time she got back to the living room it was 00.44. All the lights in the room seemed so bright. She must have been staring at the screen for too long. And she was for ever giving Kareen a row for that. The way she could sprawl forward on her bed clutching her portable's remote and channel-hop all evening, that button taking her from East Drylaw to the East End, to Manchester, to Australia.

She tidied, stuffing the *Daily Record* with the last article she'd read, entitled 'Drew Barrymore – Hollywood's Wild Child' into the bucket. She noticed the date again. Today had been St Andrew's Day. Now it was December.

She shuddered to think what Kareen thought that she might be getting for Christmas. Last year she had requested Armani jeans. Christine had sent her younger brother out for these and he had returned with a pair that were blue denim but had stated Chipie on their label. Craig had told her: 'These were seventy, Christine. And that wasn't far off *two thirds* the price those ones my daft niece was after.' Kareen had tugged them out of their wrapping with a smile right enough, but Christine had overheard her daughter on the phone a few weeks later saying: 'I know, Tara. But Chipie's well out, man!'

Christine turned to the corner where they would be putting up the tree. She felt angry and sad and frightened and suddenly shivered with the coldness that she was feeling.

So she kicked off her slippers and scurried back down the hall, barging into Kareen's room where she fell on to the bed and crawled under Kareen's covers. It smelled of sweat in here. The only thing missing were the post-coital tissues. 'Devlin. You *bastard*,' she spat out.

But all that she could think of was that she wanted to be nowhere other than underneath these covers, Kareen's covers, in Kareen's bed, keeping its warmth in. She would stay here as if cocooned, cosy beneath the poster that said in a voice that she could hear her daughter repeating: 'Cool as fuck.'

After Kareen had shoved Devlin's cassette deep into a pocket of her jeans she flipped the present tape over. The hissing from the four speakers indicated that the music to follow would be loud. Devlin turned the wheel and the car sped into the Crewe Toll roundabout. Then his foot stamped for the brake with such force that Kareen had the absurd notion that a rat had somehow got into the car and was at their feet.

As the impact came, this stuck in her mind, along with the recognition of the DJ doing this next mix: Hectic, her favourite DJ, doing her favourite dance track of all time, 'Spinning on XTC', the one she'd first heard at *9C*; her pal Tara had gone out with DJ Hectic, and once when she'd chummed Tara round to his bit at Magdalene to muck around with his new deck, they'd dropped enough mushies to get buzzed and Tara had spent two hours locked in the toilet while her and DJ Hectic, or Richard, who was famous for his spinning at 45, had spun at 69 on his settee as they'd listened to Tara's muffled singing through the door then they'd dressed and danced, really freaking out to Hectic's sounds and when Tara had reappeared she'd dyed her blonde locks red and it was still dripping down her cheeks like some vengeful Carrie until she'd caught her reflection in the mirror and decked herself and they'd joined in, Tara's face going as red as her running dye, Richard compounding her state by nashing round from his turntables to undo her bra-top under her Destroy jacket but Kareen had felt so cool and when she'd closed her eyes tightly there had been sparkling lights like along George Street at Christmas and now her thoughts were whizzing along as fast as the line of lights on the horizon was going vertical.

* * *

It was like the start of *Casualty* on TV. Flowing with this trolley, peering up at the ceiling and the faces bowing over. Something came back to her for a second: she wondered if the rat had bitten Devlin to fill him with this poison, too. The thought slipped away.

Kareen had never felt so light-headed, so out of it. She tried to make a fist; she thought that this would stop her floating along this way, it would take her back to the trolley. The trolley was solid, supporting.

She wanted to tell these men in white overcoats to release Devlin. Right now. Because she would need to be jellied for coming down from all of this.

GOD'S OWN COUNTRY

P.F. Brownsey

I saved Judy Garland by taking her hill-walking in Scotland.

See, in those days we didn't fall in love with each other in Glasgow. Oh, the guys would have, you know, sex with each other, but to *really* fall in *love* . . . well, you'd, like, go down to London, you could meet *fantastic* guys down there, and there were places you could actually dance together, too. And someone would come back and say he'd met this great guy, and they'd try to keep it going, him going down to London at weekends. Sometimes the London guy might actually come up here. But usually it fizzled out after a bit – the distance and so on.

Well, I went down for a weekend, and, yes, I met this guy, Jude. Really good-looking he was, dark hair, great dresser, really knew his way around, he had everything together. Fantastic guy, he was. So I thought. Actually his name was James, James Fairfax-Vere, but he called himself Jude because of that Beatles song, *Hey, Jude*. I met him in this pub I'd been told about and he came up and talked, so friendly, like he'd known I'd be there and he'd come there just to meet me, and he said, Wherever you thought you were going to stay tonight, forget it. You're staying with me. I'll make sure you enjoy it. When he said that he just stared at me and his eyes, you know, compelled me. Not that I didn't want to – I mean, I couldn't believe my luck. And he was a fabulous lover, just taking his time, I'd never experienced anything like it. In the past it had all been getting down to it right away, you know, getting your thrill. And after it was over he said, I'm very glad I've got you into my life, Tommy, I just know we're going to spend a lot of time together, and he tapped me on the nose, playful.

The next weekend I decided to surprise him so I 'phoned in sick at work and caught the coach down and got to his place – a really fantastic flat – on the Friday night, and I went up the stairs and rang the bell, and when he answered he didn't seem to know who I was, and I said, jokey, Remember me? It's lover-boy. And he didn't seem to know what to say, and I was standing there, smiling at him, and I was wanting him to, you know, take me in his arms, and a couple of times he started to say something and stopped, and then he said, Well, it's awfully sweet of you to look in, Billy, and then he said, Off to somewhere nice, are you? And I said I'd come to see *him*, and I thought, you know, nothing ventured, and I said it, just like that, 'I love you, Jude.'

And he said, That's good, that's good, so long as we all love each other, what else matters, hey? But he just stood there and just sort of smiled, and it was a nothing smile. And I asked him, wasn't he going to ask me in, and he said, and he really sounded sorry as he said it, Billy, I *am* sorry, I *really* am, but I've got some dreadful party to go to.

He just stood there saying nothing with that nothing smile, and I could see there was nothing more to be said, and I said, Bye for now, and he said, Ciao. And he watched me go down the stairs and gave me a little wave, which meant something, I suppose, and shut the door.

Well, I was really disappointed, but when I got down the stairs I thought I'd try again, because I loved him. And after last weekend, the previous weekend, I *knew* there was a really nice guy there, I knew he liked me, if I could just get through to him. So I thought I'd go back and say I'd just wait there in the flat, and he could go out and I'd be waiting for him when he came back. And if he came back with someone else, well, he had the right to do that, I didn't want to put any pressure on him, I'd just slip away. So I went back up but as I was going to knock I could hear his voice, he was on the 'phone, and I heard him say, Guess who has just turned up, my little gap-toothed piece of Glaswegian rough. And he said I was awfully sweet in a way but not something you went back to, and anyway Adam, I think it was, was back. And I don't mind saying I went back down the stairs and when he couldn't hear me just sat down on the carpet and had a greet. And I didn't know where I was going to go.

But then I thought he might come out to go to his party and find me there, and I wasn't going to have that, I've got my pride, so I got up and went out the door and stood on the pavement wondering what to do, it was just getting dark, and then suddenly this little woman came running along and banged into me, and she shouted, Get out of the way, motherfucker. And then she stopped and just stood there, not looking at me, just staring nowhere, and then her face sort of went, collapsed, and it was like she was in agony, all alone in agony, and she said in this really terrible voice, not saying it *to* anyone, Oh, what am I going to do? It was Judy Garland.

And I asked her, trying to be gentle and show respect, What is it, hen? And what she said was this: 'I've killed her.' And then she came out of her nowhere stare and sort of *saw* me, and she said in this pleading way, I don't know who you are, mister, but you look nice. Please help me.

Well, I couldn't resist that, and she was sobbing now, and I put my arm round her shoulders and said, Tell me all about it, I'll do anything I can to help, and she looked at me, but she didn't quite believe me yet, and she said, Will you? And it was the most fantastic story. She said she had this double, Ethel Hotchkiss, that they used for Judy in films, and this Ethel knew an awful lot about Judy, about pills and booze and drugs and bad stuff, and she'd been blackmailing

Judy. And she'd actually been up to Judy's place that night trying to get money out of her – Judy's husband then, Mickey Deans, had gone out because they'd had a blazing row about something. And this Ethel told Judy that if she told what she knew Judy'd never get her career up off the skids. Well, Judy didn't know what to do, she thought she'd have to pay up like she always did, and then she had an idea – she'd slip this Ethel something that would knock her out till Mickey came back and he could deal with her, and she gave her this drink which she'd slipped all sorts of pills and things into. Well, she'd overdone it. Ethel got ill and went to the bathroom and didn't come out and after a bit Judy sort of peeked in and there was Ethel *dead*! And now Judy was hugging me like I was her only hope and I had to protect and save her.

And then it came to me, I *could* save her. I told her, Look, Judy, if that woman's your double, this is the chance you've been waiting for. You can *really* change your life, cut loose from all your troubles. I mean, I know how it's been for you, I read the papers. But they'll think this Ethel is you, that it's Judy that's dead. So there's an end to all the pressure, and you can start your life again, quietly, and change your name, and put all the dramas and suicide attempts and pills and booze and stuff behind you and come and live with me in Glasgow, I stay by myself.

She looked a bit doubtful, so I said, It's the perfect solution. But she still didn't say anything, she just hugged me the more, like she was a kid, really, and I said, When we get to Scotland we'll go up in the hills, go hill-walking. I can show you fantastic places and views, I'd love to do that, and it'll be so good for you, the air, exercise, get all the booze and pills and pain out of your system, you'll be *happy* at last.

And she looked up and made a decision, and she just said, 'Okay, I'll try anything, I can't fight any more.'

* * *

It was a fantastic day in early May, spring, the best time for the hills, and I drove us in the van down Glen Etive, it's all sort of crowded in with big pointed hills with steep sides. And I was planning for us to go up Ben Starav, this really massive hill right on the sea's edge, you see it and you think, Christ, it goes up and *up*. But actually it doesn't take that long, there's a clear path, and the view from the top knocks you out, the top is a sort of plateau with, like, two horns, one on each side, absolutely unmistakable. But Judy just took one look – I carried the big rucksack, she had just a little one – and she said, You're crazy, I can't go up there. She'd put on shorts, blue ones, her legs were a bit white and podgy, and a headscarf and dark glasses.

I said, Yes, you can, Judy.

Then she started shouting and screaming, there at the roadside where I'd parked the van between some gorse bushes. She really lost the rag. I was a brute and a monster, she just *couldn't*, I was driving her mad, I was another fucking man fucking up her life, who did I think I was, all that kind of stuff. I grabbed her wrists and then got them into one hand, and all the time I was telling her, Judy, it's for your own good, you've *got* to do this, you'll prove to yourself that you *can* change and get out of your old ways and be on the road to happiness. She was squirming and resisting, but I had her wrists firm and then with my free hand I hit her across the face, twice, just two wee controlled slaps, really, like they do to hysterical women in films, and at once she quietened down and changed completely, and in that kind of strong voice of hers that made you feel you could really rely on her, for anything, she said, Okay, Tommy, let's go.

So off we go, and to cheer her along I talk about this and that, and it really works. I tell her something I've read somewhere that someone called Deirdre of the Sorrows lived in Glen Etive once, and she says, I've had a few sorrows myself, and I say, But they're going to be over soon just like

April showers, and she gives me such a real warm smile. She asks me about Deirdre of the Sorrows, and I don't know much, but I tell her I think she was an Irish princess hundreds of years ago who was forced to be married to some Scottish prince who lived in the glen, and then probably she had to take her husband's part in a war against her own folks and all her brothers were killed or something, and we stop, already we're high up, and look down at the long narrow loch running into the glen from the sea, and we imagine, you know, long ships like Viking boats sailing up under the mountains all those hundreds of years ago, and Deirdre standing by the mast staring out, and Judy says, 'Poor damn kid.'

On up we go, it's steep but no problem if you take it steady, and then something really nice happens. For God's sake, look at that, she says, and I look and she's pointing at a beer can someone has pressed down between two rocks – the path goes over lots of loose rocks – and she says, Why do they have to leave their frigging beer cans up here and spoil God's own country? And she says, Do you know what really gets me? – they think if they crush the damn thing with their boot first it isn't a fucking eyesore, God, sometimes I despair of people. I'm thinking, that's a good sign, she *cares* about the mountain and not spoiling things, and that means she's mending. And then she says, 'But not you, Tommy.'

And so we reach the top, it's a big area and we wander about looking at the view, there's this other hill across the loch with these sort of huge black slabs hundreds of feet high running down the sides, and everything is so tiny in the glen, it's so far below, and the sun is shining and everything is, like, clean and new and bright and vast, and there's still bits of snow here and there on the hills, and it's so white and shining like it was your heart's desire and you have this big ache to reach out to it across miles, and you see clouds, shadows of them, moving across the glen and other hills, and we have this fantastic feeling that it's good, actually *good*, to be alive, and I say, she being American, Freaks you out, doesn't it? And she takes my hand and looks at me serious and says, Tommy, you've *given* this to me, and if it wasn't for you I'd never have seen it, and it's all so real, and I can see it, really *see* it, and I'm sort of part of it, and, oh, I feel so much *peace* inside, and how can I ever thank you enough? I don't mind saying I'm in tears.

And then we find a couple of rocks as seats and we eat our food and I've brought a thermos of coffee and Judy's really enjoying herself, she says, This is the best goddam doughnut I have ever eaten in my whole goddam life, and jam sort of squirts out on to her chin, and we both laugh, and I think, I really have saved her.

And then she says something odd, but in a very ladylike way, very delicate. She says, Tommy, ever since we came up to Glasgow on the coach and I came to live with you, you've never, well, Tommy, there doesn't seem to be a lady-friend in your life.

No, I say, and I feel a bit awkward.

Tommy, she says, I don't want you to alter your life for me. I mean, if you're keeping her away because you think I'd mind, well, I know it's only a little flat but I wouldn't think my privacy was being invaded if you, you know, invited her up.

And I say, It's not like that, Judy. You see, I'm gay, the word was coming in.

At this she bursts out laughing in a way I didn't like, a bit of the old Judy returning, and she says, God, a fruit. I didn't like that. And she kept laughing. And then it, the laughing, became more friendly, and she says, Just like some of my frigging husbands, and she hugs me, and I hug her back, and we're laughing together now. And she says, Well, Tommy, I don't mind making tea for a gentleman-friend, either.

And I say, No, there's no one now, I got hurt, and I think I'm best out of it, that sort of thing, love and so on. I'd rather have you as my friend, Judy.

Ben Starav is not a totally separate, separated hill. I mean, it's joined to others along a ridge. Next along from it is a hill called Glas Bheinn Mhor. Well, as we were sitting eating and chatting I could see this tiny figure coming along the ridge from this next hill, sometimes you could see it, like a tiny ant, sometimes not, and then it would be further on again. Well, I didn't really think about it, but then Judy went off to find a place to have a pee and I stood up and started wandering about again, just looking at the view and the drop and so on, when this little figure I'd seen in the distance arrives at the top, and it's Jude Fairfax-Vere. And he says, all warm and friendly, Tommy, you're just the person I've been hoping to meet, I came up to Scotland specially to try to find you.

No problem, I tell him, you had my number.

Did I, he says, I must have lost it. Then he says, looking at me very sort of meaningfully with those, you know, compelling eyes he had, You always lose the things you value most.

I say I don't follow him.

And he says, Look, Tommy, I want to apologize, I treated you bad, real bad, I'll never forgive myself for what I did to you.

I don't quite know what to say to this, but he doesn't look for any reply, and he says, What I've come to say, Tommy, is, I love you and I want to spend my life with you more than with anyone else. He thinks this is a compliment, but I think, Ah, so there's others in for the job, too. And he steps forward as if I'm going to fall into his arms right there on top of Ben Starav with all the forest and sea and sky all around. And I tell him, It's not as simple as that, and he looks surprised. Arrogant sod, assuming all he's got to do is snap his fingers and put on that awful smooth sincere English voice and I'll come running.

And he says, and now to look at his face you'd think he was genuinely hurt, like *I'd* been bad to *him*, Tommy, what have I done?'

I'll tell you what you've done, says a voice, and there's Judy, back from doing what nobody could do for her. She says, You called the nicest, sweetest man in the whole frigging world a gap-toothed bit of Glaswegian rough and you threw him aside like a used Kleenex.

And he says, But, my God, I realize what a mistake I made, Tommy, don't you believe me? I love you, I'm desperate for you, I want you back.

But Judy says, It's too late for that. You hurt and damaged him and he doesn't want you messing him up again.

And now he ignores me and speaks to her. He says, Judy, when my father dies I shall be *Sir* James Fairfax-Vere, I shall inherit Fairfax Castle, in Suffolk or somewhere, he said. I invite you to share it with me, he says, a huge real castle, Judy, that's the setting for a star like you, not his Godforsaken hole of a city.

And now Judy really gets wild. She says, You lousy son of a bitch loser, you motherfucking English slimeball, get the hell out of here, let me tell you that not all the frigging faggotty Fairfax Castles and fucking titles in the whole goddam world could *begin* to equal the happiness, the TRUE HAPPINESS, I've found with Tommy in our little flat in Glasgow. And she starts picking up rocks and throwing them at him, raging and screaming, and one hits him in the mouth, and I think, That'll do for your beautiful good looks for a bit, maybe break one of *your* teeth, you piss-elegant shite. And he turns and runs, with Judy still shouting and chucking rocks behind him, and the last we see of him he's hurrying back the way he came, along to Glas Bheinn Mhor.

And Judy is smiling, there's, like, absolute joy on her face, joy in absolutely everything, her face is, like, purified, and she links her arm in mine and says, Well, we saw him off, Tommy, if that's the man that got away, let him go. And now there's not a thing to stop us caring for each other and being happy. Oh, I know I've been a rotten frigging bitch sometimes, Tommy, but deep down I could see you were giving me what I've always needed in my life, and I want to tell you you're the greatest and grandest fella I've ever known.

Of course, we didn't have a lot of money, because she was supposed to be dead so couldn't get at any of hers. But that didn't matter, we managed, and she said, I'd rather be happy with you, Tommy, than rich and miserable and screwed-up like I used to be. And we had happy, happy times over the years. She had a stroke a couple of years back, she recovered well but it left her a bit shaky and tottery and I couldn't afford to stop work and look after her because we only had my money, so she went into a, you know, home at Strathblane, and I go out every weekend to see her, and she's settled down there really well. The warden said a funny thing, she's quite young, just a lassie, really, but she wears these women's suits like Margaret Thatcher with a big bow in the front, they have karaoke nights at the home and Judy absolutely slays them, and this warden, she says, Your auntie's just like that Liza Minnelli.

ROSH HASHANAH

Esther Woolfson

The last time that I saw my Aunt Adele, I was fifteen. She was already in middle-age somewhere but I was never certain where. It was very difficult to tell because she had seemed for so long to hover in gold-blonde changelessness, miraculously protected against time. It must have been her wig that made it seem as though she never changed. She wore a wig because she was very religious and very religious women shave off their own hair and wear wigs instead. At the time, I didn't think much about it. It just seemed like one more thing that you were told to do and did.

In fact, Aunt Adele's wig was probably more attractive than her own hair would have been if she had let it grow. The wig at least wasn't susceptible to the changes undergone by ordinary hair, the greying and thinning which I had noticed beginning on the heads of my father and Uncle Aaron, though not yet on the head of my mother whose hair, although like Adele's an unlikely blonde, was her own.

The wig seemed to lead a life of its own, ignoring the steady back-tow of the years, spending time by itself in the local hairdresser being set while my aunt did the shopping and preparation for Shabbas. She wore her stand-in wig while it was away, a wig which looked very much like the other one except that it was a slightly different style, a little lop-sided, its gleam fainter, its air more youthful. It made me feel sad, reminded me of the way things had been when I was very small. No. 1 wig would be back in place by evening, set and golden, presiding, with my aunt, over the Friday night table.

My family, my parents and two brothers, always had Friday night dinner at Adele's house, her perfect, sparkling, gleaming, entirely, strictly, totally kosher house. Our house was kosher too, but not that kosher.

The year I'm writing about seemed at the time ordinary enough, if any year of one's life is ordinary, but looking at it now, I know it clearly to have been the year from which all things pivoted and grew, the point from which all things moved out, moved on, resisted regression.

It was, among other things, a time when an unnatural state of peace existed in the family, among the wide, extending circle of aunts and uncles, cousins and second cousins who were considered family. There were, as I remember, no quarrels outstanding, everyone being, inexplicably, on amicable terms. It happened very seldom in a family which regarded the ability to prolong a quarrel as an area of expertise. 'They didn't speak to each other for thirty years after that,' was a familiar ending to stories my parents told me.

I remember some of the stories. Mostly, they involved wills, insults, cases of unbelievable ingratitude after acts of outstanding kindness and generosity, wilful misunderstandings. Even then, I recognized their astonishing lack of objectivity. They seemed depressingly like illustrations for a catalogue of the shallower, muddier pools of human behaviour. But then, being initiated into the complexities of the universe appeared to me to be part of a whole experience, a part which went along with going to synagogue, learning Hebrew, not eating sausage rolls at parties, being careful not to say the word 'Jesus'.

If thirty years dealt with the small quarrels, there were the ones to which thirty years could bring no end. These involved marrying people who were not Jewish, becoming involved with other religions, pursuing dangerous, possibly fatal paths outside the fold. As a small child, I knew of the existence of such things though I didn't know till later what they were. I had older cousins who disappeared mysteriously, their graduation photos removed from pianos, childhood pictures quietly peeled from frames. The pictures of people who had died stayed on pianos so whatever had happened to those who disappeared was clearly worse than death.

Families appeared to me to be like minor constellations which came into equable confluence once every thirty years, entering briefly into the cold shadow of an eclipse before one element or another would toss itself, meteoric and petulant, burning fizzy like phosphorus, white, luminous, trailing burning smoke into the unknown, distant darkness.

That time was a moment of eclipse, rare, strange and passing. I felt conflicting magnetic fields claiming me, pulling at me with grim, ineluctable force.

During that year, I was becoming difficult, for myself no less than for everyone else. I was aware of it but I couldn't find a way of stopping a process that had the mean feel of the inevitable. I felt closed in by interlocking walls of family and expectations, my sole means of retreat a recourse to sullenness and showy misery. To have made a wrong move would have held the danger of binding myself in the eternal, infant docility which was the delight of many mothers I knew, including my own and Aunt Adele.

'Why can't you be like Adam Goldfarb?' they used to ask, naming a roster of boys I would have died rather than resemble, youths lacking glitz or style, failed people who had looked at puberty from afar and decided it wasn't for them.

My barmitzvah had taken place late in the previous year. My own role in it I knew had been less than distinguished. I performed the ceremonies adequately but with bad grace, awkwardly, fidgeting as I read the law, twisting the fringes of my prayer shawl round my fingers, aware only of how foolish my voice sounded there in the resonant cave of the synagogue, how high and thin and childlike, of the critical, watching presence above me in the women's gallery. I made the accepted speech beginning, 'Today, I am a man.'

At the party my parents gave for me afterwards, Aunt Adele came up to me. She had on a new, shiny blue dress and tight blue shoes.

'Vy d'you fiddle and do this?' She imitated my fringe-twisting.

'I don't know.'

'"Don't know!" "Today I am a man." Huh!'

My mother and Uncle Aaron were sister and brother. They were very close, a closeness I envied. Aaron was the kind of man whose attention everyone wanted. I envied whoever was sitting next to him at table, whoever was encompassed by the total gaze of his downward-slanting brown eyes. He was quiet and mild and witty, too subtle, I had begun to believe, too sardonic for Aunt Adele. He seemed happy though and I wondered why. I could see very few attractions in being closed tightly as he was in Adele's ordered Jewish firmament.

* * *

Aaron and Adele had two daughters, Deb and Judy. At that time, they were large, overweight girls who got on well with Ben, my older brother, but ignored me. Deb had left the previous autumn to go to university in Cardiff. At the time she left, my parents speculated on the camouflaged quick-sands of the outside world, a world of non-kosher meat stock and bacon sandwiches in which no Adele existed to interpose herself between Deb and unknown, gentile custom.

'She'll be fine,' my father said, 'she's a sensible girl.'

I felt strange and uneasy as they discussed it. I felt unprepared for the world and by no means as sensible as Deb.

My mother had always tried to teach us how to deal with awkward situations. She taught us polite excuses for occasions when we might be offered food which wasn't kosher.

'Just say, sorry, I don't eat that. I'm a vegetarian. Or say you've got an allergy. No one will mind.'

I knew they would mind. I knew they would mind that I was making up things about allergies when they knew I wasn't eating it because I was Jewish.

My cousin Judy was still at home. She was a little older than me, tall, broad, impatient, sarcastic, with huge quantities of dark, frizzy, frightening hair.

A few weeks before my barmitzvah, I began to realize for the first time that it was important, just as everyone said. I felt scared, reluctant to look at the way life would be without the Hebrew classes and barmitzvah instruction which had taken up so much time over the years. It's always been the same. I only appreciate things when they're about to end.

In the final few weeks, the classes held a new appeal, the fleeting, sudden, finite blaze of something almost over. I listened to Mr Berg with desperation. I knew I had spent all those years missing the significance of everything he had said which seemed to me suddenly to be deep and true and right.

'Why do we keep the commandments? Because God tells us to! No reasons necessary, no questions asked, understood? Because God tells us to!'

I began to envy Nathan, my younger brother who still had two years before barmitzvah. Ben had passed easily from its grip three years before. I tried to ask him about it, carefully, in a way which revealed nothing.

'Other things, my boy, other things will come into your life!' he said to me in Aunt Adele's voice. He was looking at himself in his shaving mirror. 'Look forward, my precious, look forward! Von day, you too vill look in your mirror and find you're nearly as gorgeous as me!'

Ben had begun going out on Saturday evenings, returning late looking glowing-eyed and secretive.

Straight after barmitzvah, I stopped seeing the boys from my Hebrew class. It was a decision of principle. We had spent a long time together over the years, messing about, sitting around in cafés after class, being prepared together for adulthood. I felt sad that in the first moments of adulthood, I no longer wanted to be with them. It didn't feel particularly like adulthood. Nor was it that I didn't like them, there were some I liked very much. It was simply that even the best had a feeling of the past about them.

That winter, I hung around at school longer than I needed to in the afternoons. I began playing the saxophone and took my place in the school's jazz group to squeeze out dismal, melancholy sound. Sometimes, I joined the sad band of no-hopers who kicked a football around on the huge, empty playing fields after school. It was the time when there were still the kind of fogs which got into your hair and enclosed you in a yellow-grey world of muffled loneliness. Frost rose alive and visible in the air and crept by way of your boots into your socks, stiffened your toes and tried to fix you to the hardening mud for ever. Winter made me miserable but in some perverse way justified my self-pity. It made me feel suffering and righteous.

'Look at him! White like a ghost!' Aunt Adele said on Friday nights. She used to clutch a portion of my cheek agonizingly between two bent knuckles and shake it hard.

'A ghost, Edna. Isn't he like a ghost? Aaron, what would you do with him, eh? A boy of his age shouldn't look like a ghost!'

The pain would last halfway through dinner.

That year, it had begun to be an irritation to me to go there every week, to be harassed by Aunt Adele, surrounded by her ornaments and crystal, her silver-framed photographs on the piano. It feels mean and cold and totally heartless to write that, even now, because Aunt Adele had no photographs of her own family on her piano. There were what seemed like hundreds of her children, my mother and Uncle Aaron's parents, even ones of us, Ben, Nat and me in blue shorts, white shirts and yarmulkes, fixed in perpetually embarrassing moments of untypical mellowness. Instead of Adele's family photos, there were photos of the Levenburgs, the family who took her in after her parents had sent her alone and in haste from Berlin as the war closed in. Meir Levenburg was a rabbi in a small London synagogue, the head of a household of model Jewish practice, according to Aunt Adele anyway.

The Levenburgs were the origin of a lasting antagonism between Adele and my grandmother. They argued constantly over correct procedure in matters of law and practice, my grandmother quoting long experience, her mother, her rabbi from the small town where she was born (which sometimes was in Poland and sometimes not, according to what onrush of history had recently taken place), Adele quoting the Levenburgs.

My grandmother, however, held a trump card, one I was mystified about for a long time.

'What did her family know about Judaism?' my grandmother would storm, 'they hardly even knew they were Jews. It was Hitler who taught them they were!'

I knew the Levenburg daughters, Nussa and Eve, from their annual visits to Adele. They were big, pale-faced women with thick, straight legs whose lisle stockings made them look like stuffed legs, not legs with femurs and tibias and muscles. They brought small, timid husbands and fat, religious-looking children who would never come and play noisy games with us in Adele's garden. Nussa and Eve wore wigs too but theirs were ugly, brown matted ones teased from old ship's rope or tweezed out of doormats.

It was in the spring of that year, just as the last of the fogs had trailed off into weak, grey sunshine, that a school friend, James, told me he was moving to the south of the city, a few streets away from where I lived. It must have been in the late March, early April.

James and I had begun school together on the same day shortly before we were five. That experience gives people a long shared past. You can't cry at being parted from your mother for the first time, try out new, careful friendships without forming a bond with the other weepers, the other small, sad dupes who joined you round the box of toys the teacher brought out to fool you into thinking that that was what school was all about. There was a small group of us who were there on that very day who continued through the school, into secondary and then to university. It was as if we had been in the same regiment, died on the same beaches. No one, however soon after that they joined our class, could be part of the experience.

We always had been friends but we had stopped seeing one another, the way you stop seeing the colour of your classroom walls or appreciating the view from its window. We didn't ever see each other out of school. James lived on the other side of the city, in the west. The distance between the south and the west was equivalent to the distance between the sun and the moon. You just didn't ever go there.

'We're moving out your way,' James said to me one day as we walked between classrooms.

'When?'

'End of the week after next. Do you get the 59?'

'Usually.'

'I'll get you home.'

On the day of his move, James waited for me at the street gate of the school. He was standing alone in the mesh shadow pattern cast by the wire on top of the wall, the wire that stopped old ladies being killed by footballs. He had a few carrier bags in addition to his leather school case.

'A few of my own things,' he said, indicating the bags. 'I said I'd take them myself.' I took one from his hand and carried it for him. It was oddly heavy.

'Sorry, my stone collection. Didn't trust the movers.'

We walked out into the bright throng beyond the school wall and crossed Sauchiehall Street.

'It's a bit weird.'

'Must be. Did you live in your old house for long?'

'I was born there.'

'Was it a nice house?'

James thought for a moment, as if it had never occurred to him. 'No, not specially,' he said.

We had moved house once, before I could remember, to the large, comfortable house we lived in all the rest of my childhood.

We sat at the front of the top of the bus, commanding the street traffic, the flow of activity on the wide span of brown river, the slow dredgers digging and clanking and dripping revolting river mud from the chains.

'What's making you move? My father always says that if you live in the west you always stay in the west.'

'Oh, it's not choice. If it was choice, we'd never go anywhere. My father's been given St Andrew's.'

'St Andrew's what?'

'Oh, for God's sake, Henry. St Andrew's church.'

'Oh.'

I knew St Andrew's. Nor far from where I lived, it was a large Victorian sandstone building whose shallow steps bisected a sloping lawn. It sloped in two stages, steep and very steep and must have been constructed by someone who wanted to tantalize every child who ever walked past.

'Can we roll down?' we used to say to our grandmother when she took us past it on walks.

'Of course you can't. You'll ruin your clothes. Anyway, it's a church. You wouldn't like it if you saw little goyshke children playing in front of the schule, would you?'

We wouldn't have cared. We'd have thought they were mad to have chosen to play there on a gravel and stone path with an institutional metal railing. It did in the absence of anything else during a long service, or when we were put out during the prayers for the dead on Yom Kippur, but any potential pleasure was spoiled by the people who were coming in late for the service and invariably told us off for playing on Yomtov.

'It's a nice church. Is your father pleased?'

'Very. The manse is huge. Much better really. Come round and see it.'

'I will. When you've moved in properly.'

'Come round any time.'

'Won't your mother want to get things sorted out?'

'My mother? No. Why? Should she?'

We got off the bus at the same stop and I walked a bit out of my way to take James to the corner of his street. I didn't turn the corner with him. I let him walk down the street for the first time by himself.

I waited for a few days before visiting. The bigger, better manse was in the street parallel to the one where Uncle Aaron and Aunt Adele lived, both streets of gold and fawn sandstone houses with well-cared-for gardens. James's garden was the exception in the street. The weeds formed fringes round the paths and flowerbeds, pushed up through the gravel which was all flattened into earth. Abundant moss crept on the front steps, furry, green, stealthy, a damp, growing shadow. I don't remember seeing any in the house but it may have been there too, creeping in the faint, ancient light of the hall, up the stairs, past the brown Bakelite plugs and huge brass light switches which even then were long gone out of fashion, up the brown embossed wallpaper and round the tops of the brown, varnished doors.

* * *

When I rang the doorbell, it sounded deep inside the house, as if from another age. James answered the door.

'Come up, I'm organizing my room,' he said.

James's room was a Victorian orphan's room, the room of a child sent home from India, the room of a sorrowing, homesick maid. It was small and brown, its air filled with old loneliness. James's small quantity of possessions was arranged with exquisite neatness.

'I rather like this room,' he said, 'specially the view.'

I walked across the beige lino to the window. The woodwork and frames were brown, the kind of brown that's painted deliberately to look like wood. A cluster of dead, dried flies lay in the corner between glass and sill. It smelt of warm dust. From that height, you could see down the line of gardens, over the tops of the apple trees and garden swings and stems of climbing roses just beginning to grow again in the spring light. I could see easily into Aunt Adele's garden. I pointed it out to James and told him about Adele and Aaron and Judy and Deb. I had to tell him. He'd have seen me in their garden.

'Come down and meet my mother,' James said. His voice was neutral, genuinely easy and casual. He was like that, completely lacking a certain consciousness of danger.

James's mother was a creature from another part of the jungle, a life-form I could recognize but never comprehend. My own mother used to drive into town frequently wearing a smart coat and high-heeled shoes, her hair tinted and set firm by Sheila whose idle, hairdresser's chatter was one of my mother's few windows into the non-Jewish world. James's mother was tall and very thin and wore trousers which were too short round her bony ankles, pale blue blouses with short sleeves and sandals with beige socks which belonged to

James's father. When she was 'dressed', she wore plain, shiny gored shirts, wrinkly stockings and flat, scuffed brown leather shoes. She carried bags of shopping from the bus stop and greeted me as if I were a friend of hers, not a friend of her son's.

Annie Mathieson had been born and raised in Canada and had the kind of accent and casual way of speech which disarmed you before she came in with the blow of what she was saying, her sureness and cleverness and certainty. Eventually I learned that you made no chance, flippant remarks in the presence of Annie Mathieson. Her long fair ponytail and pale, freckled skin made the girls at the tennis-courts in the park, in whom James and I were taking a distant interest, look as if they had been freshly painted, as if they were going to be my mother and Aunt Adele only were at an earlier stage of the life-cycle. I didn't understand Annie Mathieson's life-cycle. Annie's confidence was like a wall which stopped you, making you think about it before thinking about anything else, wrong-footing you, making you question deeply anything that you thought you were about to say. It showed in everything, her manner, her voice, her doctorate in Theology, her way of singing completely unselfconsciously in a loud and tuneless voice.

Annie often scared me. It was her way of talking. There was something uninhibited about Annie, something which made me fear that she was unstoppable, that she would carry on regardless to some end I wasn't capable of imagining. She had a disconcerting way of talking about God and about Jesus Christ as if they were there, both of them, in the room with you.

I used to meet Annie walking round the district. She carried an old brown shopping bag full of posies of flowers she had picked from her garden and jars of pale, lumpy marmalade she had bought at church bazaars to take to the elderly members of her husband's church. She told me she liked to sit with them, 'to share their quiet' she said, though I knew it wouldn't go on being quiet if she was there. I couldn't imagine what she said to them.

'Perhaps Henry will recite the Hebrew grace over bread,' Annie asked the first time I stayed for a meal with them. I said it, numb with the shock of the request. It wasn't even Friday.

'Don't worry, Henry,' she had said to me before we dined, 'I will make sure you are able to observe your faith. I will 'phone your mother and reassure her.'

I offered to 'phone but Annie insisted.

'I was raised a lacto-vegetarian,' I heard her say loudly, the way she conducted all her 'phone calls, 'my Daddy believed it to be God's way.'

We used to eat Annie's solid, tasteless food in the dark kitchen. It was lit by a dusty light which seemed conducted meanly, reluctantly through twists of brown, fraying corded flex. No one ever did anything about the house either after the Mathiesons moved in or in all the years I knew it. It stayed the same, brown and fixed and musty, the light falling from under burnt parchment shades on to rooms of austerity and denial, rooms which whispered to me that I was spoilt, corrupted with comfort loving. For years, James and I did our homework together in those rooms, with the crude blue and yellow painting Annie said was the Rockies on one wall and the map of the Bible lands on the other. There were shelves of books that related to Bible subjects, bibliographies, commentaries, biographies of famous missionaries. I used to take them out occasionally. They were out of date and musty-smelling, with gently browning, spotted pages. They had pictures of smiling black people, white-painted churches with bells on ropes outside, scenes of soft, rolling, empty hillsides somewhere in the vastness of Nyasaland or Zululand or Tanganyika.

At mealtimes, Annie always sang a vigorous grace. Her husband Angus and James sang quieter, more muted versions. I was called on from time to time to provide the grace over the first fruit of the season or some other part of the Jewish ritual about which Annie knew more than I. One or other Mathieson was expected to come up with an original grace from time to time. Annie awarded points for the most gracious, timely or appropriate.

'Apt, quite apt,' was Annie's line in praise.

After I got back that first time, I expected some comment from my mother, but all she asked me was if I had had a nice time.

It wasn't long after James moved that Adele first addressed the Friday-night table on the subject of my friendships.

She had lit the candles and was fussing about with plates and bread.

'I see that Henry can't find any Jewish boys to go home on the bus with. Maybe there aren't enough in this district. Or maybe they've all left his school.'

Both the school and the district were well populated by other Jews.

'No,' I said, 'they're still all there. I just don't want to get any of them home, that's all.'

* * *

I knew that Aunt Adele discouraged her daughters from having friends who weren't Jewish. She said it was easier for everyone.

'Ah, so you don't want to now,' she said.

'What does it matter who I get the bus with? James and I have been friendly for years,' I said. I wondered why I was saying something which sounded apologetic but Aunt Adele had stopped listening. She was dipping the silver ladle into the tureen of soup.

'James, nice boy. Bright. His father's minister at St Andrew's,' my father said. He was one of those people who never notices atmosphere, who blithely, innocently, plunges into conversations.

'That's a recommendation?' said Adele.

'He's a very nice fellow,' my father said in his vague way. I didn't know if he'd even heard Adele. 'I gave him a lift into town the other day. Interesting man.'

My mother and Aaron joined in and the conversation hovered a little and then turned and flew off in another direction, a direction of James's father's imagining, about some future development in physics. Judy looked at me with loathing over her plate of soup.

It wouldn't have mattered what my father had said about James. Aunt Adele couldn't recognize qualities in people who weren't Jewish. She didn't know any so she hadn't had any practice.

My parents' private conversation was always peppered with Yiddish. They spoke it quite well, though less well than their parents. My brothers and I know odd words here and there which we still use in conversation with one another. My parents always discussed certain subjects in Yiddish – gossip, how much to pay the daily, exasperation with members of the family.

'She's impossible!' they used to say on the walk back home on Friday nights, thinking that we didn't understand.

Ben, Nat and I liked the walk home, the sudden freedom, the shaking down of liver and chicken and dumplings. We hid behind trees and pounced out from dark gateways yelling. Our parents said that we sounded like the Hampden roar.

The summer of that year, we didn't go away on holiday. My father was too busy in the business. I remember sleeping late, being woken in the morning by Nat who hadn't yet succumbed to the familial torpor which affected first Ben and then me sometime after barmitzvah, making us able to sleep easily until midday.

James went to Mull with his family for a couple of weeks and then came back. The Mathiesons owned a boat, an old, wooden rowing boat of great beauty which they kept in the boat house of a church old people's home on one of the lochs to the north of the city, about an hour's drive away. They used to take me up there with them on a Saturday morning after I had assured Annie that I definitely wasn't planning to go to synagogue that morning. We drove up in their big, ancient Rover, a vehicle which smelled of leather and car oil and glinted with old chrome and walnut. It was driven by Annie with a kind of crazed determination. James's father wore old Scout shorts for these expeditions, Annie a series of flowered dresses of a style long past.

Old ladies sat in deckchairs among the trees and called out greetings as we passed, commenting as we dragged the boat out and launched it.

'That's a fine crew you have, Mr Mathieson!', 'Would you like a wee hand with the ropes there?'.

* * *

Out on the hazy, grey water, James and I lazed and read and helped his father write his sermon. I had no idea what was required, never having heard a sermon but I tried nonetheless, supplying ideas I thought useful, phrases or words which I thought might resonate suitably round St Andrew's. I remember some of the topics he worked on: development in the Third World, the season's SNO programme, the nuclear threat.

After a time, I began to recognize that as soon as his father began talking about the sermon, James prepared for a fight. He was always argumentative but with his father it felt as if something vital depended on it. I didn't really know what. Often, I had no idea what the argument was about. His father was, in his way, as implacable as Annie.

'Dad, can you really tell people not to pray selfishly? Praying is selfish.'

'Is it? I think I would disagree with you there. There's such a thing as praying for others.'

'It's still for your benefit, isn't it? You're the one who wants whatever it is, even if it is for someone else.'

'Do you think so? Don't you think that the purpose can be unselfish? What about expressing your own feelings towards God? I suppose you would say that that's selfish.'

'Yes, I would. Nobody else cares about your relationship with God. It's a contradiction really, isn't it? It's unreasonable to go on to your congregation about something they can't do.'

I rowed intently, smoothly as I could, trying to establish a rhythm of dipping and pulling, an even sound of water dripping and flowing by turns over the oars.

'Do you think my congregation would appreciate your argument, James?'

'Why not? I bet it's what they'd think themselves.'

'We'll ask your mother's opinion.'

Angus Mathieson always appeared to me to be trying very hard to be the reasonable, open, fair-minded father whose working model I, at least, could see very clearly in my mind.

Annie enjoyed points of doctrine. It was her speciality, doctrine. Annie didn't often come in the boat with us. She sat on the stony beach, her skirt up round her white legs, reading. Her books were called things like 'Challenges to the Christian Life' or 'Paul Re-considered'. When we joined her at lunchtime, we pulled the boat up on to the stones and she asked about the progress of the sermon. Annie and Angus fell to discussing the finer points while Annie lined up flasks and plastic bottles and boxes round her. They talked about denial and prayer and something they called witness which I never understood while Annie handed round sandwiches, making sure the round of ham missed me.

James and I never talked about religion.

There was one afternoon which must have been one of the last trips we made to the boat that summer. Although it was late in the season, it was a peculiarly hot day. The old ladies were fanning themselves with copies of *The People's Friend*, calling out 'What a heat!' and 'Aren't you the lucky ones!' as we passed.

We were drifting in the water, lying back in the boat, not rowing. James and Angus were discussing the sermon while I let the oars float lightly under my fingers.

I don't recall the way the discussion went, only Angus's voice, louder than usual, sharp and controlled.

'Ah, now, that's the atheist's line.'

James's voice hovered, hung a moment.

'So?' he said.

I sat up a bit to watch. Angus seemed to square off, his shoulders lifting belligerently, his brow, a bony ledge traversed by two thick, light eyebrows, lowering. He hesitated a moment, watching James, then turned in the stern to look at me.

'Well, Henry, what would your family say if you decided to abandon your religion? Would they mind?'

Suddenly, this deep water. Mind? The word seemed barely adequate.

A wind had got up. The water moved in patterns of shallow grey furrows towards us. I looked across at James whose face was tight closed, unreadable.

'I don't really know,' I said, 'they'd probably accept my decision.' For the briefest moment, something about James's face changed, some tiny part of it moved and then was still again.

I sat up and leaned over the boat's curved wooden side. I had never thought about it. I had never needed to but now I did and just thinking about being without it presaged the falling of masonry, the rising of sharp dust, the perpetual blowing of a desolate wind. I knew that I didn't know how not to be a Jew and that I'd never know how not to be one. I knew we were talking about something I was. I looked into the deep, moving shadows of the water's depth. I leaned over further and traced the boat's name with my finger, *Columba*.

Angus looked at us both, from one to the other, then silently picked up his book. James moved over and took an oar, his eyes tight, narrowed against the wind.

* * *

We talked it over a couple of days later, James and I. We had been waiting for the moment. We were at the park, sitting on a branch of the huge, dominating beech tree which was in full, glittering leaf.

'Your family would mind.'

'Of course,' I said. I hesitated a moment. 'Is he very anxious about what you believe?'

'God yes. To him atheism's like death or betrayal, a terrible abrogation.'

'Are you?'

'What? An atheist? I don't know. I suppose so. I don't even care. I'm tired of thinking about it. I'm bored. I'm just fed up, Henry.'

'Honestly? I thought you were really bound up in it all.'

'Bound up in it?' Suddenly, he let go of the branch and turned upside down, holding on with his knees and hands. He swung back and forth for a few moments. 'That's exactly it. Bound up. Like a bloody rope. So tight round you, it hurts. It's as if there's nothing else that's really important and any time spent thinking about anything else is a luxury or a waste of time. You'd go mad.'

'I would, you're right.'

James sat upright again. 'No one in your house ever mentions God.'

'They don't need to. They spend all their time worrying about whether there's gelatine in the sweets or if some joker at the abattoir has switched the meat. I don't even know what's meant to happen if he has. Anyway, I've heard your father say you can think what you like.'

James began to hang from the branch with both hands, moving along it till he was totally hidden in a gently moving ocean of deep red leaves. The branch shook and dipped dangerously low. 'He says that, just as long as I don't. And what about my mother? She couldn't even imagine one of us not believing. Doubting a bit, okay. That's one of the struggles you have to face and overcome. Not believe? Oh no.'

James re-appeared like a deep-sea diver from the depth of the leaves. Grabbing a small branch, he pulled himself up and sat beside me again.

'She's always very nice to me and I don't believe.'

'It's Christian to tolerate you, lad. You're unsaved. She might get you yet.'

'Me? Never.'

'I know that but she doesn't. People like her never know things like that. Never.'

I kept looking at people after that, wondering if they believed in God. When Uncle Aaron thanked God for the bread and wine on Friday nights, I wondered if he really, really thought there was a God. I didn't wonder so much about Adele. She was, in her way, like Annie, hand in glove with God. They were just hand in glove with different Gods.

The Jewish year ebbs and flows, as any other year, raising itself towards festivals, flattening out, going into hibernation at quiet moments, waking again towards spring. Rosh Hashanah, the beginning of the Jewish year, was late that year, well into autumn. It always felt strange, portentous and paradoxical, coming as it did in the season when everything was closing down and dying, the trees shedding, the sunlight all but gone.

That year, I had no classes to prepare me for the festival. I was a man, meant not to need them any more. I could remember dazzlingly clearly what Mr Berg had said, about how on Rosh Hashanah, God writes your name in one of two books, the book of life or the book of death, thinks about it for a few days until Yom Kippur, then seals the books.

'Those who keep God's commandments are written in the book of life. The others are not. Finish! Yom Kippur, decided! No argument!'

I never asked Mr Berg why even people like my grandmother who I was sure had in her long life, kept every single commandment, had one Yom Kippur, been written in the book of death.

I waited for Nathan to come home from his classes with Mr Berg. I took his homework away from him and held it above my head where he couldn't reach it.

'The most important blessing we say on Rosh Hashanah is the "shechechionu . . ."'

'Give it, pig,' Nat said. It was all written out neatly.

'You know that this year you've to say it in front of everyone,' I said out of malice. It wasn't true.

'I'll say it. So what? It's more than you could.'

In fact, I remembered it very well. It was a favourite.

'Blessed art thou oh Lord our God, King of the Universe, who hast kept us in life and hast preserved us and enabled us to reach this season.'

'Rosh Hashanah soon, Henry,' Annie said to me one day. We were walking home together one late Saturday afternoon having met at the shops. James and Angus were at the match, an interest I never shared. 'How are you preparing yourself?'

I had learned caution. I never knew what Annie wanted.

'Well, I've been through the bookshelves to get out the right prayer books – there are hundreds you know, special ones for Pesach and Simchat Torah and Tisha b'Av and all, and we've all got our own sets. It takes hours.'

It was as if she hadn't heard me.

'There is a common motif in all autumn worship, Henry.

New life being created from the old. Resurrection. The preparation for winter which is the preparation for death and the life to come. The preparation of both body and soul, Henry. Come in for tea, James will be home.'

Together, we turned up the weedy, darkening drive.

On the first evening of Rosh Hashanah, we walked round in the dusk to Aaron and Adele's house. We generally had dinner there on festivals too. The only colour was the tarnishing red of dry beech hedges, the thin fall of bronze and silver leaves from the branches.

It was my second walk to Adele's that day. When I got back from school, my mother asked me to go to the greengrocer's to collect the basket of fruit she had ordered for Adele and Aaron. I called in for James on the way.

The shop was a brilliant, bobbing sea of fruit baskets, an orchard of fat dusty grapes, voluminous, striated green melons, golden, rounded pears.

'For Davenstein?' The man looked in the big ledger; 'Davenstein, round the back.' A slow, pimpled youth stopped ferrying baskets out to a van and disappeared for a moment into the back shop.

Our basket burst with gilded pomegranates, velvet green russet apples, blinding oranges. I had to walk slowly to accommodate its weight, lifting my chin to see over the huge red cellophane bow.

'Explain again. You all send these to each other?'

'Yes. We got one from Aaron and Adele and one from Dad's sister in Manchester and one from his brother in Edinburgh. It's to do with eating sweet things at the New Year. We'll have apples dipped in honey this evening. Symbolic, for good luck, you know.'

'And your parents sent them ones?'

'Of course. Sometimes people send flowers but it's usually fruit.'

James hesitated at Aunt Adele's gate.

'Come with me, I'm not going in or anything.'

'Okay.'

Adele came to the door in an apron. She was wearing her old wig. She took the basket and said she'd see me later. I waited for James to mention Adele's wig but he didn't.

We were all there that evening. Deb was back, looking thinner, more like other people look. I felt a sudden lift of optimism. There seemed to be some hope for the way she might turn out. Our basket stood on a side table next to a vase of yellow-gold chrysanthemums. Everything shone and glinted and gleamed. Gilt-framed mirrors glanced fire off their edges, the reflected chandelier winked liquid drops in a dazzling infinity above us. Deb and Judy and Ben and I sat together on one of the sofas and drank sherry and giggled. I felt warm, included for once.

It was in a moment of quiet before we went in to dinner that Adele said it.

'Deborah,' she said across the room which was suddenly quiet, 'I don't know if I told you. I'm surprised your cousin Henry's here at all. He's happier spending time with his goyshke friends. He couldn't even come round with a present earlier on without one. Maybe we should feel honoured that he can bring himself to come to his aunt's house for Rosh Hashanah.'

Deb raised her eyes towards the ceiling. It was an eloquent, ambiguous gesture. I didn't know if it castigated her mother or me. Ben and Judy began giggling.

It may have been just then, or perhaps on the way into the dining-room that my neck broke out with prickly heat, or perhaps with malaria which I had heard made you go hot and cold, burning and shivering in quick succession. Uncle Aaron's voice reading the service for the eve of Rosh Hashanah came at me from far away, zoned in from distances beyond the sphere of my own small life.

Aaron's services were always democratic. He asked who wanted to say the blessing. He even let the girls say them.

'Who wants to say the blessing?'

'I will,' I said.

I stood, swaying slightly, talmudically, as I did. I held the prayer book open at the blessing.

'We thank you,' I said slowly, in English. A finger of ice wound itself round the room, through the candle flames, over the rustling flower heads, across my hot forehead, 'for all your good gifts. In Jesus' name, Amen.' Annie's workaday grace.

It's never happened to me before or since, the feeling of floating, separate from myself, out somewhere beyond, free and calm and utterly silent.

'Amen,' Uncle Aaron said, 'thank you, Henry,' and easily, he passed on.

The season was portentous. I was right that year.

About Christmas time, Uncle Aaron began to look yellow and waxy and thin and shortly after, he was found to have a liver tumour from which he died in early summer.

Uncle Aaron withered that spring, like a branch torn from a big tree. He grew smaller and drier and frailer till you feared a slight breeze would blow him, rustle him with its slightest movement.

* * *

Adele never addressed a word to me again, not over the dinner table and not when we passed in the long quiet corridors of the hospital, not even in her house during the week of mourning. A few months after Aaron died, she moved to Bournemouth to be nearer Nussa Levenburg.

'She's not even a relative!' my mother said. I wondered if she really cared. It was Aaron she missed.

After Adele moved, I never saw her again. My parents kept up contact, phoning, sending birthday cards, eventually wedding invitations.

No one ever asked me why I'd done it. My father suggested that I might write to Aunt Adele which I did, taking hours to find ways of sounding as if I was sorry without actually saying I was. I had to wait till after the two days of Rosh Hashanah in case Adele was offended by my writing on Yomtov.

I walked round to Adele's after school carrying my letter. There didn't seem to be much proof around of life beginning in the autumn. Resurrection? The leaves were curling, drying, dying under my feet, the light thinning, the cold seeping in. What kind of hope did you have to have to see life still burning?

I kept thinking about the prayer I had missed saying, '. . . who hast kept us in life and hast preserved us and enabled us to reach this season.' My footfalls fell into its rhythm and I walked the sound of the words on the blown, leafy pavement. This season where everything falls and dies and ends.

Everything was still as I walked up the path. The two sentinel lights on either side of the front door cast a greenish glow over the polished step. Judy answered the door. She was wearing her horrible purple school uniform and holding one of Adele's iced kuchen in her hand. She stood in the doorway as if she was guarding the house against me. I could see the chandeliers glittering inside.

'Could you give this to Aunt Adele?'

She held out the kuchen-free hand but didn't say anything. Her mouth was full. She took the envelope and closed the door.

I turned and crunched down the gravel path. I walked home slowly, kicking up leaves in red-orange clouds. I knew Aunt Adele would be reading my letter. I hoped she knew I wasn't sorry. Turning the corner towards home, I realized, suddenly, in one, clear moment, that I had discovered something enduring, something that could never change. Everything would always be like that. I would for ever be casting stones into voids, never hearing them crash, never knowing when they'd stopped falling.

HERON

Douglas Strang

When the lunch-bell rang, Findlay pulled himself from underneath the car he was working on and made his way across the workshop to the toilet.

'Would you look at the speed of that,' one of the mechanics shouted after him, grinning to the others. Findlay removed his overalls and scrubbed the oil from his hands and face.

'D'you think he's off to meet a lassie?'

The mechanics did not change for lunch. Their dirty overalls were a uniform, worn with pride. Every day they crossed the road to the pub, where they were served re-heated pies and pints of heavy. They ate and drank standing up, in position, at the bar.

It was raining on Dumbarton Road. Umbrellas flowered open, their colours smeared across shop windows and trampled in dirty puddles under foot. The lunch-time rush hour was on; bank clerks and secretaries cascaded down the steps of grey office blocks, swelling the flow of people on the street. Uncovered, Findlay pushed against the flow. He passed a man at a bus stop who cursed the weather and the buses. The man flapped his arms, shaking water from his coat.

Once inside the park, Findlay followed his usual path, eating his piece as he went. He had served two years of his apprenticeship, and for two years he had come to the park. He talked to no one, enjoying the solitude: an escape from the constant noise and jokes at work. The mechanics thought he was odd. They couldn't understand why he didn't come to the pub, and some of them resented him for it.

Only Angus seemed to understand.

'Leave the lad alone, he's no doing any harm,' he would say to the others, when they made fun of Findlay.

Angus MacPhail was the oldest serving mechanic in the garage. He was a big man, bald and beer-bellied. The lines chiselled across his face, and clogged with oil, were a mark of forty years in the trade. When Findlay started working there, Angus took him under his wing.

'I worked with your father at Stevenson's, back when they were still British Leyland,' he explained on that first day. 'I've promised him I'll look out for you, it's the least I can do.'

They had stopped for a tea-break; Angus perched on his tool box, and Findlay resting on the side of a car, holding its carburettor in his hands.

'How is the old man these days?'

Angus had to raise his voice above the sound of an engine being tuned, the question came out louder than he intended.

'Sorry, son, you don't have to say anything.'

'It's okay, he's no bad,' Findlay answered, his eyes fixed on the carburettor, intimidated by the precision of its valves and floats.

'The doctor wanted to get him into the hospital, but Da said he wasnae going to end his days in a ward in the Western.' Findlay shrugged. 'That was that, he'll no even give up the fags.'

Findlay followed the path which ran alongside the Kelvin, walking as far as it took for the river sound to drown the noise of traffic. In the summer, he sat beneath the trees on the river bank. He would eat his piece and then lie back, enjoying the warmth of the sun. It was too wet to sit, so he crossed the Kelvin Way and headed towards the fountain.

On dry days, the skateboarders were there. Findlay sometimes came to watch them, entranced, as they raced around the fountain; flipping and spinning their boards like acrobats; baseball-capped and brightly dressed, their jeans threadbare and torn. He imagined his father's voice:

'No son of mine'll be seen out in the street with his arse hanging out his trousers.'

Findlay knew he was no acrobat; he mended cars. Turning away from the fountain, he walked on.

A woman was waving to him, by the duck pond. He recognized her immediately, she was one of the regulars who came to the park every day.

She and her dog had first appeared on a cold day in autumn. Findlay had been sitting on a bench beneath the University tower when he noticed her. She was on the lower path. The dog, a Jack Russell, ran ahead, stopping now and then to burrow among the piled leaves. The woman who walked her dog had dark hair and a Roman nose. She was as tall as her dog was small, and she strode through the park with an ease that Findlay admired. He often looked out for her; and, though they never spoke, they nodded to each other when they passed.

She was there, by the duck pond; and she was waving him over. Findlay, confused, felt his cheeks burn.

They both stood against the fence. She grasped his arm with one hand and pointed to the island in the middle of the pond with the other, her eyes shining.

'Look, do you see it? Under the bushes.'

A heron stood in the shade, perfectly still, its sleek head tucked into its chest. It was a grey shadow, with one bright eye staring out at them.

'Can you believe it? A heron in the middle of Glasgow.'

Findlay couldn't believe it; her hair, damp, falling just like that; and so close, her hand still clutching his arm; and the heron.

'I've never seen a heron. No a real one, alive.'

'Magic, eh?' She smiled and squeezed his arm.

The dog barked. Startled by the noise, the heron lifted its head and unfurled its wings; ready to fly in an instant. She let go his arm and stood back from the fence. Calling softly to the dog, she moved away. The heron curled back in on itself. As she went, the woman who walked her dog called back to Findlay, over her shoulder:

'I'm glad you saw it too.'

Findlay ran back along Dumbarton Road. The man at the bus stop was still there, still cursing.

The foreman caught him putting on his overalls.

'Where've you been?'

Findlay apologized, out of breath.

'You'll make sure and no be late again.'

'Aye, I'll make sure.'

That afternoon he and Angus worked on a car together, fitting a new starter-motor.

'You're quiet the day, Fin, what's on your mind?'

Findlay said nothing, and then asked:

'Did you always want to be a mechanic?'

Angus laughed from beneath the car.

'No much difference now if I hadnae.'

His hand appeared up through the bowels of the engine. It was a broad hand, calloused and scarred. Findlay placed a ratchet and socket, the right size, on the open palm.

'I wanted to be a forestry man.' Angus's voice was quiet, muffled. 'Can you imagine that, eh? Me stuck in some wee hut in the middle of nowhere. Looking after bloody fir trees.'

When Angus crawled out from under the car, he threw

the ratchet into his tool box and dumped the old starter in a bin.

That night, Findlay lay in a bed that had been too small for him for years. In the room next door he could hear his father wheeze and cough; a hacking cough, trying to clear lungs that would never clear. Sleep wouldn't come, so he wrapped his quilt around his shoulders and went to the window. They lived on the top floor of a tenement, high on Maryhill Road. From his window, Findlay looked out over Glasgow. The rain clouds had passed and the sky was black, starless.

The heron would be gone by tomorrow, Findlay knew that. He imagined it rising up from the park, its beak stretched forward like the point of a compass. Silently, it would head north, wings beating steadily through the night, out and away from the city.

AND ON THE SEVENTH DAY AN ANGEL CAME

Jonathan Wood

On the bed the man turned on to his side and opened his eyes. The girl lay with her back to him, the jumble of her black hair covering the pillow and reaching down to her shoulderblades. The man moved his hand slightly and took some of the hair between his fingers. It was thick and soft and a few of the hairs divided at the ends as if frayed. Her back was long and slim, the muscles under the dark brown skin moving slightly with each shallow breath, and his eyes traced the line of her backbone down to her buttocks which were half hidden by the white cotton sheet that lay dishevelled over the lower half of the bed.

Over the curve of her hip he could see a shaft of sunlight slanting in through the fly-screen door that opened on to the fire escape. It lit up specks of dust in the air, swirling in the current of the air conditioning unit that was jammed under the lower sash of the window. The unit was not working properly and had little effect upon the hot, humid August air. The man could feel the heat of the girl's body even though they were not touching, and the sheet underneath him felt damp with perspiration.

Across the alley from the fire escape the 47th Street Evangelical Choir could be heard practising gospel in the empty church hall. The voices rose and trembled and the clapped-hands rhythm echoed a little against the hard backs of the pews. The piano was slightly out of tune but the strength and conviction of the singing was such that the discord did not seem important.

Inside the room, two flies buzzed slowly and aimlessly around the ceiling, their drone merging with the hum of the air conditioner.

Moving slowly, so as not to disturb the girl, the man rose from the bed and went to the bathroom. He stood for a few minutes under the shower, then shaved with the girl's disposable razor and towelled himself off in front of the mirror. He stood there for a moment, trying to see his body as the girl might see it. He was tall, with heavy features and coarse dark hair on his chest. The tattoo on his right upper arm showed that he had once been a State level boxer, but although he was still muscular it was obvious that he was now out of shape. He wrapped a towel around himself and went through to the kitchen where he made two cups of coffee, and then carried them back to the bedroom.

'You still here?' She was sitting up in bed, the sheet around her waist, tying her hair back with a piece of elastic. He stopped short, spilling a little of the coffee on to the bare boards of the bedroom floor. She folded her arms across her breasts and looked at him steadily, measuring him as he stood in the doorway, a cup in each hand.

'Guess I fell asleep,' he said. 'Then I woke up and it was light and I needed a coffee. Brought you one too.'

'Jees. Breakfast in bed huh? Hang out the flags.'

'I didn' know you was awake,' he said, stupidly.

'I wasn't, but I had a bad dream. How come you fell asleep?'

He grinned at her and shrugged one shoulder. 'You musta tired me out, honey.'

'Don't bull me, Marty. You gotta reason. This is the first time and I know you.'

'Honey, look . . .' He sighed. 'D'you want coffee or not?'

She hesitated, then said, 'Sure. Guess I'd better make the most of it.'

He crossed the room quickly and sat on the edge of the bed facing her, still wearing the towel. He put her coffee on the bedside table and sat back without touching her. Their eyes met and held. For a moment neither of them spoke, then the man cleared his throat and jerked his head in the direction of the window.

'Maybe I should get you a new cooler. It's hot as hell in here. I know this guy in New Jersey.'

The girl studied the chipped red varnish on her fingernails.

'Yeah. You start to notice it in the morning. It's always worse in the day than the night.'

He looked down at his coffee, and began stirring it slowly with his fingertip. She did not move. Her cup sat on the bedside table, a wisp of steam curling up from the black liquid into the hot morning air. Across the alley the choir had finished their practice and the congregation were arriving for the morning service. Out on East 47th Street car doors banged and the women's Sunday heels clicked on the concrete slabs of the sidewalk.

The girl let her hand fall into her lap and sighed.

'What you done, Marty? You got trouble?'

'No trouble, honey. I told you. I fell asleep is all.'

'Don't gimme that. You would only stay over 'cause there's a reason.'

'Jesus, Debra. You always think I got trouble. I fell asleep is all.'

'You are such a bullshitter, you know that? Margie told me Lou was at the club yesterday lookin' for you. Had Angel with him. What you done, Marty? You crossed him or what?'

'For Chrissake, Debra, I fell asleep okay? I ain't dumb enough so's I'd cross Lou. Like I told you before, Lou an' me, we're okay now. An' anyways, Lou ain't the only guy in town these days. I think maybe Lou's starting to lose it, you know?'

'Jesus, Marty . . . !'

'Listen, honey. You always complainin' about I never stay over, an' here I am. Doncha wanna spend some time, huh? You always bin saying we should spend time. Maybe even we should go away for a while. Maybe New Orleans, or the West Coast, huh? You like LA. You told me.'

The girl put her head back against the wall and looked up at the ceiling.

'I don't fuckin' believe this.' She tore the sheet aside and scrambled awkwardly from the bed.

'What the fuck you sayin', Marty? We goin' to the West Coast huh? Oh yeah? The hell we are!'

She stood over him and yelled down at him as he stared into his coffee cup, her voice becoming ugly in her rage.

'We bin together for what? Nearly three years now. You come here two, three times a week, but you never, ever stay over. We meet in a bar, we have a few drinks, then we get laid and by morning you gone. Ciao honey, thanks for the fuck. You don't call, you don't treat me natural like I was something you care about. You just expect me to say, hi, yeah, great to see you. Fuck me and forget me, why doncha. It's like that cheap lousy cooler: it ain't no damned good but you sure as hell better learn to live with it cause it's all there is and without it things is even worse. And now what? Now it's mornin' and whoa!: you still here an' you bringin' me fuckin' coffee in bed. Now you tell me you wanna spend some time. Course, there ain't nothin' wrong, but maybe now we should go away awhiles. The West Coast! You expect me to believe that bullshit? You a fuckin' liar, Marty Ross. You know that? You got trouble? You go give it to somebody else. I got plenty trouble of my own.'

She turned away and went to the chest of drawers, fumbled a cigarette from a packet, lit it and inhaled deeply, facing the wall. From the church hall the sound of the gospel singing rose and fell, and now the congregation had joined the choir the massed voices almost drowned the sound of the discordant piano.

'*And you will be my strength, sweet Jesus, standing by my side.*'

The man had not moved since the girl had left the bed, but had sat staring down into his coffee, his fingertip making small circles in the liquid's surface. Now he looked up at her where she stood with her back to him. The dark lines of her naked body stood in sharp contrast to the peeling white walls and the pale shades of the old chest of drawers. She smoked silently with her head bowed, but with her hair tied back he could see that her shoulders were shaking. He put the cup down and walked over to her and put his arms around her. The paleness of his skin against hers seemed to emphasize his embrace. He did not say anything but stood and held her closely for what seemed like a very long time.

'*For I am lost in Satan's darkness, and I am lost in the light.*
Without you as my strength, sweet Jesus, standing by my side.'

Slowly her trembling ceased. After a while she linked her fingers with his, and held on to the arms that held her. He turned her to face him. 'Honey, let's not do this.' He touched one side of her face with the backs of his fingers, wiping away the wetness from her tears. 'Let's not do this, okay?'

She buried her face in his chest. 'Jesus, Marty. Jesus. You a real dumb-ass if you crossed Lou. You don't mess with guys like Lou and then walk away. Guys like Lou they get even, that's what. You know it. What the hell you gonna do?'

'Forget about Lou, honey. There ain't no trouble with Lou. Just you an' me'll go away awhiles. That's all. We gonna spend some time, you'll see.'

'Jesus, Marty . . .' She shook her head and then looked up into his face. 'You said that at Thanksgiving. You said we would go see my sister and you lied.'

'I know honey, and I'm sorry. But that was different; and I'm here now ain't I? I'm here and it's mornin' and we're still here together.' He smiled down at her. 'And I made you coffee too.'

She pulled away from him, pouting. 'You spilt the coffee on my goddamn floor.'

'Okay, okay. I'll clean up already. Just gimme a break willya, honey. I tell you we'll spend time and we will. We'll take the car and drive clean across the country, an' we'll stop over in St Louis and say hi to your sister and we'll go up to the Grand Canyon and I'll get you one of them Indian rings like you lost before. You remember, the silver one?'

'You mean it this time? We gonna go on a vacation, like we was married or something?'

'That's it. Just like we was married.'

'Oh Marty, when? Can we leave today? I don't gotta work at the club this week on account of Julie being in town. Can't we leave today?'

'There's a coupla things I gotta take care of first in the city, honey. I figure we leave in a coupla days.'

She bit the end of her thumb and looked down at the floor.

'You lyin' to me, Marty. Just like last time. You lyin' to me.'

He spun away from her with his arms thrown wide. 'Fer Chrissake, Debra, I don't fuckin' need this. You don't want me around? Fuckin' A. I'm outta here. I'm gone.' He bent and began snatching his clothes off the chair by the bed.

'Marty! Marty please.'

She grabbed him by the arm but he stood facing away from her, holding the clothes to his chest. He could hear her breathing quickly behind him.

'I'm sorry, baby. Sure I believe you. Sure. Please stay, huh?'

Slowly he put the clothes down and turned to face her.

She was twisting some of her hair tightly round her forefinger and her dark eyes were pleading.

'You ain't gonna give me no more of this lyin' shit areya?'

'Marty, I swear. It's just I'm scared is all. I'm scared for you and I'm scared for me and I'm scared for both of us together. What'll I do if . . .?'

He took her hand, unwinding the hair and putting her forefinger to his lips.

'Listen, honey. You gonna be okay. I'm here, an' you gonna be awright.'

She put her arms around him and looked up into his face. 'Marty, I need you. I really do. Stay with me this time, okay?'

'I'll stay with you. I promise.'

She shut her eyes and held on to him as he enveloped her in his embrace. He held her like that for a moment, and then ran his hands down her back and over her buttocks. He stood caressing her for a while and she pressed herself against him, then he picked her up and carried her to the bed. She pulled the towel from around his waist and lay back, smiling at him with her wide, bright eyes. Across the alley the gospel singing increased in volume as the hymn drew to a close.

'And I will weather the storm, sweet Jesus, and I can stem the tide,

For you are now my strength, sweet Jesus, standing by my side.'

They made love with an ease born of confidence and familiarity. She moved with a languorous grace, secure in her body and her ability to satisfy its desires. He held himself over her, looking down at her sinuous motion as they moved rhythmically together, slowly at first and then gradually increasing in tempo and in force, bonded together with common purpose and a single mind and carried up and over by the rush of their desire until she gasped and her body arched up from the bed and his strength gave way and he fell forward and they held each other as their climax shuddered and shook them into that peaceful place beyond.

Afterwards they lay together on the bed, she asleep while he lay with his head on her stomach looking up at the flies that still flew in lazy, pointless circles around the ceiling. The air conditioner had been switched off and the room was hot and still, but quieter without the machine's constant futile humming.

Outside in the alley someone had opened the side door of the church to let in some air, and the tremulous voice of the preacher could be heard reverberating from the alley walls.

'And in this world of pain and suffering we all need to seek the comfort and strength of our brothers and our sisters, for loneliness is nothing but a state of mind.'

On East 47th Street a trolley car rumbled past on its downtown run and the house shook slightly at its passing. As the sound died away a shadow appeared on the fly-screen door, and then the door opened very quickly and a man stepped noiselessly in from the fire escape and closed the door behind him. He was short and fat, and his skin was completely hairless with the pink smoothness of alopecia. He wore a white T-shirt and baggy white trousers stretched tightly over his round stomach. In his left hand he carried a large white handkerchief, while his right hand held a silenced automatic pistol. The hard black metal looked incongruous against the white clothes and the puffy pink flesh.

'So do not stand alone in the midst of the crowd. Open your hearts to those around you and be loved and give love.'

The man on the bed started up, but stopped halfway to his feet when he saw the gun. He froze on the edge of the bed with one foot already on the floor, and stared first at the gun and then at the smooth, cherubic face of the man who held it. On the bed the girl murmured and shifted a little in her sleep. The fat man raised the gun slightly and shot her once in the head.

'Lou says to say hello,' he said in a soft, high-pitched voice.

The man on the bed looked down at the girl's body. The bullet had entered cleanly at the temple and exited into the pillow. She lay as she had been sleeping, and apart from the spreading blood on the pillowcase she looked almost peaceful.

The man began to stammer.

'Angel, look . . . I . . . Jesus . . . listen to me. Angel!' But the gunman put his finger to his lips.

'Quiet, Marty. The preacher man's talking.'

'*But the most powerful love of all is that of the Lord God, and without His love and His strength we are as nothing in the face of Satan's power.*'

The two men faced each other, separated by a few feet and the silenced barrel of the pistol. The man on the edge of the bed crouched motionless, his teeth bared and his breath coming in short gasps. His eyes were wide and staring as they fixed on the gunman's face.

'*For Satan works to close our hearts and our minds to our own love; to our compassion and the need of those around us.*'

The gunman stood relaxed, his face impassive as he held the man in the gaze of the gun. A bead of sweat slipped slowly down his smooth pink cheek and he dabbed at it delicately with a corner of the handkerchief. Then raised the gun and pointed it at the man's head. The man stopped breathing abruptly, and urinated on to the floor. The gunman looked down at the wetness, shook his head and clicked his tongue disapprovingly.

'*And so I ask you now to kneel in this house and pray to the Lord in Jesus' name that He will walk beside you and guide your footsteps on the path of love and righteousness.*'

The gunman's eyes widened as he raised what would have been his eyebrows.

'Too late,' he said. Then he smiled and shot the man in the middle of the forehead.

BIOGRAPHICAL NOTES

PAUL BROWNSEY has lived in Scotland since 1972. After leaving school, he became a newspaper reporter and later studied at the Universities of Keele and Oxford and at Swarthmore College, Pennsylvania. He is now a lecturer in philosophy at Glasgow University and lives in Bearsden.

ELIZABETH BURNS's work has been included in previous volumes of *Scottish Short Stories*, and a collection of poetry, *Ophelia and Other Poems*, has been published by Polygon. She lives in Edinburgh.

JOHN CUNNINGHAM was born in Edinburgh in 1934 and now lives in Glasgow. His novel *Leeds to Christmas* was published by Polygon in 1990.

STUART DAVID was born in 1969 and lives in Alexandria. He is a singer/songwriter with his own band and is the author of three novels. 'The Unlocked Door' is his first published work.

ALI DUNCAN was born on Valentine's Day 1958. He started writing four years ago, and works as a scientific officer in an agricultural college. 'Mirror Image' is his first published story.

HAL DUNCAN is twenty-two and lives in Glasgow with his dog, Kore. He has a degree in English and is currently training as a press photographer. He is a member of the Glasgow Science Fiction Writers' Circle.

MARK FLEMING was born in 1962 in Edinburgh and has always lived in the capital. His short stories have appeared in many publications, from football fanzines to *Scottish Child* Magazine and *The Big Issue* in Scotland.

JANE HARRIS was Writer in Residence at MMP Durham from 1992–1994. Her work appears in various publications including *New*

Writing 3 (Minerva); *Chapman*, *Stand*, *New Writing Scotland* and *Scottish Short Stories 1993*.

GORDON LEGGE is the author of two novels, *The Shoe* and *I Love Me, Who Do You Love?*, and a collection of stories, *In Between Talking About the Football*. He lives in Edinburgh.

ANNE MACLEOD is a dermatologist and lives in Ross-shire with her four children. Her poetry has been published in *Cencrastus*, *Lines Review*, *Chapman*, *Original Prints IV*, *Second Shift* and *Northwords*; her short stories have appeared in the *Aberdeen University Review* and in such anthologies as *The Junkie's Christmas* (Serpent's Tail) and *Meantime* (Polygon/Women 2000). She is currently working on her first novel.

HUGH MCMILLAN teaches History in Dumfries. He has published two books of poetry, *Tramontana* (Dog & Bone, Glasgow, 1990) and *Harridge* (Chapman Writing Series, 1994). A third, *Aphrodite's Anorak*, will be published by Peterloo in Autumn 1995. He has just completed his first novel.

CANDIA MCWILLIAM was born in Edinburgh in 1955. She has published three novels, *A Case of Knives*, *A Little Stranger* and *Debatable Land*. She has three children.

DILYS ROSE lives in Edinburgh with her family. She has published two collections of poems, *Beauty is a Dangerous Thing* and *Madame Doubtfire's Dilemma*, and two of short stories, *Our Lady of the Pickpockets* and *Red Tides*.

ALI SMITH was born in Inverness, has lived in Aberdeen and Edinburgh and now lives in Cambridge, where she writes and teaches. She has published drama, short fiction, poetry, criticism and reviews in a number of books and magazines. A collection of her short stories, *Free Love* was published in May 1995, by Virago.

IAIN CRICHTON SMITH is a poet, novelist and short story writer. He was born in 1928, spent his first twenty years in Lewis and now lives with his wife in Taynuilt.

DOUGLAS STRANG was born in Glasgow in 1966. After leaving school he worked in the motor trade for five years, then worked as a gardener on Iona for three years. He is now a mature student studying Scottish Ethnology and Literature at Edinburgh University. 'Heron' is his first published work.

JONATHAN WOOD was born in Edinburgh in 1958, studied first Architecture and later Psychology at the University of Edinburgh, and completed his postgraduate studies at Oxford. After several periods spent working and travelling abroad and in London he now lives in Edinburgh where he tries to fit writing around his professional work as a design management consultant.

ESTHER WOOLFSON was born in Glasgow and was educated at the Hebrew University of Jerusalem and Edinburgh University. She now lives in Aberdeen. 'Rosh Hashanah' is her sixth story to be published in this collection.

Marcel Möring

The Great Longing

'A desperate and powerful vision of love.'
PETER HØEG, author of *Miss Smilla's Feeling for Snow*

Twins Sam and Lisa and their older brother, Raph, are orphaned when their parents die in a car crash. Dispersed to various foster homes, they lose touch, re-uniting when the twins reach adulthood.

On the surface, all three have taken very different paths in life: Sam, sad and solitary, works as an archivist; Lisa is a painter, desperately unable to love her husband; and Raph, wild and resilient, always seeks the limit. What unites this strange, restless trio is their ever-present sense of what they lost when their parents died – a connectedness with their fellow men and the innocent, unconditional love of the family. Attempts to satiate their 'great longing' take all three on a journey back to the lost paradise of childhood, where memory has become myth and hidden truths await discovery.

A bestselling novel and a masterpiece of European fiction, *The Great Longing* has taken Holland by storm. Critically acclaimed and winner of the prestigious AKO prize, it has already established itself as one of the country's great works of literature.

'Poetically slim, modern in tone, the novel deals with timeless things: sex and love, destiny, memory . . . so compelling a novel guarantees a long life in English translation.' *The Times*

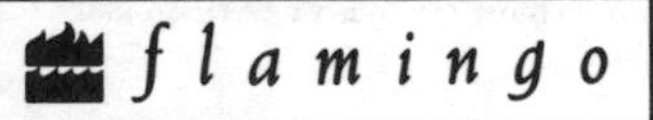

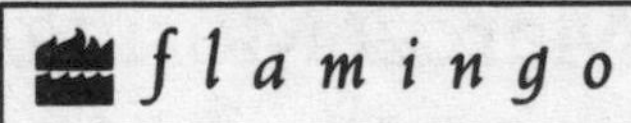